Mommy Minds

S.S. Zemke

Published by S.S. Zemke, 2024.

Blessings!
-S.S. Zemke

MOMMY MINDS

First edition. September 2, 2024.

ISBN: 979-8227053022

Written by S.S. Zemke.

Special thanks first to the Lord for putting this message on my heart. To my mom and husband and other family members for all of their support with my writing adventures. Thank you to my writers group Footprints, Glynn, Janice, Rhonda, Frances, Kate, Lindsey, Fran, and Lorrie for critiquing parts of the book and encouraging me.

Cast of Characters

Chloe......Mother expecting a baby, employee at Marsha's bakery

Missy......Co-worker of Chloe

Marsha......Owner and operator of The Sunflower Bakery and Restaurant

Kate ......Friend of Chloe from Los Angeles

Jesse.......Midwife for Chloe and mother of two teenage girls

Chapter One

Chloe

Spring Mountain, Montana

Pregnant. Two empty pregnancy test packages were strewn over the bathroom counter. I sat on the floor leaning against the white wall, clutching my fists full of hair. Wringing my hands, I glanced at the time on my cell phone, realizing it was my husband Peter's usual time to get home from work. Curling my legs up, I buried my head between my knees, waiting for the sudden wave of nausea to pass.

Five minutes later there was a tap at the door. "Please hurry. I gotta go really bad," Peter complained.

"Just give me a minute," I croaked. Tossing the pregnancy tests into a plastic grocery bag, I shoved it underneath the bathroom sink behind some cleaning chemicals.

Standing over the sink, I wasn't sure if I was nauseous because of morning sickness or from nerves. I hadn't expected to get pregnant that soon. There was no way we could afford the medical bills and other expenses.

I opened the door and trudged to the kitchen. "What's for dinner?" Peter walked in just as I was filling my water bottle. I stopped and stared at him.

"Really? Do I have to make dinner for you every night? Are you not even capable of getting yourself something?" I stomped back into the bathroom to get ready for work. Marsha had asked if I could come into the restaurant for a couple hours that night, since they were short-handed.

Peter stood in the doorway to the bathroom, his arms crossed. He was wearing his lumberjack-looking shirt again with a red plaid jacket and jeans. His beard hadn't been trimmed in months. "You don't have to be rude. I just asked you a simple question," he grumbled.

I continued to apply my mascara, hoping he would go away but he continued staring at me, waiting for an explanation.

"I have to get to work. Someone at the restaurant went home sick and I was asked if I could pick up extra hours. We need the money," I growled.

"You are always worried about money, aren't you? Why don't you just give it a break?" Peter rolled his eyes.

"Why don't you work more hours?

"Why? We have enough to get by. I'm already working overtime. You're the one who wanted to live here. The rent on this place is way too expensive."

"If it was up to you, we'd be in that crappy trailer next to a meth lab."

"No matter where we live, you always find something wrong." Peter's face turned red, his fists clenching.

Applying deodorant, I pushed him off to the side, making my way to the bedroom to find my comfortable work shoes. Tying my shoelaces in a hurry, I then grabbed my black sweater, keys, and raced out the door.

The crisp air blew loose strands of brown hair into my face. I didn't have time to curl it, so I just tossed it up into a messy bun. Fiddling with the keys, my hands were still shaking from the news on the pregnancy test. How was I going to tell Peter?

The car wouldn't start, and I stopped myself from heading back and asking Peter for help. Remembering it was only five blocks away, I set out walking. The small town of Spring Mountain was quiet as I trudged through the sleepy streets. Making it a game, I counted the pumpkins in people's yards, trying to distract my mind. During tourist season, each street was bustling with visitors, touring the shops or during the winter season, people were on their way to the local ski resort.

Finally reaching the restaurant, I spied Missy standing behind the cash register, handing an older gentleman back his change. My heart sank. It was going to be a long night working with a crabby coworker.

My job description included wearing many hats at the restaurant, but tonight I was a waitress. During the dinner rush, the place was full of customers ordering the special-Marsha's pot roast, garlic mashed potatoes, and roasted asparagus with a side of her secret sauce. It was something I had to recite over and over again.

"What can I get for you this evening?" I said in my cheerful voice, although I was feeling the exact opposite.

"I'm just having dessert tonight," the young man said. "Peach pie with whipped cream, of course." Nodding my head, I told him it was a good choice.

Out of the corner of my eye, I spotted a familiar plaid shirt. Thankful to be headed to the kitchen, I ducked behind a wooden beam, hoping Peter wouldn't see me, but it was too late.

"Just what is your problem, Chloe? I can't figure you out. Why did you walk and not take the car?"

"I'm in a hurry. Let me through," I hissed. "And what are you doing here?"

"Thought I would get some pot roast, since there's nothing in the fridge," Peter said.

"There's sandwich stuff, you big baby." It was a challenge keeping my voice quiet, as others were eating at the booths near us.

"I won't let you get back to work till you tell me what's bothering you. I know you. There's something going on."

Annoyed, I moved to step around him, but he blocked the way.

"Okay! I'm pregnant, alright? That's what's going on. There. You happy?" Every person in the restaurant stopped to look.

Chapter Two

Missy

Spring Mountain, Montana

The Sunflower Restaurant and Bakery

This is just not working out. Clicking out of my text messages, I slammed the phone on one of the new tables Marsha had just bought for the restaurant. Another breakup. This had been what? my fourth relationship since high school. The breakups were always about the same thing. The secret I had been carrying around for years, the baggage I brought into every relationship, no matter how much I tried to hide it.

"You doing okay?" One of my drinking buddies, Candace, walked into the restaurant. I had texted her earlier that day, letting her know what time my lunch break was.

"Do I look like I'm doing okay?" I sneered down at my phone.

"Your hair looks extra red to me for some reason. You want to head downtown to the brewery after you get off? I hear it's trivia night," Candace said.

"No, I don't. Just leave me alone." It was easy to close my eyes, wishing she would walk away.

"You're the one that asked me to come here. I know you're always this grouchy, but did something happen today I don't know about?" It was the first time I'd ever seen Candace look concerned.

"I hate this day. I always seem to be the one who gets the rude customers who don't care about anything but looking good for their friends. They come into the restaurant or whatever this place is and order a bunch of stuff and get mad if you do one little thing wrong. It's never ending." I kept the subject off the breakup, not wanting to talk about it yet. Or maybe ever. Besides, Candice was only my friend because she liked to go out drinking with me. We didn't talk about the deep stuff very often, and that was fine with me.

"And ugghhh! That woman I work with. I found out her name is Chloe. I've worked with her how long? and just found out her name. They don't make us wear name tags and I honestly didn't care to ask. All she ever talks about is her pregnancy and babies."

"You've talked about her before." Candace chewed her nails. "You guys used to get along."

"I was so close to just telling her I really didn't care. I don't give a hoot that she's planning on having a midwife deliver her baby. Or that she's having random cravings for cinnamon bread. And her outfits. I mean come on. Are clothes that limited in town that all she can ever wear are the same stupid shirts over and over? How lame is that?"

"Is Chloe around here?" Candace asked, spitting her fingernails out to the side of the table.

I cringed. "No. She went home. And even if she was here, I wouldn't care if she heard me. What a loser."

"Wow. She really gets under your skin, doesn't she?" Candace said.

I rolled my eyes. "Obviously. She's also one of those people who try and shove their beliefs down your throat. Prayer this and prayer that. If I hear her talk about it one more time, I'm gonna tell her off."

Candace laughed. "Why does it surprise me that you haven't already done that?"

Ignoring her, I stared at the turkey sandwich on rye with extra mayo. It didn't sound good anymore.

Candace shook her head as she studied a menu. Without even saying goodbye, I headed to the back room for a bag to store my lunch in for later. I was glad my shift was only a couple more hours. My head was pounding, and my stomach held sharp pains. I dragged through the rest of work, gritting my teeth and clenching my fists. I even scared one of the customers off with my impatience waiting for them to order. It wasn't my fault they were so indecisive.

At the end of my shift, I walked home grumbling under my breath. Snow came down and the wind was blowing hard. I didn't have the right clothing, thinking there was going to be at least a month more of fall. My pack only held a light gray jacket and a baseball cap. Shielding my face with my hands, I pressed against the cold. My long, red hair whipped across the side of my face, and I thought my hat would blow away.

Slamming my apartment door behind me, I found my favorite fuzzy blanket and slipped into the cold bed. With my nightstand beside me, I reached over and pulled out an old journal from several years before. A picture fell out from the first page. My heart sank, remembering what it was.

Laura Beth, 2 days old. The back said. My sweet baby was wrapped in a pink and white blanket, a little bow in her reddish-brown hair. It had been the first time we caught her with her eyes open long enough to take a good picture. A smile tickled her face. Head pounding, I laid the picture beside me, buried my head under the blanket, and struggled to fall asleep. My baby girl would be almost three now. A tear rolled down my cheek. Three next Tuesday.

Chapter Three

Marsha

Washing my hands at the bathroom sink, I studied myself in the mirror. *You were a failure as a mother.* It had been years since I had those thoughts. And they were back to haunt me.

My granddaughter Maggie was waiting in the living room for a visit. I ran my hand down my face, feeling tired. Although I was sixty years old, many would tell me how good I looked for my age. I would thank them and give credit to my hairdresser for keeping my hair cut and dyed, and most knew staying in shape with swimming was how I kept up with the employees at my restaurant and bakery. Today though, my age could be felt. Dragging to the living room, I slumped down in a chair next to Maggie.

"Grandma, tell us some of your stories," Maggie said. She was 16 years old, but still requested tales about the days of my youth. She wanted to pass the stories down to her children one day. Thankful for the distraction, I smiled and grabbed my steaming cup of hot chocolate off the kitchen counter.

"I can remember back to when these streets in Spring Mountain were even more busy and booming. The town can still get busy, but back in those days, there was a huge clothing factory. It provided most of the jobs in town at the time but had to shut down in the early 2000s for reasons I'm still not sure about. Grandpa worked there awhile, all while I was raising the family."

"What was that like?" Maggie sat down on the floor next to the fireplace, crossing her legs just like when she was a young kid, and we'd gather for story time.

"Times back then were so hard. People in town could barely afford rent, but somehow were able to make ends meet. The pay checks were never big, but we always had the things that we needed.

Raising a family was probably one of the hardest things I ever had to do in my sixty years, but I loved it and would do it all over again."

Maggie smiled as I told stories, even though she'd probably heard them so many times. "Each of my children are so unique. The two older ones loved being inside and helping with the cooking and cleaning, and my two younger ones enjoyed playing outside in the creek and playing baseball with the neighbor kids. I was blessed by each one. As you know, now they're grown and none of them live close by. Most decided to go off to a bigger area, where the jobs are plentiful. I don't blame them. Around Spring Mountain, certain jobs can be scarce, but I see each year how it's getting better. Maybe someday one of my kids will move back here."

"Do you think my dad will ever move back here, Grandma?"

Unfortunately, I already knew the answer to that. My son had been having marriage problems for a long time and wanted to hide from the family.

"I hate to say this, but I saw some papers out on my dad's desk the other day. He didn't know that I was snooping around in his office. They were divorce papers. I'm praying so hard right now, Grandma. More than anything, I want them to stay together. I never imagined they would end up this way," Maggie said.

"I'm praying too, Mags. That's all we can do right now." Wanting to push the thoughts away about being a failure, I blinked back tears. No use upsetting Maggie even more.

Once my granddaughter saw the look on my face, she changed the subject.

"Can I show you my new phone that I bought the other day, Granny?"

"Young people I know are so wrapped up in technology these days," I laughed. "My grandkids must fill me in with some of the newer things going on."

"What is the name of that thing they use on the phones now? Snapchat and Insta what? I can't keep up with it. Your aunt wanted to buy me one of those Smartphones, but I turned her down. My landline is just fine for what I need. I prefer the simpler life. And not be bothered with all that news. Getting lost in my cooking and baking is what I'd rather do."

"Speaking of that, I wanted to try my hand at baking again, Grandma. You think you could show me some tricks? Maybe take me to your bakery tomorrow?" Maggie said.

"I would love that. The bakery is my happy place. I'll also show you my collection of books we keep out for the customers too. You'll love it."

Thinking of how much Maggie loved to read, I grabbed the collection of classic stories I read to her when she was little and opened to the first page. We both soaked up each word, hoping to dwell on happier thoughts. It was what we both needed.

Chapter Four

Kate

Los Angeles, California

Although exhaustion had its grip on me, the batter mixing had to continue. My arm felt as if it was going to pop off any moment. Wiping my hand on the apron, gooey cupcake mix smeared all over. It was time to let my arm rest.

"I'm so stressed out. I don't know how we're going to get this cupcake order out to Mr. Jenkins in time. He said he'd be here before eight and then he has to drive to his son's baseball game," I grumbled. Los Angeles traffic was always terrible.

"We'll get it mom, it's not a big deal. He's a pretty cool teacher. I'd doubt he'd be angry if he just had to wait a few minutes," my son Brock said. He was a sixth grader, always wise beyond his years.

I sighed, then mixed the batter again. "I should have known better than to put this order off. We should have done it last night," I complained. It was early in the morning, and we had a hard time sleeping the night before.

Brock grabbed the first batch out of the oven. We'd have to let it cool before decorating it with the team colors blue and gold and a soft cream cheese frosting topped with baseball-shaped candies. He had asked for three dozen to take with him to the game.

"How long have you had the baking business again?" Brock asked as he licked a mixing spoon.

"This will be my fourth year." I couldn't believe it. Brock had been beside me since he was eight years old, helping me with my creations. What started as a baking hobby for just a few friends, turned into a word-of-mouth business for a small crowd of people around L.A. My friend Louise was to thank for that. She told other moms about the cakes I made, and soon they were calling me to help with weddings, birthdays, and other events.

"I'm afraid I can't keep up with the orders. This business has grown so much." I popped the next batch into the oven. Between taking care of kids, being a wife, and doing my cupcake business on the side, I was overwhelmed and drained and couldn't remember the last time I had been on a trip or gone far from the house.

"Thanks, Kate." My husband Mark strolled into the kitchen and grabbed a cupcake off the counter and shoved it into his mouth. Before I could protest, he was already out the door. No hugs. No kisses like he when we were first married.

I hardly saw him anymore, since he started his new job a couple months before. He would stay late at the office to finish work so he wouldn't be distracted by all the chaos at home. I prayed it wouldn't always be that way.

"What was it like running your own restaurant?" Brock's eyes sparkled. Whenever we talked about making food or people starting their own business, he would get excited. He always told me he wanted to run his own restaurant someday.

"It was a ton of work. I was glad I didn't have to do it on my own, though. But I loved it. It was a lot of fun to run that place with your dad."

It was a joy taking a walk down memory lane. I had worked for Mark's mom as a waitress at her restaurant when I was a teenager, and after college I came back to help run the place. It was then Mark and I started dating.

After the cupcakes cooled, I sat down at the table and added the colored frosting. The year before, Brock had first started helping with the decorating part of the business. It was hard for him at first, but he can now be trusted to make an entire batch on his own, from start to finish. We worked non-stop until Mr. Jenkins rang the doorbell. Brock and I both sighed in relief. The order was ready.

"Kate, I have a huge order for you," Mr. Jenkins said the moment I opened the door. "My older daughter is turning 16 and we're having a birthday party for her next week. She doesn't know about it yet. I told my wife I would have you make a big batch for the party."

I gulped. There were already eight other orders for the next week. Where would the time come from?

"Sure. What day do you need them by?" Inside, I scolded myself for not knowing how to say no. I smiled my prize-winning smile, but in reality, wanted to scream.

Mr. Jenkins gave me the details and his wife's number to call in case we had any more questions. After helping him carry his order to the car, Brock shut the front door behind him. Sighing, I rolled onto the floor and prayed for guidance. In my head, I prayed for my marriage and when Brock leaned down to pray with me, we asked if another person would be sent somehow to help with the baking business.

"At least you get a little break here soon, mom," Brock said after we were finished praying.

I smiled, remembering my promise to my best friend Chloe to come visit her and welcome the arrival of her first baby. Yes, it would be a much-needed break indeed. I was looking forward to it.

Chapter Five

Jesse

The Midwife

Standing by the front door, I pictured my teenage daughter as a little girl of only two years old. She was wearing pigtails, overalls, and a pink cowgirl hat. It was going to be Halloween and I was preparing to take her out trick-or-treating. We had been standing at that exact spot. I teared up thinking about it as she stood before me in real time—sixteen, wearing eyeliner and mascara, begging to go over to a boy's house. Arms folded, she did the typical teenage eye roll as I explained to her this outing was not going to happen. Why did she have to be so much like I had been as a teenager?

"His older brother is going to be at his house, too," Haley explained.

"I don't know his older brother and you are not going over to their house without an adult there," I said. Fists clenched, I took a deep breath to stop from an explosion. My husband liked to joke that my dark brown hair would turn fiery red and my brown eyes turn yellow when I was angry. He said my tattoos were already intimidating enough.

"His brother is eighteen, mom." Haley put her hand on her hip.

"It doesn't matter. I know his mom, but not the brother. Next time she's over there, I'll think about letting you go."

"My friend Tammy goes over to her boyfriend's house when nobody's home," Haley countered.

"And Tammy will probably end up pregnant," I mumbled under my breath, heading into the kitchen to load the dishwasher. The kitchen was a complete disaster, but finally, I had a moment of silence away from the nagging teenager.

Just as I was about to load the last dish, Haley stomped into the kitchen, veins bulging out of her forehead. Her hands were stretched out behind her back. Oh boy. Ready for attack.

"I can not believe this, mom! I just got a text from my boyfriend that said you're not going to allow me over there at all anymore. What is he talking about? I thought you said I could if his mom was there."

I stopped to think. When was the last time I had talked to the mother and what did we talk about? The days were mixing. I had helped with three home births that week, and two of them had been at night. That explained why my thinking wasn't clear.

I scratched my head. "Oh yeah. I do remember having a conversation last week with her. I forgot. Sorry," I said while wiping down the counter.

"What did you guys talk about?" Haley scowled.

I searched for the right words, hoping to soften the blow. How could this have been forgotten?

"Basically, we've decided that..." My cell phone rang. It was the other midwife I worked with, Lily. "Sorry, Haley. I gotta take this. Just one minute." Haley turned and stomped out of the room and up the stairs to her bedroom.

"And once again, our lives have to be put on hold for a stupid birth," Haley said loud enough for me to hear all the way down the stairs. Her sister was up in her room, probably lost in her own world of music.

"Hey, Lily," I said, holding back the tears.

"Hey, Jess. Mary's been texting me. She's ready to come into the birthing center. Her contractions are close enough together," Lily said. It sounded like the wind picked up on the other side of the phone.

"Why didn't she text both of us?"

"She forgot, I guess. I'm still in Hamilton, but I'll be leaving soon. Need anything when I get into town?" Lily knew just what to say at the right moment.

"The regular," I sighed.

"Got it. See you in a few." Lily hung up. My regular was a hot vanilla steamer from The Sunflower Restaurant and Bakery. Marsha sure knew how to make a good one. Whenever it was time for a birth, it calmed my nerves being able to have a huge mug of it around. With the weather getting colder, I craved it more than anything else. Imagining holding the warm mug between my palms, I hoped it would warm me up inside too. I could only hope. Balancing work and home life was never easy, especially with teenagers.

Chapter Six

Missy

"Are you kidding me right now?" I screamed to no one in particular. That day at work in a moment of rage, I threw a bucket of water across the kitchen floor. It took me a great deal of the afternoon to clean it up. One of my incompetent coworkers had the nerve to leave me a huge mess and didn't finish mopping up the floor before they left. He had skipped out early to attend the football game.

It sure had been a long frustrating day. I couldn't believe how slow it was. We usually had a steady trickle of people, but I think because of the high school football game, most were there cheering and didn't have time to stop by the restaurant. There was one guy that I specifically remember coming in that I won't ever forget.

"I'll have the usual."

"The usual? And what would that be?" I snapped.

"You don't know what my usual is?" The guy replied. It seemed his eyes were smiling.

"Ummm....no. I've never seen you here before," I said with extra attitude. I didn't feel in the mood to play any games.

"Good. Because I've never been here before. And if you had, it must have been someone who looks just like me. I have always wanted to say that to someone at a restaurant. It makes me sound like I'm sophisticated enough to eat out all the time and have a usual."

I couldn't help but laugh a little at his comment. Secretly, I was glad to be the first employee to meet him, although I wasn't in the mood for this at first.

"So what'll it be?" I asked in a more cheerful tone.

"Hmm. What's your usual?" I studied the baseball cap he was wearing. It was black with no visible writing on it.

"I really like the steamers if you're looking for a warm drink. We have one with pumpkin that we serve year-round. I would also get Marsha's dessert of the day for breakfast, which is a cinnamon roll with special homemade icing."

"Mmmm. That sounds good actually. I'll have that."

It was hard to not notice his smile and calm demeanor. This made me feel at ease, which didn't happen too often. He didn't seem to be in any big hurry like some customers.

While I made up his drink, instead of tapping his foot and waiting while glancing at his phone as many do, he looked around then walked straight to the books. Looking up and down the bookshelves, he studied each title and grabbed one off the shelf. It was Charles Dickens's book *The Christmas Carol.* He leaned down and sat on the floor, his back facing the fireplace, and stretched out his legs. Glancing over, I could see him opening the book and flipping through, touching each of the pages as if he had just found a treasure. He moved his hand down the page and paused to study it a bit. A smile lit up his face.

When he glanced up, I looked away, not wanting him to see he had amused me. I went back to making his drink, grabbing out our thick glass plates for those eating in, and dug a generous sized cinnamon roll out of our display case. It had just been baked less than half an hour before, and I could feel it was still warm from the oven. The smell made its way up to my nostrils, making my stomach growl. For sure our new customer could hear it, but he kept reading his book. I could have left him there for hours and he wouldn't have even noticed. After I finished his steamer, I headed over to bring him his cinnamon roll, placing it on the coffee table in front of him.

"Can I get you anything else?" I asked. He didn't even glance up from his book.

"Nope. This should be good. Thank you." He grinned and kept on reading.

I walked away, a little disappointed he didn't order anything else or even look up at me. He seemed too preoccupied. What was it about that book that made him pick it up and start reading it? Everyone knew the story, right?

Sighing, I walked back to the display case I'd left open. I had been craving a roll and thought about getting one out but argued with myself for a while whether to take one. It was too hard to resist. Why did I always seem to allow myself to give in to temptation?

I grabbed one of the rolls with my bare hands this time. The thinly sliced almonds slipped off, but I didn't care. Hunger overcame me.

"We need more cinnamon rolls?" Marsha walked in then, her hands full of freshly baked pastries. She caught me just as I was getting ready to take a bite.

"Mmm...umm...no we have plenty," I muttered. Marsha had always been kind to me, even on days when my attitude flared up. One of the nice things about working at The Sunflower was Marsha had her workers eat for a very low price, as long as we let her know if something was getting low in stock for the customers. She made sure we wrote it down and delivered it to her, running the place with a lot of sticky notes. On more than one occasion, I'd thought about writing on a sticky note how grateful I was for her adopting me into her family. The Sunflower was like a family to me. But I'll be the last one to actually admit that out loud.

Chapter Seven

Jesse

Tuesday and Wednesday I had a grand total of three births. The last was in the middle of the night. Haley was angry she was woken up for me to ask where she had put my car keys. She still hadn't forgiven me about the new rule of not going over to her boyfriend's house and didn't tell me where the keys were. I finally found them under a pile of her homework on the kitchen table.

Opening the front door, I felt a gust of the cold night wind and grabbed my heavier coat and mittens, then rushed to the car. The steering wheel felt frosty despite the gloves covering my hands. I drove the half hour to the birthing center, whispering a prayer about Haley.

Lord, you know Haley better than I do. You know just what she needs and when. Please show me what to do as I raise her during these crazy teenage years. I'm so lost.

The driving time flew by and soon enough the car reached the birthing center parking lot. Turning off the car, the silence was embraced with the warmth leftover from the heater. Wishing I could keep driving and praying, reluctance came to leave my sanctuary. If the walls of my car could talk, what would they say about the countless prayers I had prayed about everything from handling births, to making life decisions about my teenage daughters?

An hour later during the birth, the mother was already at the transitional stage. "Alright Angie, you've got to really try hard. I know you're tired but put your all into this," I encouraged, clutching her hand. Angie sighed and nodded her head. She was between contractions, grateful for a well-deserved break.

"I don't know if I can do this!" Angie said. Lily wiped her sweat with a towel.

"Yes, you can. Angie, look right here," I pointed to her eyes and then mine. It was a comfort remembering my own birth, my doula doing that for me, and it making a world of difference. It gave me a sense of empowerment, as if I could do anything. Angie followed my directions. We guided her through some breathing and counting to help her along, having more breaks in between.

"One. Two. Three. Okay go. Push! Come on, Angie. You can do this. You're going to meet your baby soon. Keep going." She pushed so hard, and I could see beads of sweat dripping down her red face. Our intern was nearby so I asked her to wipe Angie's face. She was towards the end. We grabbed the roll-away full-length mirror that was nearby so that she could see her progress.

"Angie, reach down and touch your baby. The head is out!" I said. Dark circles encased Angie's eyes. Weary, she reached down.

"You're doing great," Lily said as she held Angie's hand. During each contraction, Angie would squeeze her hand tight while her face turned bright red.

Twenty minutes later the baby was out and with gentle hands, I laid him in Angie's arms, wrapped in a blanket. She put him right to her chest and he latched on right away. The room was silent for a moment, except for the sound of Angie whispering to the baby, "I love you." My heart soared. Seeing the new mother hold her baby is the best part of my job. Without warning, I thought of the moment I held Haley when she was first born. If there hadn't been more work to be done, I would have wept right there on the floor.

"Where's her husband?" I asked, helping with cleanup.

Lily smiled. "The poor guy. He was a little queasy during the birth, so I sent him out to the front room to relax." She peeked around the corner. "Yup. He's still there. Holding his head and chewing a peppermint candy. It happens sometimes with the first baby."

"That's not the worst we've seen. Remember the husband who passed out towards the end of his wife giving birth? His arm even bled from hitting it on the side of the bed," I said, distracting myself with chatting.

"Oh yeah. How could I forget that one?" Both Lily and I looked over at Angie. She was holding the baby's fingers. I held back tears.

"You okay, Jess?" Lily asked as she changed the top blankets on the bed. We had moved Angie over to the comfortable recliner so she could rock the baby.

I pointed to the other room, motioning for her to follow me. I waited until we were out of earshot to speak. "It's Haley. She hates me so much."

Lily was aware of what I had been going through the past couple of years with Haley. She had even witnessed a couple outbursts. "She doesn't hate you. Haley just doesn't understand what it's like being a mom. When she has her own kids, I'm sure she'll see what you're doing. Right now, it's just hard. She's a teenager. It comes with the territory."

"In some ways she's also jealous of my work. A lot of times I either have a prenatal appointment or a birth. She's mentioned how much I'm gone. I thought she would be glad I was out of her hair."

"No. She wants you there." Lily stopped to think. "I have an idea. Why don't you take some time off, Jess? It'll be good for you and your family. We have my other midwife friend from Billings coming next week. She even talked about helping out while she was here."

I considered it for a moment. Haley's hurtful words from the week before came to my mind about how she wished she had a different mother. "I don't think it's a good idea. Maybe down the road after the psycho at home cools off." I hear the door to our clinic open, but I don't stop to see who it is. With my back to the door, I continued my rant. "Right now, work is an escape for me. You know. A way to get away from a spoiled, bratty teenager for a while. You understand this. You have a couple of your own at home. I wouldn't mind trading if you want."

Lily stopped and stared toward the front door. I turned around to see who she was looking at, surprised to see Haley standing in the doorway, eyes wide.

Chapter Eight

Kate

Flying to the mountains from where I lived in California was exhilarating. Chloe was there to greet me at the airport, enthusiastic as ever. She asked right away if I could take her Taurus to the tire store though, while she did some last-minute grocery shopping next door for her guest.

The waiting room was full, and a lady nearby told me a story about her children. "I walked back into the living room after loading the washer, and both my two and three-year-old were gone!"

"What happened?" I gasped.

"Turns out I'd accidentally left the front door open. I found them outside in our front yard playing with their new toys. Thankfully, the neighbor was standing nearby and said my boys had come over to her front porch a few minutes before. I'm just grateful they didn't stray out to the highway."

Sadly, I knew I could relate to this story. There had been times like this raising my kids where I didn't know where they were. It turned out fine in the end, but it sure did give me a scare.

It's amazing how many instant friends a mother can make. That day, I had several conversations related to motherhood with four different women in the waiting room at the tire store.

My phone rang. It was my husband, Mark. I sighed and put my hand to my head, staring at the caller ID for quite some time before answering. Good thing the lady I was talking with already had walked away to the counter to pick up her car. At least someone's tires were finished.

"Hello?" It seemed everyone in the waiting room was listening. I imagined their ears perking up as they eavesdropped on my conversation, so I stepped outside.

"I don't think this trip was a good idea," Mark snapped.

"Is Ethan crying again?" Ethan was our three-year-old. I attempted to keep my voice calm.

"Like you wouldn't believe," Mark hissed.

"Did you play the song for him I told you about?" I gazed into the distance, wishing the conversation was already over.

"What's it called again?" He huffed.

"Maggie's Lullaby. Something like that. It's on the playlist." I kept my voice even.

"When does your flight get back again?" I could hear the aggravation building even more in his voice.

"I'll send the info to your phone."

"And why does it seem like your friend is more important than us?"

Caught a little off guard, I knew better than to argue when he was in a mood like that. "I'll be home before you know it. Your parents are going to help too."

I wondered why he'd give me a hard time for visiting one of my best friends. He wasn't even going to be watching the kids most of the time I was gone. It's not like he was ever around anyways. He was married to his job.

"You know your friends have always been more of a priority than me. You shouldn't have bought that plane ticket. At least not until Ethan gets past whatever phase this is. I told you that, but you bought the ticket anyway. Of course, what I say doesn't matter. And I'm the bad guy for getting angry," he spewed. It wasn't often Mark exploded. What was going on?

Silence. I could feel the tears form in my eyes. I took a slow, deep breath. "I got to go, Mark. I'll talk to you later." That was the truth. A man who worked at the front counter of the tire store had opened the door and waved me down. Chloe's tires were finally done. Perfect timing.

Father, sometimes I don't know how to communicate. Marriage can be so hard and frustrating. Please help change my perspective. Change my heart. I want to be a loving and supportive wife for my husband, but it's so hard when his attitude can get me down and I don't know how to respond. I need your strength. I feel myself carrying all this bitterness around from things he's said and for being gone so much. I need your help to let it go. You're the only one who can help me right now. Please just give me your peace at this moment. Help Mark have peace too. Amen.

Chapter Nine

Marsha

While my granddaughter Maggie was here visiting, I pulled out the quilt my grandmother made. It was multi-colored including my favorites—red, white, and blue. I ran my hand across the most perfect stitched masterpiece I'd ever seen.

"This is so beautiful!" Maggie's eyes grew wide. We sat on the bed in the guest room, the one she always stayed in when she came to visit. It was still full of toys she used to play with when her cousins would come over, including a homemade wooden dollhouse, baby dolls, a Pocahontas Barbie, and a miniature farm scene.

"Each square in the quilt has a story that goes along with it. Reminds me of one of my favorite books I read to you when you were in second grade." I stood, spreading the quilt on the bed so we could see each square better.

"Grandma's Attic!" Maggie exclaimed, not missing a beat.

"That's the one," I smiled. "I remember one patch was from when Grandma Viola fell from a tree as a little girl and tore her dress. She fell out because her foot got caught in her skirt, and she twisted her ankle. Ohh! Landed in a bad way. It was the first time she decided to make the quilt. Her mother was always good at making them, and said it was something she just picked up while watching her." I imagined my grandmother, sitting at her favorite chair, working on this quilt.

"Did you ever think of adding your own stuff to the quilt?" Maggie asked.

"Never. I love it just the way it is." I stared at it, daydreaming about the times I would play at my grandmother's as a little girl. "And I know just who I'm going to give it to." I smoothed my hand again over a section of the quilt.

Maggie's eyes lit up even more. "I am so..."

"My friend Chloe over at the bakery is going to love this for her baby shower. I just got the invitation in the mail today," I said, excitement rising in my voice. "She's just like family. Wait till you meet her, Maggs. You're going to love her."

Maggie turned and stared out the window, then cast her eyes down. Did I hear a sigh?

"Oh, yeah. Chloe. She sounds great, Granny," Maggie mumbled and then changed the subject. "I really wish Dad was here right now. I'm sure he would love hearing the stories from the quilt." Tears pooled in her eyes. She was trying to hold them back.

"Me too. Even though my kids are grown, I still think about them all the time and worry about how they're doing." I folded the quilt and laid it back in the hope chest next to the bed.

"Still no word from him. The last time I talked to Dad, he mentioned how he married young and fast, and that was one reason his marriage isn't working out. He said he was stupid and didn't know any better."

I shake my head. "There's more to it than that, I'm sure. Now days it seems most marry when they're around twenty-five. Doesn't mean their marriage will last. It really depends on the people. I married young and fast and don't regret a minute of it. There's other couples that would say the same."

"That's good to hear." Maggie kicked her shoes off then snuggled under the top blanket of the bed.

"Chloe, the one getting ready to have a baby, was married at twenty. That's young, compared to others these days. I remember she told me her family didn't approve. Times were just different when I was that age. Folks didn't seem to care about how old people were when they married, or it could have just been the crowd I was around. There were hard-working farmers around us who were just known for marrying early. I say as long as you love someone and are able to support yourselves, why not?" I kicked my house shoes off, following Maggie's example.

"So you don't think Dad marrying young has anything to do with the problems they're having now?" Maggie seemed to really consider this.

"It doesn't matter how old he was when he married. People can date for years and get married when they're older and still have serious problems. Anyways, it's about time your dad fights for his marriage. I don't want to see him give up. I have never been one to meddle, but I think it's about time I give him a call."

A smile formed on Maggie's face; it must have reached her bright hazel eyes.

"You go, Granny." She sat up in the bed and handed me her cell phone from the nightstand beside her. "He hasn't answered for me. But go ahead. Leave a message."

Chapter Ten

Missy

I cannot believe I was invited to that stupid baby shower. How lame are those parties anyways? They spend an hour playing these cheesy games and open presents that are supposed to be "really cute" for the baby. They eat totally crummy snacks like cheese with a dumb hat. I guess I'll be going though. Marsha mentioned it in a quick meeting we had in the back of the restaurant, during Chloe's break outside.

"I wanted to mention this to all of you during Chloe's break. I heard that her friend invited all of you to her baby shower, and I think it would be a sweet gesture if we could be there to support her. It's important to attend events like this as a team. She's had some hard times, and it would be helpful if we each brought a small gift. Let me know if any of you want to pitch in and get something bigger. I'm not sure how those online registry things work, so don't be surprised if I ask one of you to help me with that," Marsha said.

"I can help I guess." I grumbled, raising my hand. Everyone looked at me, shocked.

What made me say that to Marsha, when I really didn't give a hoot about the shower? Could be that I just liked her. Some days she was my only friend amid my crazy life. Besides, I was decent with technology, and I thought Marsha could help me with gift ideas since she was asking us to go anyways.

"Oh. Thank you, dear." Marsha said, studying me. Was she surprised by my random outburst of wanting to help? I can be cool at times, right? I'm not always a jerk. I glanced around, betting a few of the staff members disagreed with that.

Later in the back of the restaurant right before closing time, I helped Marsha navigate the internet. She told me her grandson gave her a new laptop, and she had been waiting for the right moment to ask for help. I scrolled through Chloe's registry and noticed she entered some bigger things like a crib. Those items were not in my budget, but some of the small knick knacks like the little blanket or the pacifiers were.

Caught off guard, an image of a family flashed through my mind as I sat there at the back desk. That's what I deserved, for volunteering to help. Mushy stuff like baby showers could spur this on. It was my secret, but I often daydreamed about a family. I shook this thought away, turning back to the task in front of me.

I heard the front bell chime on the door to the restaurant, even though it was approaching closing time. Glad for the interruption, I hopped up to take their order. Watching to see who it was, my legs responded by jumping back. The man who had been reading *The Christmas Carol* approached the counter. I'd learned his name was Shawn. Oh dear. My hair was a wreck and I hoped it wasn't sticking up and out like it had been that morning.

"What can I get for you?" I asked him in a more polite voice than our first encounter.

He scratched his head. "I'll have the usual," he said, showing his perfect white teeth.

"Cinnamon roll?" I asked, nodding over to the display case.

"You know it. These are the best. Since coming here, I haven't stopped thinking about those rolls."

"Well, they aren't fresh this time, but I can heat one up for you if you'd like."

"That sounds great. Thank you so much, Missy."

I didn't know how he knew my name, since we don't wear name tags. Did he ask someone else what it was? Pondering this, I prepared the cinnamon roll and thought about my short story waiting for me at home. Another secret I kept from the world. Maybe I could scratch my original idea about the adventure story out in nature and write instead about a stalker who knew the protagonist's name.

After the cinnamon roll was heated, I brought it up to the counter, but Shawn was nowhere in sight. It was too cold outside, otherwise I'd have checked there. I shrugged my shoulders, then plopped on the new couch by the fireplace. This was one of the many attractions that brought people in during dinner time. I picked up Roald Dahl's *Matilda* off the shelf that I had read before and skimmed the pages. Maybe I could squeeze a few minutes of reading before cleaning up and shutting the place down. Another secret I kept from the world was my addiction to reading. Seemed there was a lot of secrets. Did anybody really know me?

About a page in, I heard a voice and jumped in my seat out of surprise. "That's one of my favorites. Good choice." Shawn's head peeked around the couch I was sitting on. He had been lounging on the floor around the corner, a book in his hands.

Chapter Eleven

Marsha

Approaching the big table at Chloe's baby shower with all the balloons, I noticed Missy standing off to the side, her arms crossed. She relaxed when she spotted me. Clutching my favorite necklace from my mother, I beamed. She had been the one to encourage me and told me I had a gift for making people feel comfortable and welcome. The necklace helped me feel close to her. She had passed away many years before.

"Come sit with me," I said, patting a chair next to me.

"Hey, Marsha. I was beginning to wonder if you were coming," Missy said.

From our spot, I observed more people coming through the front door. I knew about every family in our community and waved at several when they arrived. My good friend Mary, one of our most faithful customers at the restaurant, stopped by our table.

"Mary, I want to introduce you to Missy. She works at the bakery and is like a granddaughter to me. I'm sure you've seen her there when you've came in." I glanced over at Missy and saw her beaming. This was a rare occasion for her.

As the baby shower began, I listened to Chloe's sister-in-law stand up and introduce the first game of the afternoon. I'd been to so many baby showers, but maybe this was a game I still needed to learn.

"For this first game, we have three suitcases at the very end of the room. Inside you will find various articles of clothing. Some of them you will notice have something to do with babies. Your job is to run to the suitcases, put on everything you see in the suitcase, then run back," she pointed over at the other side of the room. "Then you pass the items to the next person in line, who does the same thing, only carrying it back to the suitcase and they start all over again. The first team to make it through everybody wins a prize," she explained.

I expected Missy's eye roll as the directions were presented. Sure enough, it came. She crossed her arms again. At work, she always had a frown on her face when Chloe acknowledged her. Chloe had kept her distance to give her some space, but still attempted to make Missy feel welcome at the restaurant, which I appreciated. Chloe knows well how I want the workers at my restaurant to be like a family.

"Alright! The first game. Let me just split everybody into teams," the host exclaimed.

Chloe's sister-in-law split us up into three equal teams. I told her that Missy and I would be on a team together. Missy gave me a disapproving look, but didn't protest about playing the game, to my relief.

There was a mixture of people on my team for this first game. A few ladies were wearing yoga pants and work out shirts, and looked as if they would be in shape for the running part of the game. I talked to a middle-aged lady on my team who told me she was a little worried she couldn't run very fast, but seemed excited to be there.

"When I say 'go,' you guys run as fast as you can across the room to the other side, and start putting on all the articles of clothing."

As she told us the instructions, I saw a young man named Shawn from my church, standing off to the side. He was assigned to my team. While I thought it was kind of funny and untraditional to see a man at a baby shower, I smiled. Not only does he attend my church, but he's also the man who had been hanging around the restaurant and couldn't put down Charles Dickens' *A Christmas Carol*. He had a sparkle in his eye, and I could tell he was enjoying being one of the only guys there, the other one being Chloe's husband.

I glanced over again at Missy, and maybe it was just my imagination, but she was gazing at this young man from the restaurant. When one gets to be my age, you realize these subtle things. I've seen plenty of this in my day.

"Hey, honey. Who's that guy who is here beside Chloe's husband? I've seen him in the restaurant before. Usually I know everyone's name that comes into the bakery." I said a silent prayer and asked forgiveness for lying. I knew a great deal about Shawn. Clutching my necklace, I hoped I could help Missy feel even more comfortable and at ease.

Missy changed positions and shrugged when I mentioned him. "Oh, him? That's just Shawn. He's been in the restaurant a time or two. Kinda weird that he's here at a baby shower."

As we continued the game, I observed how Missy kept her eyes on Shawn as he played. While most of the items in the suitcases included things related to a baby, the host threw in some high-heeled shoes. This made me laugh when it was Shawn's turn to run. He put on the high heels with no hesitation. He took off his shoes and then peeled off his socks, revealing his hairy feet.

"Whose shoes are these?" he said with a dimpled grin. It reminded me so much of my grandson. Honestly, I wouldn't mind if Shawn were my grandson as well. Maybe he could be like an adopted grandson. The more the merrier.

"They'll stink after this round, so not sure if anyone else wants to put them on. People may at least want to keep their socks on if they have any." He smiled again, and hurried down the floor.

It turned out to be quite the afternoon. I had mixed emotions about Missy and Shawn. Part of me enjoyed the thought of Missy taking a liking to him, and the other was worried. Very worried.

Chapter Twelve

Jesse

I spotted one of my old clients on the other side of the grocery store. Ducking behind a stack of bread, I remembered her making comments on all my tattoos when I first met her at our clinic. She held her nose up in the air, telling me how much tattoos were disgusting. Normally, it felt nice to see the mothers I'd helped around town with their babies. This time, I was in a big hurry and didn't feel like being judged. On top of it, Haley overhearing me tell Lily what a pain she was, really upset her. It made me physically ill, the more I thought about the silent treatment she was giving me yet again. Not to mention I had witnessed a birth that ended up in an emergency C-section.

To my disappointment, my old client somehow spotted me hiding behind the groceries.

"How are you, Jesse? Been delivering a lot of babies this month?" The woman asked, her eyes scanning me up and down. I smiled a fake smile.

"Oh, not a lot. We just have three mothers who are due this month. So mainly just appointments and such. They are all due around the end of the month."

"Wow. Hopefully you guys can both be there for each of the births," the woman said as she grabbed baby formula off the shelf. Hadn't I advised her about that type of formula? That kind was terrible for a baby. I wondered how her milk supply was doing.

"Yeah. Hopefully we don't have to use our back up room. That is always so overwhelming running back and forth between the two rooms," I rambled on. "I have my assistant, but Lily and I like to spend time with our patients, even if they are going through delivery at the same exact time. Let's just hope that no one else wants to have their baby at home that day, but wants to use the center. I doubt it, but you never know." I placed some chocolate bars into my grocery basket. Knowing I'd regret the calories later, I justified it in my mind by thinking about how it would take my mind off the troubles with Haley. Or maybe a good workout at the gym could make up for the indulgence.

"The baby is so excited to be out of the house," the woman said, changing the subject. "She loves just looking around the store, taking it all in." I saw the dazzle in her eyes from being a new parent. She smiled as she held her baby and she cooed back at her. The baby had some large dimples. Right then I could only see one side.

Grinning at the sweet baby I'd delivered only months before, it made me sad, having flashbacks of Haley. She was growing up way too fast for me.

"I gotta grab us some things for dinner and rush home. But I'll hopefully see you around." The woman waved again. Did she sneer at my tattoos again? Or did I just imagine it?

"See ya," I mumbled, waving. I walked away down one of the deserted aisles. Being at the store stressed me out with how busy it was, so walking down one of the quiet aisles brought great relief. That day it was especially hard to talk to people.

That morning I'd witnessed a birth that didn't go the way I had planned. She started out fine, and it turned out she had to be transported to the hospital. She ended up having a C-section, due to distress with the baby and being exhausted. It was taking her too long, one of the other midwives at the hospital had claimed.

My blood boiling from all that was going on in life, I drove the half hour back home. It was time to get my car fixed. Sounded like something was about to fall off, and I didn't know what was wrong with it. Driving in the dark had always been a challenge for me, since deer were too hard to spot.

Thankful to reach home, I lugged the groceries through the front door, the lights in the front room dim. I threw the groceries to the middle of the kitchen floor, hoping the eggs didn't happen to be in one of those bags. Worried I'd broken something, I turned on the kitchen light to check. I was startled, turning to see Haley sitting on the couch close to her boyfriend. She pulled him close and kissed him long and hard. My head grew hot, not wanting to give into her little games. She was getting back at me for what I had said to Lily. The rules were clear: no guys over at anyone's house. Shutting the door to the master bathroom, I sat down on the lid of the toilet to catch my breath. Flashbacks of when I was teenager came to me. I'd been that girl who had made mistakes, gotten pregnant from being unresponsible. Now in my thirties, I knew guys were not to be messed with. I didn't want her to regret anything, just like I had.

If I let her continue on with this behavior, I couldn't live with myself. If I stood up to her and demanded that he leave, it could end up in another huge fight, several of which we'd had through the rocky teenage years. Finally, after stewing awhile, a thought came to me. I wasn't going to scream or yell at her or kick the boyfriend out. It was time for a whole new approach.

I marched straight to the kitchen, grabbed some cookies from the cookie jar that I'd allowed myself to indulge on the weekends, and snatched up the throw blanket from the back of the couch. Although it wasn't the weekend, I decided this was a special occasion for the cookies. Haley and her boyfriend were still sitting on the couch and kissing. Making myself as comfortable as possible on the other side of the couch, I propped my feet up on the coffee table and grabbed the remote. It was fun crunching the cookies as loud as possible, leaving all the crumbs.

"Want one?" I asked, stuffing a chocolate chip cookie in my mouth. The couple had stopped kissing and were staring at me, dumbfounded. I scooted closer to her boyfriend on the couch, then rested my head on his shoulder.

"Isn't this a nice evening? I'm glad you could make it." I peered over at Haley on the other side. Was that a small smile or was it just the lighting on her face?

Chapter Thirteen

Marsha

One crisp cool Friday evening an event took place a week after the baby shower in Spring Mountain in which tons of people from all over the country came and watched logger sports. It had been going on for three days, and business was extra busy at the restaurant. It's very rare to encounter rude customers, but one older gentleman must have been having a terrible day.

"What can I get for you today, sir?" I asked, glancing up at the clock on the wall. Two more hours till closing time.

"Get for me?" he snapped out of a daydream. Most of the time I'm behind the scenes baking or cooking for the restaurant, but sometimes scheduled time to be out with the customers is important to me, so the owner's not a stranger. This has really paid off over the years, as I know just about everybody who comes into my restaurant. That is, until there is a huge event in town. Then everything is a jumble.

The man had been staring at the menu for quite some time. He was holding up the line, and I could tell some of the other customers were getting impatient. Many had to get back to one of the logger events, and had planned to grab a quick meal in between the festivities. Little did they know, the restaurant was running behind.

"Oh. Ummm..." He cleared his deep voice. The man ran his hand through his long whiskers, which was mixed with some grays. His attire was something I would never think of someone wearing to a logger sports event. He had on a very expensive suit and shoes that made him look taller than he already was. His eyes were glazed over, as if he had just woken up and hadn't had his morning coffee yet.

"Get me one of them cinnamon rolls," he snapped.

"Okay, sir. No problem," I said, knowing something must be going on. I hoped the food would cheer him up.

"Boy, you're awfully cheerful today, lady," he frowned.

I didn't know what to say. Isn't that what servers are supposed to do for their customers? The man tapped his fingers on the counter and grumbled under his breath. It reminded me a little of Fred Mertz from The *I Love Lucy Show.*

"Hurry it up. I can't wait all day," he said loud enough for everyone to hear. "Don't you have some hot fresh coffee? It looks like it's been sitting out. I need it hot."

"I brewed that about 10 minutes ago, sir." I said, pointing over to the coffee machine.

"Stop calling me sir! I don't care if you brewed it 5 minutes ago, I want some made right now," he said, pounding his fist on the counter.

Studying him, it was clear his face was cherry red and his eyes tired. I felt my blood pressure rise a little by the sound of his voice. But looking at him, it was obvious something was very wrong. Maybe this man had been through something hard and it was fresh on his mind. Was it his family? I was tempted to close down the line and sit with him at a booth with a cup of hot tea.

"I'll be right back with your coffee. How do you like it?" I said.

The man huffed and puffed. "Black. Straight black. And hurry it up."

"I'll have it in no time. Now if you wouldn't mind just stepping over here and waiting while I get one of my employees up here to take the next order."

The man huffed again, but at least he moved to the side.

While walking to the back of the bakery to grab what I needed to brew fresh coffee, an idea came to me. Chloe was there visiting with another employee who was on their break. I tapped her on the shoulder.

"Chloe," I whispered. "I need you to do something for me. There's a man out there who is off to the side and I'm getting his coffee right now. He's having a really bad day. Please tell him he's the hundredth customer and he will get his meal free and can order anything he wants. It's on the house. Then grab Larry from the back. Another man might be able to help him with his bad day or whatever's going on with him."

Chloe didn't hesitate. She marched right up to the man and made the announcement.

"Eh. Don't care," he said, shrugging his shoulders.

"Either way, you get a free meal. You can use it now or maybe another time that you come in." Chloe's voice was soothing.

"I don't want to come in here again," he snapped. Chloe stopped. I could see the expression on her face as I brought the hot cup of coffee out to him. She was at a loss for words.

"Here we are," I said, presenting the coffee to him. Larry had just walked in, so Chloe waved him down. We headed to the back for a chat, as Chloe worked on finishing up another order.

"What's the matter?" Larry asked.

"The man ordering right now as had a very bad day. I think he needs another man to cheer him up," I whispered.

Larry considered this for a moment. "Anything in particular I should talk about?"

"Hmm. Maybe grab him out of line and tell him about the tool sale down the road. Every man gets excited about tools, right?" I said.

Larry studied me for a moment, then slowly made his way to the disgruntled man. All those years of being a youth leader, Larry was used to helping others. I remembered back to all the times in the grocery store he would see someone for the first time and say something like, "You heard about Jesus?" And it would be the most natural thing. He had a gift.

Larry somehow was able to talk to the grumpy man in line, serve him a hot meal, and chat with him about his life. I grinned ear to ear the entire time they sat at the corner booth. The man's defenses had come down. He relaxed in the booth, and had even slipped off his shoes.

After the restaurant closed, Larry informed me of his evening with the man. "Sounds like you were right, Marsha. There was something very wrong. He had just lost his wife a couple of days before he came into our store." Larry pulled my waist, bringing me into a hug.

"Oh no," I sighed. "I had suspected something like that. I can see why he seemed so tired and on edge. He had just been through a ton."

"It shows us that sometimes people act the way they do for a reason. Not excusing that kind of behavior, but it does help explain why." Larry hugged me for a long time and stroked my hair. Reminded me of our wedding day so long before.

"Thank you for talking to him. It seemed the more and more I talked and tried to serve him, the angrier he became." I pulled away and finished wiping down the counters.

"He explained that to me. He said later he felt terrible for the way he treated you. You remind him of his daughter, which reminded him of his wife again and...anyways, I could tell he felt really bad about it. He kept mentioning it." Larry grabbed a rag to help me clean. "Turns out he wants us over sometime for dinner to make it up to us. He used to be a chef at a fancy restaurant back east and just moved here to be closer to his sister. He's thinking about opening his own restaurant in a nearby town, where there's more people, but he hasn't quite found the right place yet.

"Wait...he thought I reminded him of his daughter?" I paused.

Larry chuckled. "Out of everything I just said, that's what you're stuck on?" He grinned. He was probably wondering if I'd catch that part of it.

"Well of course. Everyone thinks you are younger than you are."

"Fiddlesticks!" I giggled. "If anyone looks like they are 60 years old, it's me. Now come on. What did he really say?"

"Okay. He thought you were so old that...you fart dust," Larry said with a straight face.

I pretended to throw the wet rag at him. All those years of marriage, and I'm glad we still knew how to tease.

Chapter 14

Jesse

The Midwife

"I think my water just broke," Chloe said into the phone. Her voice sounded nervous.

"Okay. Explain what happened."

"I was sitting on the couch watching a movie and all of the sudden I felt this gush. The water keeps coming. I've felt like I've soaked some of my clothes already," Chloe confessed.

"Alright. You need to eat something and get some sleep so you'll have energy for when the baby comes. Get as much rest as you can," I said.

"Okay. I'll try." Chloe sounded anxious.

"Then call or text me to let me know how it's going later on. I'm at another birth right now, but I'll have my phone on me." I adjusted the phone to the other side as I prepared some decaf tea for my client. She was soothing her contractions in the tub.

"Okay, thanks." Chloe hung up.

I refocused my attention on the patient in front of me. She came from England and moved to the states after she married.

"How much longer do you think it will be?" she asked in her English accent. I was having her breathe through the contractions, encouraging her along the way.

"Don't worry about how long it's going to take. Each person's body is different. Just do your best to relax and not let yourself get stressed out. Your body was made to do this." I don't know how many times I've said those words to birthing mothers. But every single time, I mean every word.

"Look forward to those breaks," Lily told her after she had a long contraction. They were getting close together. The woman looked exhausted, yet so beautiful. I grabbed the shawl she'd made for me nearby. Although she was hot and sweaty, I felt so cold. She had been so kind to have made a shawl for Lily and I as a thank you gift for taking care of her. Such vibrant colors, including yellow, which is my favorite.

When the birth was almost over, I received a text from Chloe. It was around three or four in the morning, and I'd been up all night.

"The contractions are close together. I think it's time," Chloe texted.

Messaging her back, I let her know how long it would be for me to get to the birthing center. Lily went home to get some rest, and the hope was that she could take over for me later in the day.

When Chloe pulled up, I was grabbing some clean blankets from our storage upstairs, wondering in the back of my mind if I'd be sending her home that morning. We'd seen several times where the mothers were sent home because they weren't ready yet, although many were convinced they were. It would be disappointing for Chloe, but part of me felt relieved if that happened. It would have allowed me to drive home and get some sleep before things picked up even more.

I peered at Chloe's black bag, which was overflowing with clothes, electrolyte drinks, and CDs. She had her husband Peter carry it in for her. He looked calm and collected at that moment. Over those past few months, I was able to befriend Chloe and the appointments she would attend by herself were often a time of venting. She shared with me her worries about money, and her fears of parenting, especially since her dad had left their family when she was young.

Chloe lay on the bed for an examination, her eyes closing, on the verge of sleep. The bag of waters had broken in a spot where the test I administered did not show there was amniotic fluid. She'd be sent back home, at least until she was further along. Chloe's face turned into a frown.

"I don't want you to feel disappointed or discouraged. This happens sometimes. You did the right thing by telling me you felt it was time to come in. At least now you can go back to the comforts of your own home as you go through early labor some more." I tucked some loose clothes into Chloe's bag and handed it to Peter.

Chloe nodded, her eyes puffy and red.

"You can take the sleeping things I told you about that are safe for the baby. Try to get sleep if possible. You'll definitely need it later."

Peter reloaded their car as Chloe dressed. I helped put her arm into her jacket.

"I'll have Lily check in with you later this afternoon to see how you're doing. Hang in there. You're strong," I squeezed her left shoulder.

Chloe smiled and said, "thank you so much, Jesse."

As they walked out the door, I prepared everything for the next round of appointments that Lily would be doing. She only had a few scheduled that day, and she'd be hoping afterwards Chloe would have made a little more progress.

Later that afternoon Lily texted Chloe to see how she was. She responded that the contractions were closer together and felt like she had to keep using the restroom. Typical first-time mom descriptions.

Lily asked her if she was ready to come over for an examination to see how she was progressing.

"I'll be over soon with my husband," she messaged.

As soon as she came back to the center, Lily told her she would be having the baby that day. She had a nurse come over and give her the first round of antibiotics, since Chloe had tested positive for Group B strep and part of her bag of waters had broken.

"We have a nurse come in to do it, since it's the law. We know how, but for some reason the state says that a registered active nurse from the hospital has to administer the antibiotics, since we are a free-standing birth center," Lily informed Chloe.

After the first round of antibiotics, we asked her if she wanted to get into the tub.

"Wow. Really? I'm already at that point?" Chloe sounded surprised.

"Yeah. You can make yourself comfortable in there, and it helps ease the contractions." In the birthing classes a doula had told her we save the tub for the most intense part of birth. She wasn't all the way there yet, but I could see she was having a hard time with them and the water could soothe her aching body. Several midwives I knew called the water in the tub nature's epidural.

As Chloe sat in the water, we left her there for a while to hang out with her husband and listen to the calm music playing. "I don't want you to feel like we're abandoning you. We're just giving you some space, since sometimes people crowding around can slow down the labor process. Please let us know if you need anything," I said.

"Oh. I don't feel like you guys are abandoning me. It's kind of nice. Thank you," Chloe said. I thought about the transitional stage of birth. She wouldn't sound as calm as evening approached.

A while later, Lily grabbed the baby doppler and placed it in the water so she could hear the baby's heart rate.

"Wow. I didn't know you could put those in the water," Chloe said.

"Yep. Pretty cool, huh?" Lily said. "Hmm...There is a little hesitation there with the baby. We'll keep monitoring him."

Chloe raised one eyebrow. Would her baby be okay?

As she continued to labor in the tub, she finally decided she was ready to hop out.

"You want to try some different laboring positions?" our assistant Madison asked.

"Sure. It was getting a little uncomfortable in the tub," Chloe said.

"How about we try the ball?" Madison grabbed a big blue yoga ball over in the corner, next to the toiletries.

"I could try that."

We left the room and Chloe changed into dry clothes. Madison prepared some of her special herbal tea.

“Here’s to the calm before the storm,” Madison lifted her mug into the air.

Chapter 15

Chloe

At home before contractions started-8:00 pm

"What would you guys like to have for dinner tonight? Homemade ravioli or a casserole?" I peered into the fridge, grateful some friends had thought to bring meals while we waited for the arrival of my baby. My stepmom Rory and sister Lucy were also in town visiting.

"Hot dish sounds the best," Rory said.

I peeled the foil off the casserole, realizing it had broccoli, which Rory hated. Grabbing the ravioli, I preheated a pan on the stove and glanced out the window to see the sunset.

When dinner was served at the table, we sat in silence awhile, staring out at the sun setting behind the mountain.

"We never talked about that email I sent you that day," Rory blurted.

I thought about the email and how I'd wanted to talk to Kate about it, but never had the chance. Rory had said some hurtful things. I looked over at Lucy as if to say, "Oh boy. Here we go." She gave me a look of sympathy.

Good thing Peter had stepped out for some groceries. He would have joined in on any arguing. I wanted to run far away from family feuds as possible. Lucy knew this about me, so she grabbed my hand. "You guys gotta work this out," she whispered. "Don't run from your problems, Chloe. I know through the years that's what you've always done."

"Why did you have to go and marry a man with no money? He barely has two pennies to rub together. Just look at this place you're living in. It's filthy and no place to bring a newborn baby." Rory pointed at the tiny back yard. We hadn't had time to clean up the trash yet left by the owners when we'd moved in.

My mouth dropped open. I had a feeling Rory felt this way about my marriage and home, but it was surprising to bring it up when I was so close to having a baby.

"You should have married Daniel, like your father and I wanted for you. At least you would have lived in a decent place, and closer to us," Rory said.

I clenched my teeth to stop from screaming. *Lord, how should I even respond to that? Will you please give me the words to speak?*

Lucy's eyes pleaded with me to respond and resolve the argument. Knowing Rory, she must have vented a lot about it on the long drive up to visit.

I couldn't take it anymore. Rory had crossed a line. It was time for me to bury the shy, timid Chloe everyone knew. "I live up here in the mountains. Get over it. And it's none of your business how much money we have. It's not like you're my real mom anyways. You're just the woman dad had an affair with. He only married you because he thought you were pregnant," I blurted.

Rory put down her napkin beside the plate and stood. "You ingrateful brat. After all the things your father and I have done for you over the years, and this is how you treat me?" Rory pushed away from the table.

She didn't know about the anxiety attacks I'd had the night I found out about her and Dad so many years before. Or the night I went to the ER because the stress had taken its toll on my health. I hadn't told her about the low self-esteem I'd lived with all these years. All because of her poor decisions. I stood from the table and clenched my fists.

"Get out of here!" I screamed. "Leave Lucy here."

I felt a sudden gush, and wondered if my water had just broke.

My face turned red. I peered over at Rory. "Um...I think my water just broke," I said.

"What?" Rory stared at me, taking a step closer. The anger had gone from her eyes.

"Yeah. I think it just broke."

I headed to the bathroom to change, then out the back door to the car to call the midwife. I didn't want to make a huge deal out of it, but I wanted to let them know that my water broke and that labor was probably coming soon.

"Can you explain to me what happened?" Jesse asked.

As I explained, Jesse told me to eat then get as much rest as I could. I felt like a nervous wreck. I expected birth was going to be the worst physical pain I had ever experienced in my life. How could I simply sleep when the baby would be coming soon? To top it all off, I had just exploded at my stepmom. How was I going to deal with all the stress? I walked back into the house, feeling awkward. Rory and Lucy had popped in a DVD and were just sitting on the couch. I was surprised Rory hadn't left.

"What was that all about?" Lucy asked.

"My water just broke. I called the midwife and she told me to get as much rest as I can, so I'm going to bed. Mom's on her way. She should be here around 10:00 tonight." I stared at Rory. Surely that would get her off the couch and heading to a motel far on the other side of town. She wasn't welcome in my home anymore.

"Okay." Rory gazed at me with excitement, her expression soft. I was surprised she had changed her tune so fast and didn't rip into me. But then again, I was about to give birth to her first sort of grandbaby.

I turned to Lucy to ask a favor, distracting me from the way Rory was acting. "Would you mind writing some memory verses on these note cards for me to read later? I have a couple of Bibles here."

"Sure. That's a good idea." Lucy grabbed the notecards from me and sat in the blue rocking chair.

Rory even joined in. I changed into pajamas and laid down in the guest bedroom, since our room was so messy. We were wanting to rearrange everything before the baby came but didn't complete it.

I tossed and turned and tried to sleep, but how could anyone possibly do that when they were about to go through a ton of pain and water was gushing all over the place? Rolling out of bed, I inched back to the living room, wondering if my Rory and Lucy went out to get a motel room, but they hadn't. They were still sitting on the couch, writing memory verses on the notecards. I smiled, grateful Lucy willing to go along with my ideas.

"Hey. Mom should be here really soon."

"Okay." Rory didn't seem phased by that statement, like I thought she would be. I figured she would want to be long gone, by the time my mom arrived. There had been many hurtful words exchanged between them over the years.

"Thank you for writing those for me, guys." I sat down on the floor next to the wall and sighed. "I'm so nervous."

"Would you say this is the most important day of your life?" Rory's voice was soothing and understanding. She talked about how I needed to get some rest too, because I started talking to them at 90 miles an hour about the upcoming birth.

Finally, I slowed down. "Well...goodnight you guys. I will try and text you and keep you updated about what's going on."

"Alright. Love you." Lucy smiled. In a way, I was so glad they were there with me, despite the blow out earlier. I don't know what I would have done without someone there with me.

Back in bed, I dozed in and out, then felt the contractions come. As early morning approached, I could feel they were close together, but the midwife told me to wait. I dragged out of bed to take a warm shower.

Mom arrived the night prior around 10:00, like we were expecting. She kept calling me along the way, updating about their travel stories of how they needed to get their trailer fixed, and some people saw them in the parking lot and offered to come and help with the tools they had. My mom had bought this little trailer "pod" as she called it, and she insisted bringing it up, since we didn't have much room in our house.

Mom said she prayed and prayed she could make it before the baby came. She never was able to see me in person with my pregnant belly, and for some reason, really wanted to. She'd gotten her wish and made it just in time. Approaching my bedside with a giant stuffed llama, she presented me the gift and talked about how I should name it for the baby. I held it, daydreaming about the baby that would soon be born. What would he be like?

Chapter 16

Missy

Although it was my day off, I headed to the restaurant.

"Hey, Missy. How are you doing this morning? Let me put these muffins in the oven a bit longer and then I'll be right out." Marsha disappeared before I had a chance to answer.

I didn't feel like spending my day off around the stupid, smelly old apartment. It was time to just get out.

"Were you wanting to pick up some extra hours today?" Marsha asked as she wiped her hands on her apron.

"No. I wanted to see if we could talk maybe on your next break. I have some things rolling around in my mind," I said, fiddling with my hair. My palms felt sweaty, even though it wasn't hot in the room.

"That would be great, Missy. After the breakfast rush dies down, I'll put someone else in charge for a bit, and then we can go talk back in the Sunflower Room."

"That would be great. I'll just wait in there." I pasted on a smile.

As Marsha busied herself with greeting customers and running the cash register, I grabbed a book off the shelf before heading to the Sunflower Room.

The room was down a wide hallway, right behind the restaurant. It was open sometimes for special occasions and had two glass doors with soft wooden trim. Guests could see the large square tables and embroidered sunflower tablecloths Marsha made herself. The wallpaper even matched. The spacious room had a stage at the front of it. I knew the town used it sometimes for gatherings, small birthday parties, and meetings. In the quiet of that moment, I noticed all the little details Marsha took special care to put together, such as little place cards.

"Laughter is great medicine," I read off one of the cards placed on the table.

"He leads me beside still waters," another one said.

Taking a seat at one of the tables, I opened the book I'd picked out to the first page. It was Anne of Green Gables by L.M. Montgomery. I was halfway through the first chapter when there was a loud knock at the door. Thinking it was Marsha, I placed a bookmark in the pages and closed it. Looking up, I realized instead it was Shawn standing in the doorway. The book lover.

He cleared his throat. "There's a meeting in here today," he said in a rude tone. "They'll be here in about ten minutes, so I suggest you move your stuff out."

Wow. That wasn't what I was expecting at all.

"Excuse me?" I barked. "I'm in here waiting on Marsha. I'll move when I want to." I turned around and opened my book back up, refusing to move. He cleared his throat again. Shawn sounded hoarse. Maybe he had a cold.

"I don't feel like arguing with you right now. Just please be out when they get here." He slammed the door.

I thought about staying planted and even sitting through the meeting, just to get back at him for being rude. It didn't seem like the Shawn I'd met before. The man who came to order coffee and cinnamon rolls at the front counter seemed fun and humorous. What had happened? I was the only one allowed to be grumpy around there.

I watched Marsha walk through the door a minute later. "I am so sorry, Missy. I forgot there is going to be a town meeting in here today. We'll just have our little chat in the back kitchen. I'm baking some muffins there. It's not as nice of a spot, but we can be away from everyone in there."

I just nodded my head, still thinking about Shawn. He seemed like such a nice guy when I'd seen him in the restaurant. Why the sudden outburst?

I followed Marsha into the back kitchen where all the ovens were full. There were several dozen muffins in each oven, including blueberry, poppy seed, and banana nut. The aroma filled my senses with its comforting smell. She led me to a back wooden table with fruit, then laid a small plate in front of me with a hot steaming poppyseed muffin with gobs of butter dripping off the sides. I could still see the steam coming off the top. My stomach growled since I'd skipped breakfast that morning, but the muffin needed to cool.

Marsha pulled up a chair beside me. "What's on your mind today, Missy?" Marsha said in a gentle voice as she pulled the butter closer to her to place some on her own blueberry muffin. Her voice was soft and even as she buttered the muffin. She seemed in no hurry at all.

I gulped. It would be the first time I had talked to anybody about my little girl since she had been born. Other than the boyfriends I had in the past, of course. How could I put all of it into words?

"I feel like I've been carrying this huge weight around for so long. I just need to talk to you about it. Honestly..." I paused, searching for the right words. "I feel at this point in my life, you're my only real friend. The one I know who seems to truly care," I said, picking at my half-chewed fingernails. Marsha gave me her full attention. I glanced around to make sure no one could hear.

Sighing, I pushed back the tears. It was difficult rehashing the memories. "Back when I was 16, I met a guy at a party who was from out of town. It only took that one night, and I found out later I was pregnant. When I went to find the guy, he had already left town. Nobody knew what happened to him."

Marsha reached for my hand. "That would be so hard."

I pulled my hand away. "When it happened, I didn't tell anybody outside my family about the pregnancy, except one of my friends at the time. She thought I should abort the baby, but I couldn't do it. I put the baby up for adoption instead."

"That was a very smart choice, Missy," Marsha said.

I shrugged my shoulders. "I'm glad I had the baby. Just wish I'd have kept her." I bowed my head. "I wonder about her all the time. If it had been an open adoption, would it have made it easier or worse? I just wish I would have done things differently."

Marsha reached for my hand again. That time, I didn't pull away. Tears pooled in my eyes.

"What is her name?" Marsha whispered.

"Laura Beth. I miss her so much." There was silence between us awhile. "Every boyfriend I've ever had broke up with me because of this. Or that was at least one reason. It seemed I just couldn't move on, and it consumed my thoughts and conversations. They were tired of me obsessing over it, I guess."

"It's not an easy thing you went through, and any man who isn't considerate of that isn't worth your time," Marsha said.

I nodded my head, pushing down thoughts of the recent breakup, hoping I could move on.

"Want another muffin?" Marsha nodded as she opened an oven that held the banana nut muffins.

"Maybe just one more. With the butter of course." I couldn't resist.

The warmth comforted me, while savoring every bite. Finishing the muffin, I pushed the plate aside and wiped my hands on my shirt. "Marsha," I hesitated. "Have you ever seen a child who didn't have their biological mom or dad with them turn out...normal?

Marsha looked up at me, empathy in her eyes. "Oh, Missy." Marsha stood from her chair and walked over to embrace me. I let the tears flow. I'd had so much worry for my daughter, not knowing how she was doing.

After the last sob, Marsha sat back in her chair. "Not many know this, Missy, but one of my good friends was adopted by a loving family. He'd been with them since he was two years old and then moved out of the house at 18 to attend college."

"What is he like?"

"A very successful young man. Honest, caring, compassionate. A hard-worker. Oh, he had a time of questioning in his teens and wondered about his biological parents, but he knows where his true identity comes from."

"So, he doesn't seem messed up because his real parents abandoned him? What do you mean he knows where his true identity comes from?"

"Just like anyone, adopted or not, he had to do some soul searching. Naturally, a child wonders about their family and where they come from. But, like with my friend, he discovered his identity doesn't come from who his parents are. It comes from Him." Marsha pointed up.

"Him?" I felt so lost as to what Marsha was saying.

"He found out his identity comes from the Lord."

"Oh," I sighed. Since working at the restaurant, Marsha had spoken of God many times. Most of the time I just rolled my eyes. This time, I stared straight ahead in silence. I didn't understand what God had to do with anything. And what did she mean by identity?

Marsha stood to grab a cloth to wipe the table down. "You're like a daughter to me, Missy. I hope you know that. I care so much about you." She stopped wiping the table and ran her hand down my cheek. "Don't feel like a failure because you gave your baby up for adoption. She's in the Lord's hands. She'll be just fine."

In that moment, I let the tears and the memories from all those years before wash over me. It was comforting to hear someone else say my baby girl would be alright.

"Maybe you could meet my friend who was adopted sometime," Marsha said as she went back to wiping the table down.

"Hmm. You think that would be a good idea?"

"Sure. You could just hang out and be friends. I know a lot of other young people who also attend my church, if you want a friend to cruise around town with. But I bet he would love to talk about his journey with you, if you're interested."

"Umm....I don't know." I felt it would be embarrassing to open up to a random stranger about my past.

"It was just a thought. If you ever change your mind and just need a friend your age, let me know." Marsha searched my eyes. "Also, Larry and I would love to have you over for dinner really soon. Larry's been helping me tweak recipes for years, but it's always nice to have someone else outside the family try them. And I trust your judgement."

"That sounds great. Thanks."

"I consider you one of my friends, Missy. I love you so much." Marsha offered another soft smile.

"That's one reason I came to you. Thanks for letting me share part of my past and for serving the muffins."

"I'm here whenever you need me. Truly. Don't hesitate to come talk with me anytime."

Chapter 17

Kate

I'd been in Spring Mountain awhile, waiting for Chloe's baby to be born and desired to explore the ins and outs of the quaint and beautiful town. Back home in L.A., it took me an hour just to get through the traffic to the grocery store that I wanted. But in Spring Mountain, everything was within walking distance.

Strolling through the streets, I thought about how I really liked the town. It was the perfect spot for a little getaway. The more I pondered it, the more I wished Mark was there. We'd been married over fifteen years. After several kids and the craziness of life, the truth was that I didn't see him much anymore, and it really put a strain on our marriage. He had switched jobs in the fall and was working for a new big company. He told me making the switch from his old job to the new one would help us get out of debt faster. I was on board at the time but didn't realize he would have to be spending so much time away from home.

He'd usually get home at nine, then the kids would have to get to bed since they had school the next day. Some nights he wouldn't get in until midnight, because he was out working on a new project or deadline. I'd so much to talk to him about it but wasn't sure how to say it. I knew he'd been out working so hard to provide for our family, but at that point I wished he had his old job and schedule. He may have earned way less money, but to me, it was worth having the time with him and the kids together.

Scolding myself, I thought about how I grateful I should be. A month earlier, his parents offered to watch the kids while we went on a little weekend getaway to celebrate a late anniversary. They even paid for most of it, which was sweet. We went to a cabin that had a tiny kitchen, a huge king size bed, and a beautiful front porch that overlooked the lake. It was the most time we had spent together in a long time, and I loved every moment of it. When the weekend ended, I was disappointed.

Approaching the Spring Mountain Bookstore, I glanced inside the windows and decided to go inside. Everything was decorated in lighthouses, with soft blues and ocean wallpaper. There were sound effects of the ocean waves playing through some speakers. Browsing the store, I realized it was more than just a bookstore. A pharmacy was in the back, and a little bar area where people could order Italian sodas with mouth-watering flavors. My choice included peach with whipped cream, and a macadamia nut cookie. After ordering, I recalled Chloe telling me about the bakery where she worked, and how it was the best place in town to get baked goods and breakfast but said it could get busy at times.

I watched a couple stroll by the front of the store, stopping near the door and kissing. They looked young, perhaps in their mid-twenties. Assuming they were dating or engaged, I didn't want them to catch me staring. Hopefully their marriage wouldn't fall apart like mine was doing at that moment. The longer the couple stood by the window, the more I imagined steam coming out my ears. They held hands and the bells on the door chimed. Oh, great. Exactly what I needed. Just a couple of young love birds kissing in front of me while my marriage was in shambles. My heart ached, bitterness creeping in like sudden darkness on a winter night. Was the bitterness towards Mark? Or was it towards myself for not knowing how to discuss our problems with him? Maybe a bit of both.

The couple circled through the store a couple times, browsing at the books and whispering. A few times, they'd stop and laugh at some inside joke. I'd had enough. I waved at the cashier and thanked her. The rain was picking up outside and, in the distance, lightening brightened the dark cloudy sky. Picking up the pace, the rain came harder and harder.

After walking three blocks, I was out of breath from the fast pace. My stomach was churning in knots. I ignored it and focused on getting back, but the longer the walk, the more my stomach hurt. At the end of the eighth block, I clutched my stomach and fell over in someone's lawn, the rain coming at a steady pace. Mud puddles surrounded me. I hoped the residents were not home to see me sprawled out in their yard. My body sobbed and shook as I clutched my stomach, throwing up right in their front lawn. Embarrassed, I heard the front door open. An older man came onto the porch. At the corner of my eye, he didn't appear to be angry. He watched me for a minute, then called out through the rain, "Are you okay, ma'am?" I nodded my head and continued to lose my breakfast in his yard. Out of exhaustion, I laid my head down for a moment in the soaked grass, then pulled myself up out of the yard. Looking up, the man was gone.

I was relieved he'd left, and embarrassed he saw me at all. I'd wondered at first if there was any way to clean up the mess I had just made, but watched how the rain was picking up even more, and knew it should clean off the lawn in no time.

Pondering why I'd been sick, in my mind it was attributed to stress and all the thinking I had been doing back at the bookstore. Sometimes stress could wreak havoc on a person's stomach. Either that or the little shop had just served a bad Italian soda. I felt the world spin and my vision give out. I fell to the ground again, blacking out in the yard.

Chapter Eighteen

Marsha

Larry was just getting over a cold. Handing over the phone, he reached to grab a tissue. "Here, Marsha. Penny's on the phone for you," he said.

"Penny? I've been meaning to give her a call. It's been a few months since I've last talked to her," I smiled. Penny was one of my good friends from way back in college.

Penny lived in Mexico near the border. Her husband ran a mission with her, where people from all over the United States traveled to help build houses for locals and make meals. The facilities were set up like a camp and provided a place for volunteers and other workers to come stay and help with building projects. They had a few bunk houses and a large dining hall for people who came through. In the five years that Penny had been helping to run the mission, I had visited twice and fell in love with Mexico and the people they served.

"Hey, Penny! How are things going?" I sang into the phone.

"Marsha. They are going well. My daughter just had a baby boy in Tennessee. I'm officially a grandmother!"

"Congratulations, Penny! That's so exciting. You'll have to mail me some pictures." I fiddled with the spices in the cabinet, rearranging them back into alphabetical order.

"I can do better than that. I can send them to you through my new Smartphone. My granddaughter is making sure I keep up with the latest technology. I was against it at first, but now I like it, even though I'm old," she laughed.

"But I'll always be older," I joked back. "I still haven't given in to the latest technology. I'm just fine with my land line phone. I think that's all I'll ever need. Sorry you won't be able to send me the pictures through a cell phone. Guess you'll just have to resort to good old-fashioned mail delivery," I chuckled.

"I guess I'll have to," Penny joked in her pretend sad voice. "Hey, I called to tell you about the baby, but I also wanted to let you know some other news." I could hear the excitement in her voice.

"Did you guys get in another vacation to the Swiss Alps?"

"No way. That was a one-time gift from a friend. We'd never be able to afford that."

"I'm dying to know your news," I said, grabbing the salt and pepper and putting it at the forefront of the spice cabinet.

"Ever since we found out about my daughter and the baby, we thought about moving closer to her in Tennessee. My husband pursued the idea, and he just had an interview a couple days ago for a job at one of the churches. He also interviewed at a local car place, and he was offered both," she said. The excitement rose even more in her voice. "I'm excited to be moving over in about a month."

"You guys had been thinking about giving up the mission? I didn't even know."

"Well, it was just a thought when we first found out. I knew that he was going to apply for jobs, but I had no idea he was going to get it. And that's not only the half of it."

"What did the head of the camp say when you told him you would be moving on?"

"We haven't mentioned it to him yet. We have been talking about it being a possibility for a couple of months, but I don't think he took us seriously. I even kept him updated about the interviews. He told us he hoped that we didn't get it, because losing us would be too hard. But I think he would understand. That's what I also wanted to talk to you about, Marsha."

"About your boss?" Tired, I pulled up a folding chair to sit and listen.

"I did mention to him about you, and he said he remembered you coming to visit those couple of times. I told him how you and your husband always wanted to be missionaries and help other people in that way. That you loved helping with the houses and the food when you were here. He even remembered your cooking and how much he wanted to take some home to his family. The last time I talked about you, he asked if you would ever be interested in joining their staff. He said you were a great cook and that your husband was a master jack of all trades."

"Wow. Cross-cultural work has always been on my list of things to do before I die," I said.

"I know. And now with my husband and I moving to Tennessee, that opens even more opportunity for you guys. I was the head baker and cook for the camp, and Jeff helped with building the houses and maintenance around the facilities. He pretty much did it all. He is so good at it, but I think he prefers working on cars. This job in Tennessee will be a good fit for him and he will also have time to be on staff part time and help at the church with their youth group. I think it will be the perfect fit."

I had so much to process with Penny's proposition. Leave my business of almost forty years? The one Larry and I had built from the ground up?

"I don't know, Penny. I have my bakery here. I couldn't imagine selling it or moving away from the home I've always known. But on the other hand, the idea of a new adventure does appeal to me." I wrapped the phone cord around my fingers.

"Exactly. I knew you would be open to it. Just let me tell my boss about the new jobs and then I'll let him know you're interested."

"Hold it hold it," I almost yelled into the phone. "I haven't given you an answer yet. You don't know how much thought goes into something like this. I must talk to Larry and I'm not even sure if this is something I should pursue. It's so much change. I'm still trying to process all of it. So don't tell your boss anything yet. Give me a week to think about it and pray. Maybe even a month."

"Come on, Marsha! What happened to your sense of adventure? You told me how you needed to reach out of your comfort zone and how much it's always been your dream to help here. Well, here's your opportunity. I wish I could be there right beside you, but we want so much to be close to our new granddaughter."

"I know. But it's not just my decision. We need time to think and pray about it. If I were to ever do this, I'd also need to find someone to run the bakery. I couldn't ever just let my business die. Larry would agree with me that we want this restaurant to carry on. There's just so much to think about." I remembered then how Penny had been very impulsive in our college days. She hadn't changed a bit.

"I say you should put it up for sale and move over here. You don't even have to wait for the sell. It can sell while you're down here."

"Penny..."

"What? You have plenty of money in savings, right? You're one of the most frugal people I know. And besides, you would probably get your first paycheck in a month within arriving. Not that it pays a ton."

"Penny, I just don't know. I can't tell you yes or no right on the spot. This would be a huge life change." I felt she was being too pushy, but part of me really wanted what she was offering. "Are you sure they wouldn't want some people way younger than us? I mean, we are kinda older folks to be taking on a whole camp."

"Well they had us, didn't they? Oh, and it wouldn't be just you guys. There are other folks around here who are on staff, and they are going to be hiring another guy to help with what my husband did. I think they saw it was too much for one person. Besides, I'm not that much younger than you and they kept me on staff all this time, right?"

"Well, I guess."

"These positions are for anyone willing to serve the Lord. It's a great opportunity, Marsha. I don't think you'll want to let this one go. You have so much experience and you're an expert at baking and running things."

"I think you want to have me come so that you don't feel so bad telling your boss that you're leaving. You want him to know there is someone ready to go that you suggested."

"No. Not at all. I've been wanting you to come on staff for a long time. I see this as better timing than before."

I sighed. "Again, what a lot to process."

"I know. But isn't it exciting? A new adventure in Mexico? And you love it here. The staff people are nice, it's beautiful. Serving here is very fulfilling work."

"I don't even speak Spanish."

"There are interpreters. And you'll mainly be with the volunteers anyways. They speak English. And you'll pick it up soon enough in case you go out."

"How do you even know he'll hire me? Don't I have to go through a long process of interviewing?"

"Trust me. Since you have my recommendation and he's already met you, the hiring process won't take long. You were voted one of the top bakers in the west. That says a lot."

"Hmmm."

"Just think about it, Marsh. It's a great opporunity for you here. But I want you to see that too. Anyways, I have to go. Love you, Marsh." Penny hung up the phone.

"Love you, Penny," I said. She did have some good points to make. It's always been on my list of things to do before I go to be with the Lord in Heaven. And if not then, when would I get another chance to do it? I was already sixty years old. The longer I thought about it, the more I grew attached to the idea. But when I imagined the people I would be leaving behind and the years it took to build the bakery into what it was, I felt sadness. How could I leave everything I'd known? Wasn't it too late in life to make such a huge decision? What would Larry think?

I gathered the ingredients for my favorite tea and planned to sit down with a good book to get my mind off things for a while. Later I could process everything by doing a pro and con list, but for that moment, my brain needed to relax before diving back into it.

It was Sunday, so the bakery was closed. The staff had set it up so there was no work to do, unless I wanted to get a head start on baking. Usually, I woke up at 3:30 to head into the shop and bake.

I heated up bottled water on the stove and found raspberry tea bags with a hint of lemon. The book I'd been reading was next to my rocking chair. It was about a woman who started her own cupcake business and wanted to invest in a food truck to sell her homemade goods. It reminded me a lot of when I first started out my own business. Fresh tears fell down my cheek, and I wiped it away. How could I give up this place? It had been a part of my life for such a long time. But what if somewhere else could be my home? I'd always loved warmer weather, despite living in Montana my whole life. Would Larry like it there?

Chapter Nineteen

Chloe

Early in the morning, Jesse told me to have Peter drive me over to the birthing center. After her examination, she told me her test wasn't showing any amniotic fluid. She sent me home. I felt disappointed, since I'd hoped the baby would come soon. I had so much to learn about birth. What did she mean her test wasn't showing amniotic fluid? There had been leaking throughout the night. Her test must have been wrong. I knew my water had broke.

I found out later I actually had a partial break, and it could have been a hind-water leak. The midwife said that meant the water broke a little in a certain spot and the amniotic fluid sometimes will stop coming after a while because the two layers of membrane within the sac slip back over each other to reseal the hole. She said some women notice a dribble of fluid and then nothing more until later when the fore-waters, or part of the sac in front of the baby's head breaks.

Instead of heading home where my mom and stepdad were, Peter and I decided to stay in a hotel as I experienced more early labor.

Peter pulled into the parking lot of one of the fancy hotels in Spring Mountain, located on the main road coming into town.

"How about this one?" He glanced over at me holding my belly.

"I don't really care. Just something that will let us in now," I snapped.

"Okay. Okay. Let's go in and see if they have anything."

I breathed harder, as I felt another contraction. How could I possibly waddle into the hotel? Was he crazy? My guess was he didn't want to leave me alone for too long. He opened the car door for me and offered his hand.

The man behind the desk was ready. He looked to see if any rooms were open at that moment, but informed us it wouldn't be ready for another couple hours.

I shook my head. "I need something now," I winced.

He turned back to the hotel clerk. "Okay. I guess not today. Thank you, though."

I wanted to run out the front door and get away from all the people in the lobby. I felt like a middle schooler again, thinking all eyes were on me.

"What do you want to do now?" Peter asked as he opened the car door for me again.

"I'm not sure. I don't want to go home, since everyone is there. It would just make me anxious. But then I feel bad for blowing money on a hotel." I teared up again. Finances were something I was always worried about.

"Don't feel bad. It's just for today. This way, you'll be able to get some rest before you have to go back into the birthing center." I was glad Peter understood. I didn't always feel we were on the same page.

"Okay. Maybe try the hotel across the road. I don't care where it is, as long as they have a room available now."

He drove across the street to a dilapidated looking hotel. I worried for our safety, but almost didn't care, since I felt another contraction coming on.

"Ohhhhhhh!" I clutched my side.

"Are you okay?" Peter asked me, his hand on my shoulder.

"Yeah," I said through clenched teeth. "Maybe just you better go in this time. I'll wait here in the car."

"Okay. I'll try and be quick."

Relieved he didn't argue with me, I tried not to draw attention to myself as I finished out the last contraction. I felt like I had to go to the bathroom. And quickly. I really hoped he was able to get a room right away. Before I knew it, Peter showed up at the car with two room keys. I sighed with relief.

"They did have one available. They warned me that it used to be a smoking room, though. It's upstairs."

"Oh, great. Now I get to walk up two flights of stairs while having contractions," I mumbled.

"Do you still want the room?"

I cringed my nose, thinking of how it used to be a smoking room. That was one of my biggest pet peeves, but I was desperate. "I guess. Let's just go. I need to get to the bathroom. Like right now!"

"I'll walk you up there and then come back and grab the stuff. You want anything for breakfast?"

"Let's get up there first and then I'll think about it."

He grabbed my right arm and we trudged up the stairs. I was grateful that a contraction wasn't coming. People were loud at the hotel. It was nearing late morning, but I hoped they were quiet soon so I could finally take a cat nap.

"The midwife said it was okay to take those sleeping tablets. I think you should take one to help you get some sleep. I'll run over and get us some breakfast burritos. You want anything else?"

"No. Just two burritos sound good. And some water. Thank you."

I waddled to the bathroom.

"Okay. Lock and chain the door. I'll be right back. Make sure you have your phone by you in case you need anything."

"Alright. I will."

I thought about how grateful I was to have the privacy at the hotel, and not have to be at home with family gawking at me, waiting for the baby to come.

Peter came back with some burritos, water, and orange juice. He usually liked to watch something on T.V. when we ate, so he channel-surfed while we ate the breakfast burritos. I'd been hungrier than I thought. He stopped on a documentary about turtles, and five minutes later I was ready to sleep.

"Okay, I'll turn this off," Peter said. I prayed that after the baby came the T.V. watching would be almost non-existent.

Turning over on my side, I hoped for sleep to come. Peter changed into pajama pants and I sat up, remembering the sleeping aide Jesse swore was safe for the baby.

After chewing the tablet, my eyes closed and I dozed off, but then a huge contraction washed over me. Determined not to make much noise, I knew Peter didn't sleep much either the night before, since I was in early labor starting at home.

The pain shot up my side. Lily had once described it like a menstrual cramp that shoots up in a big wave and then increases. That's what it felt like. Very intense. Over and over, I felt I had to use the bathroom, so I waddled in there, turned on the light and sat for quite some time, just waiting. Hadn't I heard somewhere you weren't supposed to push till they told you so during intense labor? What would happen if you pushed at the wrong time? I still had so much to learn, with it being my first birth.

I laid back down, ignoring the slight smell of smoke from the room and was able to doze in and out. Lily, the other midwife, has sent me texts asking how it was going. I explained how there was some blood, as well as how close together the contractions were. She asked if I wanted to come in and see how I was making progress, and I agreed to be there within a half hour. Peter woke up and he packed everything for us to leave. When I thought I was ready to walk out the door, another contraction came on, this time more intense.

"I'm glad we're going in now," I said.

The drive over to the birthing center felt like eternity. When we arrived, Lily did a quick exam.

"You are going to have this baby today," she said, a huge smile on her face.

I gazed at Peter.

"Should Peter check us out of our hotel?" I asked. She knew how we had family over and needed the personal space.

"Yes, I would say go ahead and check out of your hotel."

He went right away to take care of it, while Lily called the nurse to come over and put in my IV.

"It's one of those things they won't let freestanding midwives do. They have us call in a nurse, even though we are fully capable of inserting an IV. It's kind of silly, but oh well." Lily rolled her eyes.

The nurse came over and gave me the first round of antibiotics. I didn't want to do it because I knew antibiotics could kill good bacteria, but because of my water breaking partially and having Group B strep, the midwives wanted to make sure everything was okay and play it on the safe side. Lily was finally able to adjust things to where the IV could hang by the bed. I thought maybe they did this often, but perhaps most of their patients didn't need an IV, and that's why all the hassle.

I sipped on the drinks Peter had convinced me to buy for birth that were supposed to give energy. One tasted like watermelon and Lily brought me a straw to place in the bottle. She asked me if I wanted to be in the tub, which I thought they saved for the most intense part of labor.

"You mean I'm already at that point?" Lily didn't seem to know what I meant, but I complied.

It felt so uncomfortable soaking in the tub, since I didn't know how to position my legs. They brought out the Doppler to measure the baby's heart rate again, and it showed some distress. I was worried but trusted their judgment. After another hour, and checking the heart rate often, Lily informed me we would have to be transferred to the hospital.

"I would never put you or your baby at risk. I just want to make sure you are being monitored and play it safe."

My heart sank. I gave Lily a disappointed look, dreading going to the hospital, but knew it was for the best. Jesse showed up and hopped in the back of the car with us to head to the hospital.

"No contractions?" she asked while we were in the car.

"Nope. No contractions." My mind was wandering. "I know this shouldn't matter but...I am in my nighty and not dressed very well. But that's just a part of it, I guess." I wondered if I was the most modest patient they ever had.

"This is birth. There are many people who walk in there naked," she said boldly.

"Wow," I smiled.

We arrived at the hospital. Jesse led me to a room that was all set up.

"Here's the trooper!" Jesse exclaimed to one of the nurses in the room.

I smiled, thankful for the complement, and felt strong again after her comment.

Chatting with the midwives, I mentioned how much I hoped there would be no males around during the birthing process. To myself, I thought about how I wished I wasn't so modest and easily embarrassed. My sister-in-law said when a woman gives birth, she really doesn't care who is around, but with me, it was different. I had been voted the shyest person in my class senior year of high school for a reason.

"Oh, there are no males today. Just all females," the nurse said.

I used the restroom and laid on the bed and a nurse checked the baby's heart rate again. I was thankful the midwife in the hospital introduced herself and also seemed really sweet. She offered me a yoga ball to place on the bed so that I could lean on it while having contractions.

Time passed by fast. Before I knew it, it was evening and almost time to push. I was at the stage of labor where the contractions were so close together, and they had taken away the yoga ball, to my disappointment. A midwife told me to push, and I was still on all fours, but instead, I asked Peter to grab me a barf bag. After, she had me turn to my back, and brought up the hospital bed so I was partially sitting up. This position was uncomfortable for me, but I knew it must be easier for them to help.

They counted as I had each contraction. The hospital had allowed both my regular midwives in the room to help. Their intern was also off to the side and offered her help at times. I'd told the hospital staff I wanted the least amount of people as possible, mainly the three ladies I was used to. They agreed to this, but then let me know that during the actual birth, there would be more people that would have to attend. Some were students. My face turned red. While most women wouldn't mind, I tended to get anxious if too many spectators were nearby.

I refocused my attention on the task at hand, and just closed my eyes. I was exhausted from not sleeping the night before and hardly any at the hotel earlier. I heard the nurses around me talking but felt like I was half asleep and it was hard to put all my energy into the pushing. After a while, the hospital midwife told me I really needed to wake up and focus, and then threatened a C-section if I couldn't get the baby out in a certain amount of time. Part of me didn't care, because I was just so tired, but I tried a little harder. I pushed and pushed and there was a moment where my body decided it needed a break. The staff watched the monitors for what seemed like a long time, waiting for the next contraction to come.

They talked about giving me Pitocin. I had forgotten what that was, but Lily explained. She didn't seem opposed to it and told me how it would make the contractions stronger and help to get the baby out. I reasoned that it would help give me a boost since I was so weak and tired. After waiting more, a contraction came. Lily offered me the mirror, since the baby's head was crowning, and they wanted me to see progress. All I wanted to do was shut my eyes and focus on the pushing, and nothing else around me. I thought of something to motivate myself to wake up more. What could it be?

I decided my motivation was sleep. If I could just get the baby out, then maybe I would be able to finally get some rest. Something inside me switched, and I was able to do all the midwives asked. They had me perform weird breathing exercises to help me through it, and it helped. My regular midwives had said there was no reason to practice the breathing beforehand. Their coaching through the birth was what really counted. I squeezed Peter's hand and prepared myself to meet my baby boy.

Chapter Twenty

Jesse

Chloe's birth went well, besides the fact she was transported to the hospital and didn't want to be. The umbilical cord was wrapped around the baby's neck twice, but we all worked together as a team and were able to deliver the baby safely.

I was finally able to get some sleep, as did Lily. Sometimes as midwives, we must expect one birth right after the other and run on very little sleep. I'm grateful my husband is supportive of this about my career, and how willing he is to help with our girls and do things like dinner or starting the dishwasher for me, since sometimes I get a call late in the day and am working till early morning.

The week after Chloe's birth I took my planned summer break and journeyed into the mountains to visit one of my best friends. It had been about a year since I'd been able to spend time with her, with our busy schedules and all. She had invited me up to her cabin. It wasn't where she lived full time, but a home she had bought with her husband a few years before as an investment. They fixed it up and used it as their getaway for mini vacations until they were ready to sell it.

The directions to the cabin were a little unclear, but I was finally able to hash through my handwritten notes, and found it tucked back in the woods. It reminded me of a scene out of a magazine, with beautifully done landscapes. There were flowers all around the front of the cabin, as well as a huge walkway with some of every color beside it. The cabin had a bit of green trimming and matched the perfectly mowed grass that was encased all around. As I strolled down the little pathway to the house, taking everything in, I could hear the creek out in the back.

It all reminded me a little of our birthing center and what we had originally envisioned. I noticed the properties around her cabin were very different compared to hers. The houses looked old and run down, and their yards not well kept. I knew my friend Abigail and her husband were very good at restoring houses and wondered if this place had looked like the others around it when they first bought it. They restored houses for a living, and I was amazed every time they showed me one of them. I wondered why we didn't ask them to help us fix up the birthing center when we first bought the property. I could've learned a lot from Abigail.

"Jesse!" Abigail opened the door and stepped onto the front porch, even before I was able to knock.

"Abby! I missed you so much," I said, walking up the steps to give her a big hug.

Abigail was barefoot and wore the cutest short-sleeved purple blouse, blue jeans with the bottoms rolled up, and her hair up in a ponytail. It had been so long since I'd seen her and could tell her hair had grown out quite a bit.

"Come on in. Sorry I'm a mess. The kids and I just came in from playing in the creek. Emmett caught three frogs, and Molly saw a little Garter snake. Emmett teased her with it, so I had to go and break up the dramatic scene of Molly breaking into tears and Emmett denying there ever was a snake," Abby said.

"I would have died," I said.

"Thankfully, I saw it from where I was picking weeds, and was able to call out his lie. Emmett is up in the office writing an apology letter, and when his dad gets here, he's going to confess everything," she sighed. "Ohhhh the joys of parenthood," she smiled. "And here I am just talking your ear off. Why don't you come on in and we can get some of those homemade cookies my mom made for us?"

I remembered how Abigail claimed she wasn't a very good cook. Usually, she would talk her mother into baking something for her kids now and again, so they could enjoy the sweets she grew up with.

"I would love to taste them," I said, slipping off my shoes. The white carpet looked very new, and I didn't want to track in any mud. Why would anyone pick white for their carpet?

Abby led us to a nice leather sofa, big enough for a football team. "Tell me how things have been going at work," Abby said, leaning over to grab one of her mother's homemade chocolate chip cookies. She took a big bite, and some fell on the floor. She didn't seem to mind.

"Oh, it's going okay. We had another round where we were running on very little sleep. One of the babies had the cord wrapped around the neck again, but we were able to get him out safely. Mother and baby are doing well. And I totally forgot to tell you..." I hesitated as the bad memories came back to mind. A nasty taste popped into my mouth. "A couple weeks ago, we met a lady who wanted to have her baby with us, and then after her third appointment, she said she didn't want to anymore. A friend of hers told me she felt we didn't mesh well with our personalities and the family wanted a midwife with more experience, who didn't look like she was eighteen years old," I said.

"You're kidding. She really said that?" Abby's mouth dropped open.

"That's what I heard," I said, crossing my arms.

"Why would her friend even mention that to you? That seems rude. I mean, she could have just bowed out and didn't have to mention all those things. Why would the friend just go off like that and tell you what she said?"

"I ripped it out of her. I have known this woman for a long time, and I told her I wanted the full truth. I thought maybe there was something we said that had offended the client, and I wanted to see what it was. You know, so as not to make the same mistake twice. Turns out she was going based off my looks and didn't even care to ask how much experience I actually had, or how old I really was. Why are people so stupid?" I shook my head, looking down at the floor. "It really hurt too, when she said that. I've gotten grief before for looking so young, but not quite in this way."

"That is harsh. At least the lady didn't tell you that to your face. You squeezed it out of someone else."

"Yeah I guess so. It hurts just the same, though," I said, grabbing another cookie.

"Don't let it. You are a professional who has been doing this for years. Why should you let what one lady says ruin how you think about yourself?"

"Because I feel like everybody thinks that about me," I said.

"So what if they do? Just wait until you're an old lady. You'll be glad you look ten years younger. Everyone your age will be walking around with old wrinkles and canes, and you'll be over there with your hair nicely done, no wrinkles, and in tip top shape. Everyone will be jealous. Besides, remember what Paul told Timothy in the Bible? Not to let people look down on him just because he was young. These men were able to make a huge difference in the world, no matter their age."

"I guess so." Abby was right. I was taking it too much to heart. But what about the other things she said?

"But then she also said our personalities don't mesh well. What does that even mean?" I fiddled with a hangnail.

"Maybe because she thought that you were so young, you couldn't possibly have anything in common," Abby glanced out the window.

"I don't even know. I can only remember being very professional to her, giving her the facts, you know? I don't recall anything out of the ordinary."

"Sounds like this lady was just picky and didn't know better. Come on, Jesse. Cheer up. Look at all the success stories you've had being a midwife. Don't just focus on this one. It's one out of hundreds."

"You're right. I shouldn't dwell on it," I said, and reached to grab one more cookie. I had hoped it would help take my mind off my troubles.

The cookie was absolutely melt-in-your-mouth delicious. Even with them sitting out while we are talking, they still seemed gooey and fresh.

"Anyways, how's the house buying and selling business going?" I asked.

"It's alright. We're having trouble selling a house over on Cherry Street. We just redid the outside with a couple fresh coats of paint, did a little yard work, and we got calls on it almost right away when we put it on the market. It just seems like several people had to walk away for one reason or another."

"If I could afford it, I'd buy one of your houses. They're always nicely done," I said.

"Well, let me know if you hear of someone looking. Don really wants to sell this one. It's been on his list for a while."

"At least in your profession, people can't really cut you down to your face," I said, rehashing everything all over again.

Abby shook her head. "That's not always true. I've had people approach me about houses we were in the middle of doing. They wanted to put their two cents in. Some of the others who live in the neighborhoods where we buy the properties have even had the nerve to come knock on our door and try and tell us what to fix. They say they know so-and-so and that they would suggest hiring a specific professional to do the job."

"What do you usually say to them?" I asked.

"Usually, Don deals with them. He's a little nicer than I can be. I tell them that we are professionals who have done this sort of thing for years. The hard part is Don is in the middle of working on something, and he has people walk by and talk about how he's doing it all wrong."

"Wow. I would have never thought."

"I know, right? It can be annoying. I think some folks are just being busy body neighbors and have nothing else to do. They're mostly older, retired folks who don't get out much," Abby said.

"I'm just amazed by what Don can do. He does electrical, plumbing, roofing, painting...What can he not do?" I asked in amazement.

"He pretty much knows how to do it all. He did have to hire a contractor to redo the heating and air conditioning in an older house he bought, but other than that, he does it all. He learned from his dad and grandpa, plus went to school a little to learn better how to do electrical stuff. I've worked alongside him on a lot of projects, but I wouldn't have a clue on how to do the electrical and plumbing stuff. I'm usually the painter and help occasionally with the carpeting."

"One thing's for sure. We should have hired you guys to help us with the birthing center when we were renovating it. Lily has had a lot of experience with that kind of stuff, but she was also busy at the time with family. I helped where I could but felt more like I was getting in the way. When it came to the decorating part, though, that's where I was able to help out more."

"You should have told us. We would have done it for free."

"If we ever have another project like that one, I definitely know who I'm calling," I said.

Abby grinned as she picked up the plate of cookies. I followed her into the kitchen as she showed me the different projects Don, her husband did with the cabinets and counter. I did my best to pay attention, but in the back of my mind, I was still stewing over what happened at work the other day. I kept telling myself it was ridiculous, and how it was time to move on. My little pep talk seemed to work, until it was time to go to bed.

I'd stayed up late with Abby chatting and eating junk food, and when we finally decided to quit, I thought I was ready to fall asleep, but my mind raced. I bit my nails and picked the skin around them, something often done while either boredom or anxiousness had settled in. This lasted until three in the morning, and then I finally was able to doze off till the sun awoke me. Despite going to bed late, I felt refreshed and ready for another day with Abby. But as I looked over at the clock, it was one o'clock in the afternoon. No wonder I felt refreshed. Feeling bad for sleeping in, I quickly dressed and brushed my teeth, deciding to skip the shower until later.

"Hey, Jesse. I was just about to head across the way to give my neighbor some cookies too. She's expecting a baby soon, and I imagine she's having some cravings," Abby laughed. "I'll be right back. Brunch is on the counter. My kids just ate and are out playing in the backyard and my husband is working on one of the houses today. So, it will be just you for brunch."

"Did you already eat?" I asked with a twinge of guilt from oversleeping.

"Yeah. Sorry. I would have waited, but my kids get up early normally, and I need energy to get through the mornings. I'm surprised you didn't hear them with all that noise they were making."

"I was so out of it. I didn't hear a peep. Sorry I overslept," I said, stretching.

"Don't be sorry at all. You're our guest. You can do whatever you want. We love having you." She turned to walk out the front door with a huge plate of cookies in her hands covered with Saran Wrap.

On top of the marble counter, Abby had placed fresh fruit, croissants, bagels and cream cheese, and sandwiches. I mixed my breakfast and lunch and made up a bagel and cream cheese with turkey meat, cheddar cheese, and salad. It was my attempt at eating healthy, after all the junk food the night before. With as much as we ate, I was surprised we were hungry at all.

Chapter Twenty-One

Kate

An older gentleman with glasses peered down at me, the sun behind him. "How are you feeling?" He seemed genuinely concerned. I recognized him as the man who had been standing on his front porch earlier. The one who saw me laying in his yard getting sick just a moment before.

"Okay, I think," I mumbled and sat up, rubbing the back of my head.

"Looks like you took a little fall." The man reached out his hand to offer help getting me off the ground.

"Yeah, I don't know what happened. I just started feeling lousy all the sudden today. Sorry I got sick in your yard back there."

"Don't be sorry. It's just grass and dirt. You didn't hurt a thing. I just hope you're okay. I didn't want to scare you by following you, but once I saw you had been sick, I went for a little walk myself shortly after, just to be sure you were alright. Then I saw you over here laying on the side of the road. Thankfully this part of town is never that busy with cars. I thought about calling an ambulance for you."

"That won't be necessary," I said, brushing off my clothes from the dirt on the road. My face turned bright red. He probably thought I was drunk or something equally humiliating.

"Do you need anything? Want me to walk with you? Or maybe I can get my wife to lead you home," the man paused, shielding his eyes from the sun. I was glad the rain clouds had moved.

"No. I'm fine. I feel so much better now."

"Well, I hope you have a good day. And that you figure out whatever is ailing you." He waved as he walked away, hesitant. He still looked concerned.

"Thank you," I waved weakly as he strolled back toward his house.

I remember back in middle school blacking out on the bleachers during a concert, after I had locked my knees. Everyone had gathered around me, ready to call an ambulance. At least this time there weren't as many spectators.

After walking three blocks out of the way, I circled back to the store where I'd grabbed the hot chocolate, not sure what to do next. As I was about to walk through the door, I saw Chloe's parents pull suddenly off to the side of the road and they shouted out the window, "Chloe is having her baby!"

I stopped, not expecting this. "What?! Why didn't anybody call me to let me know it was happening? I am supposed to be there for the birth!"

I glanced down at my phone to check it. It was still on silent and showed eight missed calls. Six of them were from Chloe's phone, and the other two were from her parents.

"Why aren't you guys there with her right now?" I asked.

"She just wants the midwives there with her now. We were going to go over soon to wait for when the baby comes. It may still be a little while, but we'll see. We were told you went out for a walk, so we drove around town to find you. We had to kill a little time anyways."

"Oh. Thanks for coming after me," I muttered, embarrassed for accusing them of not trying to get ahold of me. Swinging my purse over my right shoulder, I ducked into the dark blue Ford Explorer, shutting the door just as the rain picked up again.

"Are you alright?" Chloe's mom turned to look behind her seat. She had the same look on her face as the man whose yard I'd thrown up in.

I must have looked like I'd been hit by a train. After getting sick in a muddy lawn and passing out on the side of the road, my appearance could have scared anybody. I peeked in the driver's mirror before putting on my seat belt. My hair was all in tangles, the ponytail coming out, and several smudge marks aligned my face. Mascara, the only make up I had put on that morning, smeared down the sides of my face. Chloe's parents must have been horrified.

"I'm fine. Let's just get to the birthing center so we can see Chloe."

"Birthing center? Oh. Actually, she was transported to the hospital."

"Hospital? What happened?" I shrieked, knowing that was the last place Chloe wanted to have her baby. Something must have been seriously wrong. I felt guilty I hadn't even thought of checking my phone. Had I really wasted that much time moping around town?

"Everything is fine, Kate. She's in good hands. She did start out at the birthing center, but the midwives realized the baby's heart rate wasn't what it should be, so they transported her to the hospital. They were able to stay with her through the whole thing. They think the baby may have the cord wrapped around his neck a couple of times; but not to worry. The midwives are taking care of it, and mother and baby are healthy. Now we just have to wait until they are all ready, and we can go in for our visit."

"I wish so much I could have been there when it all started. When did she start going into early labor? Why didn't she call me then?"

"She started around eight last night but left it up to us to get ahold of you. We're so sorry we didn't call you until this morning. By the time we thought of calling last night, it was really late, and we didn't want to wake you up."

"I wouldn't have minded." I rolled my eyes, annoyed by their remarks. I hope they didn't see me in the mirrors. They were just trying to be polite and thoughtful to their daughter's friend.

"Thank you," I said. "Sorry I left my phone on silent and you guys weren't able to get ahold of me. I saw Chloe had tried to call me too a bit ago. I just got so distracted, not even thinking about the baby coming today."

"We still have some time. How about we drive you by where you're staying, and you can freshen up? We have some phone calls to make anyways. Chloe told us to tell some other family members, and I'm sure they would want to hear how she's doing."

"That would be so good. Yes. I'll take you guys up on that." They pulled into the driveway minutes later as I managed to crawl out the back door. I still felt funny, but so much better than before. Chloe and her baby were such a good distraction. I couldn't be more excited to see them both.

Pushing through the front door, I rustled through my bathroom bag for my toothbrush and toothpaste, and brushed my teeth to get the scent of any vomit off my breath. No use scaring anymore people. When I'd slid into the car, Chloe's parents seemed to cringe. Had I smell that bad? I gave my clothes a sniff, and decided I better take a quick shower and change into clean clothes before going over to the hospital. The rain made me chilly anyways, and the thought of a nice warm shower sounded heavenly.

The warmth felt so nice against my goose-bumped skin. I didn't want to leave, and then remembered how Chloe's parents were outside waiting. Not wanting to cause any more of a ruckus for them, I dressed quickly and skipped the blow drying.

After bolting into the back seat again, Chloe's mom still held the phone, chatting away with some distant relative. Her dad was on his phone too, probably texting people pictures of his adventures. Waiting patiently for them, I almost wanted to run back in and do my hair and makeup, but then Chloe's dad finally put down his phone and pulled back on the seat belt. He backed out of the parking slot. It must have been a mixture of the car's motion and my texting on the phone, but the nausea came on again. Chloe's dad was good driver, but there were a lot of turns to get to the hospital. I put my phone down to look up, attempted to get the bad feelings to pass. I felt even more nauseous.

"Ummm...Could you pull over? I feel like I have to throw up."

Chloe's dad pressed on the brakes, then pulled to the side of the road. I rolled out the car door then shut it to muffle the sounds they could hear of me getting sick again.

"Why don't you go check on her?" I could hear Chloe's dad through his rolled down window. I wondered why his window was down when it was still sprinkling outside, and it was chilly. The last thing I wanted was for someone else to see me like that again. What was going on with me? I hadn't gotten sick like that in a long time.

After five minutes, I slipped back into the car, shivering from the light rain on my clothes.

Before Chloe's dad drove off, he kindly asked if I would like him to take me to a gas station bathroom, or even back to the house to lay down before going to see Chloe.

"No. I feel much better. Must have been car sickness. Not from your driving. It was my fault for looking at my phone while doing all those twists and turns. It could have made anybody sick." He nodded his head. I looked over at Chloe's mom, wondering why her parents were in the same car together. They had divorced when she was sixteen. Maybe they were planning something together for the arrival of the baby? Turning my attention to the route, I hoped watching the road would help prevent any further sickness. I welcomed sleep and rested my head on the door, dozing in and out.

A gasp came from the front seat, awakening me. "She could be pregnant," Chloe's mom whispered. They thought I was still asleep. Some more words were muttered I couldn't understand. Did I hear her right? Were they talking about me or someone else they knew?

Chapter Twenty-Two

Marsha

The night Penny called me about the job opportunity in Mexico, I couldn't sleep, but had done my normal nighttime routine of drinking a glass of warm milk and honey while taking a bath, then brushing my teeth, and ending with reading in bed. My routine usually helped me fall asleep, and almost never failed. I'd been doing it for years, but that night it was different. My latest obsession with Mexico even made its way into my dreams.

I didn't get to talk to Larry much after he came home. I'd mentioned the phone call to him and the offer Penny made. His body language told me the discussion was something he wanted to tackle later. He'd been distracted with the bakery, working on expanding some of the Sunflower Room and repairing the roof where we noticed it leaking one day after it rained. He had to assess the extent of the damage and I appreciated his hard work. But more than anything, my wish was to talk to him without distractions. Not knowing the future stressed me out. I worried I'd get an ulcer again.

The bakery had been a part of my life for so long, it was hard to imagine doing anything else. And with Larry's renovations, it would be difficult to say goodbye. Yet I also thought about the flip side of the coin. We had poured so much of our own money into the bakery, and I knew that if it did sell, all that labor would not be in vain. I could remember back to when we first bought the bakery. It didn't look like much then, but we had big dreams for it. Sure enough, it came true.

The bakery became the busiest place in town, and tourists flocked to it when they came through. It was rated one of the top restaurant and bakeries in a travel magazine. Our business had far exceeded my expectations, and I had loved every moment of it. I had a flashback of sitting in the middle of the floor, holding Larry's hands and praying over the new place. We prayed that we could serve each person who walked into our doors and share the light the Lord had given in our hearts. Our mission from the start was to serve people more than just bakery items and coffee. We wanted to touch lives and see people brought to Christ through the store. And sure enough, there were many we were able to see come to know Him through our friendship.

The thought of moving to Mexico and leaving our work here behind was bittersweet. Bitter because of all we had poured into the place, and sweet because the thought of helping others in a different location and culture sounded like quite the adventure. I just couldn't figure out which feelings were stronger. The bitter, or the sweet.

That next morning, I made Larry's coffee just the way he liked it. Black. He was silent, but I couldn't take it any longer. "Have you thought any about Penny's offer?" I asked excitedly. I knew most likely he would be annoyed I hadn't given him much time to think about it, and tell me to back off in his own way.

"Not really, Marsha. I just woke up. I haven't had time to think much about anything." Sometimes Larry could be so predictable. I suppose it was all those years being married. We knew each other well.

"Right. It's just that...you did say we could talk about it in the morning."

"Maybe give me a little time to wake up. Then we can talk about it over breakfast."

Sighing, I went to work making breakfast extra special. It was normal for me to get excited about things sometimes, causing me to rush into decisions. I crisped the bacon the way Larry liked it, added an omelet with mushrooms, onion, and cheese, along with several pumpkin pancakes on the side with real maple syrup. He'd need a lot of energy, working on projects at the bakery for me. That was a day we both went in a little later than usual, which would hopefully give us time to talk.

Finally, breakfast was served. I moved the flowers sitting on the windowsill over to the middle of the table, where we could see them better. This occasion called for something festive.

"So, what did Penny say on the phone yesterday? Start from the very beginning," Larry said with a fork full of pancakes in his mouth. He chewed, with some of the syrup sticking to the side of his beard and he grabbed a napkin to wipe it off.

I proceeded to tell him about Penny's phone call and her new granddaughter and wanting to move to Tennessee, along with the job openings down at the mission in Mexico.

"What are the jobs that would be open?"

"Penny was one of the head cooks and her husband was the lead maintenance guy. He did just about everything, but she also said they would be hiring another person to help, so that all doesn't fall on just one person's shoulders.

"When did she say the positions would be open?" Larry mumbled between bites. I couldn't tell if he was angry, annoyed, or just wanted me to leave him alone to eat his breakfast. The tension built in my stomach. Maybe he was overwhelmed with all the projects going on.

"Penny plans on moving to Tennessee within the next month or so. They'll probably be looking for someone as soon as possible."

"That's pretty quick. I do remember when you went over there to visit and how much you enjoyed it there. It sounds like a wonderful opportunity." Larry surprised me with this comment.

"Do you think it's something for us? I know we would have to put the bakery up for sale, either that or find someone to run it for us while we're gone. We both have talked about traveling the world and helping others in different places other than here."

"That's true. Hmm. Let's pray about it together and think some more. Maybe we ought to sleep on it for a few weeks. It is a very big decision to make. We've lived here a very long time, and there is a lot that goes into selling a place. Or even finding someone to run it for us. There are still some things I want to fix up. That will take some time."

"I was afraid of that," I sighed. "They would need someone very soon, and if we wait too long, the opportunity may pass."

"I'm not saying no, but I'm also not saying yes. When does she need to know by?"

"She told me to think and pray about it this week, but I don't remember her giving me a time frame. I can ask her, though."

"That would be good." Larry shoveled a few more bites of the omelet into his mouth. "I'm going to go in earlier than normal. There are a lot of things I want to get done with the roof today. I have a couple guys who are coming later this afternoon to help me with some of the work, and I want to have everything ready for when they get there."

I frowned as I picked up the dishes from breakfast. My food hadn't even been touched; I'd been so nervous. Expecting a response right away had been foolish of me. It would have helped if I'd asked Penny when she needed to know our answer. Wondering how the application process would look, I gave Penny a call right after Larry left to work on repairs at the restaurant. She picked up on the second ring.

"Hey, Penny. It's Marsha."

"I was just thinking about you. What did Larry say about the job opportunity? Did you get a chance to talk to him?"

"He said we need to think and pray about it some more. We were just both wondering when you need to know our answer by."

"Well, I did inform my boss about us leaving. We have one more month on staff here before we move to Tennessee. He's going to be taking applications right away, and you both are highly recommended. He would like you to fill out the application and said to do one for you and one for Larry," Penny's voice sounded excited. "He'd be happy to do an interview on the phone or even on a face chat, so it feels like it's more in person. He just wants to give everyone a fair chance. There are a couple other people who are also interested in the positions. But, between you and me, it sounds like he has his heart set on you guys. They love it when couples come to the camp to serve together."

"Can you send me the applications in the mail?"

"I'll give you the website and you'll be able to either print it out from there and mail it to us, or you can send it to my boss through email."

"Okay," I sighed. Was this really happening?

"I think it would be good for you to explore their website, find even more information about them, and this will help you when they do your interview and also help make your decision about if this is something you guys want."

"Alright. I'll give it a shot. Thanks for all your help, Penny."

"Just go ahead and send in your applications. They want to try and hire someone before we even move, but we'll see how it goes. If you guys decide it's something you don't want to do, you can always ask for your application to be taken out."

"That's true. Better to apply and back out if we need to, then let the opportunity go."

"My advice is to take it. It's what you've always wanted. Maybe if Larry doesn't want to go, you could come down anyways," Penny added.

My stomach twisted like a pretzel. Leave Larry behind?

"I gotta go, Marsha. I'll be praying for you and Larry as you ask for direction. They would be so blessed to have you guys on board."

"Thanks, Penny. Bye." On my computer, I pulled up the website, wanting to read the application right away. Penny's words gnawed through my mind. *Leave Larry behind and come anyways. It's what you've always wanted.*

Chapter Twenty-Three

Chloe

Birth was the most physical pain I had ever felt in my entire life, besides some severe back pain I had experienced earlier that year. But it was also not as bad as I had imagined.

At one point, the midwife of the hospital told me if I couldn't get the baby out shortly, I'd have to have a C-section. Exhaustion overwhelmed me, and the thought didn't really matter to me about having surgery. It turned out that I had the baby naturally, with only Pitocin to help the contractions move along faster.

A smile came to my face when I saw my sweet little baby for the first time. The midwife handed him right to me. He was crying and I whispered, "It's okay." Surprisingly, he gazed up at me and stopped crying instantly. I hadn't expected that. We messaged the family that he was born, and his name would be Isaiah Paul.

He latched on right away, and I'll never forget that moment. The midwife stitched me up, since there had been some bad tearing. I could feel the pulling and tugging, and although uncomfortable, Isaiah was a good distraction for me.

Kate came to mind, and I knew how much she really wanted to be there all through the birth. She probably was distracted, which was okay. I'd been in such good hands and was excited for her to come meet Baby Isaiah.

Anxious for my family to meet Isaiah, I hurried in the bathroom to clean up a little by changing into better clothes and brushing my hair and teeth. A nurse weighed and measured him and told me family could visit after they moved me to the recovery room.

Kate came in next shortly after the family left. She looked very excited to see the baby and asked to hold him right away. There was something different about her, but I couldn't quite put my finger on it.

"Oh my gosh! He is so stinking adorable! What a treasure." Kate placed her face up to his, and I could see tears falling down her cheeks.

"I know. We are super blessed," I smiled.

"Can you believe you just went through birth!?" Kate punched me lightly in the arm.

"It all seems like a dream in a way. I can't believe I just went through all that, and now it's over."

"It's one of the most amazing things you will ever experience. I can remember looking back at my first birth and thinking 'Wow! I did *that*?' Kate smiled at me. She looked so happy to be there, always knowing how to light up a whole room.

"I remember being so tired through the whole thing, but now that it's over, I'm actually feeling much more awake and like I have all this adrenaline running through me," I said.

"It's a great feeling. After the baby comes, wanting to show him off to the world. He will bring so much joy to so many people. I can tell already."

"Thanks, Kate." I thought about what to say next. I didn't want to make her feel bad for not being able to come to the birth, but wanted to show I was thinking about her. "So how are you doing, Kate? I heard you weren't feeling too well earlier. Are you better now?"

Kate's face quickly transformed from a smile to a frown in less than a second. My stomach churned. What was going on?

"Yes. I'm okay. I am so sorry I didn't make it to the birth. You even had me written into your birth plan. I feel like an awful friend and can't believe my phone was on silent after all that time. I explored downtown a bit and went for a walk, which was great. Just wish I would have been here on time."

"It's all okay. Please don't worry. You were here in spirit, and I used all the techniques that you suggested. It really helped me out when it came to pushing."

Kate grinned and shortly after I could see she was turning green. What was going on?

"I'm going to use your bathroom real quick." Kate quickly slid across the floor before I could respond and shut the door in a flash. I could tell she was trying to be quiet, but could hear her coughing and gagging. Poor gal.

While Kate camped in the bathroom awhile, I heard a light knock at the door. I'm so modest, I considered unlatching the baby, but since I'd just started to nurse, I threw on a baby blanket instead.

"Come in!" I said.

Marsha entered the room, holding a beautiful bouquet of flowers. I saw white ones, along with sunflowers, one of my favorites.

"I thought maybe you would like these. They could remind you of the plains where you grew up."

I grabbed the bouquet with my free hand to smell them, breathing in the scent deeply. Although the sunflowers were fake and the white ones were real, I was appreciative for the reminder of my childhood home.

"I absolutely love these. How did you know sunflowers were one of my favorites?" I teased.

"Just a guess." She reached for my hand. "How are you doing, sweetie? Other than being transported to the hospital, was the birth everything you dreamed it would be?"

"Hmmm... I guess I didn't really know what to expect, this being my first and all. But I am so happy I went through that, to meet this precious baby boy."

Marsha let go of my hand and reclined on a nearby chair. "In the first year, they change so much. I could have sworn that someone had replaced my baby overnight with a different one, when I was a first-time mother. Your whole life will now feel like it revolves around them. Sometimes you make a lot of sacrifices, but it's so worth it. Children are a blessing from the Lord. The fruit of the womb is a reward."

"I remember that verse. I came across it the other day. What a great reminder."

Finally, Kate opened the bathroom door. Marsha and I stared. Her face was flushed and embarrassed, so I looked away and pretended to be distracted with adjusting the baby blanket.

"It's so good to see you, Marsha." Kate finally said.

"How are things going, Kate?"

"They're okay, I guess. I am so excited the baby is finally here."

"Oh, yes. A very precious gift for all of us."

Kate plopped down in another hospital chair. She still didn't look well, but some of the green had vanished.

"Are you okay, Kate? Do you need to lie down somewhere? Because I can get the nurse to get you..."

"No, thanks." She quickly cut me off. "I'm fine."

"You've been sick so much today, I'm starting to wonder if you are expecting a baby." I laughed, but then stopped after I saw the look on Kate's face. Maybe I shouldn't have said it. I knew right away I was correct in my assumptions.

"Oh Kate! Are you...?" I stopped. She didn't respond. After a moment, a smile came to her face again. Marsha and I both waited in anticipation.

"I did take a test before I came over. After your parents and I drove over here, they came right up to see you, and I ran to the corner store to see what tests they had. I checked out and then tried it in the bathroom, and sure enough."

"What? Are you serious?" I laughed excitedly. One of my very best friends was expecting a baby again!

"Shhh Shhhh Shhhh!" Kate said. "I don't want anyone to know."

"Well, does your husband know?" I unlatched the baby. I'm surprised he didn't wake up from the noise we were making.

"I did call him right away. I didn't want to tell him over the phone, but I knew he would have work off today and he'd be more available."

"How did he react?"

"He was speechless at first, and then he sounded like I was trying to pull a prank on him. I think it just took him a while for it to sink in."

"You told him over the phone?" I frowned. "How unromantic. You should have waited till you got home, made him a nice dinner at the very least, and told him over candlelight."

"Why, is that how you told your husband about your baby?" Kate crossed her arms.

I chuckled. "Oddly enough, it was actually at the Sunflower Restaurant, and we had been fighting, and I yelled it out to him in front of a big crowd."

"Wow," Kate said. "That's quite the story," she laughed.

I laughed with her at the memory.

"I didn't know that's how you told him about the baby. I must have been in the bathroom or something," Marsha said.

We all laughed at the same time, imagining the whole room staring at Peter and I.

"So you get on to me for telling my husband on the phone, when you told your husband in the middle of a fight at a crowded restaurant?" Kate put a hand on her hip.

"I thought about it afterwards. If I had to do it over, I would have done the candlelight idea."

"Get real." Kate rolled her eyes. "You are so not romantic and you know it."

"What?" I smiled back at her. "I so am. You know that the dinner idea is good."

"No. It's not. It's so cliche."

"Oh it is, is it? Well then, Ms. Romance. Tell me how you would break the news to your husband, if you had to do it over again?"

"Right in the middle of a dance. We would be doing a waltz or some dance like that, and I would tell him. Right there in the middle of the dance floor. I would whisper it in his ear, so no one else could hear. And then he would stop with me right there in his arms."

"Cheesy!" I said, holding the baby out to Marsha, inviting her to hold him. I dragged out of bed and walked around the hospital room a little. It felt good to be out and about. Staring out the window, I wanted to go outside.

"It is not cheesy. I happen to think it's very romantic!" Kate said.

"I guess everyone's idea of romance can be different sometimes," Marsha said while bouncing Isaiah up and down. He was taking a liking to her.

"Yeah I guess so. I think that swimming under the stars is pretty romantic, but some people don't think so," Kate added.

"I think pretty much anything under the stars can be romantic, as long as your husband is with you," I said.

"Okay. You got me there." Kate put her hands up, surrendering to the idea. "Anyways, other than him, you guys are the only ones I've told. So don't go telling anyone else, okay? It's top-secret news."

There was another knock at the door. It seemed the hospital staff came and went so often from the room, sometimes it was annoying, unless it was a visitor of course. I was glad to see it was Peter.

"What's top secret news?" he asked. He held out chocolates in front of him for me to grab. Very sweet. No pun intended.

Kate frowned. "Um, just how much did you hear?" she asked Peter.

Peter smiled his big smile, as if showing that he knew our little secret. Maybe the cat was out of the bag.

Chapter Twenty-Four

Missy

Marsha called me while she was sitting in the hospital room with Chloe, so I drove over since I wasn't working. Hospital visits are never something that interests me, but I did it to see Marsha. Walking in through the front sliding doors, I realized I hadn't brought over a present for the baby. Isn't that what you're supposed to do when you visit someone at the hospital who just gave birth? I didn't know the rules, but it bugged me through the whole visit. It was quick and boring to be honest.

Marsha asked Chloe to tell the birthing story from the beginning, which didn't interest me at all. It sickened me. I was glad when she finally wrapped it up. Hundreds of pins felt stuck in the sides of my stomach. It brought memories of when I had my little girl, and I didn't want to think about it. The green monster of jealousy threatened to burst out and come running with its claws. At least Chloe was keeping her baby. The familiar feeling of regret churned inside of me.

After spending time at the hospital, I headed home, plopped down on the sofa, and gorged on Ben and Jerry's while flipping through the stations, hoping to find something good on T.V. to distract me. The phone rang.

"Missy. How are you doing?"

"Oh, hey Marsha. Are you still over at the hospital with Chloe?"

"I'm on my way out to the car. Remember how I was talking to you about meeting some people from my church? You know, just to make friends and get to know people in town?"

"Yeah. I remember." I rolled my eyes. At least she couldn't see me.

"I have someone I'd like you to meet. They're really sweet and I think you guys would get along really well."

"No pushing, right? I mean, they aren't going to try and convert me to be a church person or anything like that, are they?"

Marsha laughed. "No, sweetie. It's just so you can make friends, remember? I just got off the phone and they were excited about the idea of meeting you. They were thinking the coffee shop over on the corner on Main Street tomorrow after you get off work. Does that sound okay for you?"

"Uh, yeah. That should work. Thanks, Marsha." I shrugged my shoulders. It was no use arguing ith her. Might as well give it a shot.

"No problem, sweetie. Talk to you later."

"Later." Hanging up the phone, worry overcame me. What was I getting myself into? Maybe this woman was one of those church goers who try to convert people, but say they aren't. That was probably what Marsha wanted. It was all a big scheme to get me converted and go to church with her. She just didn't want to be the one to ask me, so she found someone else to do the dirty work. But then again, she did assure me it was just to make friends. What harm could be in that? Maybe it would be nice for a change to not hang out with someone who just wanted to be a drinking buddy.

The next morning, I prepared for work quickly, since I'd accidentally hit snooze on my alarm too many times. Breakfast consisted of pop tarts thrown in the toaster and a glass of milk.

Work went fast since it was busy, which I always liked. Driving home afterwards, I realized the time we'd set for me to meet Marsha's friend was at four o'clock. It was 15 minutes before. Glancing in the mirror, my hair shined with grease and there was no hat in sight to cover it up. A blemish was forming by the right side of my lip, and what little mascara there was on my eyelashes had been smeared. Must have been from helping bake in the kitchen. It had been awfully hot back there, and I wondered if that made my face sweat, smearing my mascara as a result. Oh well. Marsha's friend would just have to deal.

Vanilla chai was my choice of drink while I waited at a tall table next to the door. Marsha said this new friend would be wearing a purple baseball cap and a matching jacket, so I'd know who to look for. Several came in with baseball caps, but not one of them had even a hint of purple. I sat and people-watched out the window, sipping on my chai.

Ten minutes after, I checked my watch and almost decided to give up, when in walked that same rude guy, Shawn, that sometimes hung out at the bakery. My face formed into a frown. I secretly hoped that time he didn't notice me and would just get his order and leave.

Instead, he glanced around the coffee shop, as if he was looking for someone. Then he spotted me over by the door. I noticed then he was wearing a black hat with a purple cat on it, along with a matching jacket. It's the local team's colors. Oh boy.

He smiled at me and sat down. Before I could say anything or dash out the door, he reached to shake my hand.

"You're Missy, right?" He acted like he'd never seen me before.

"Yes," I mumbled.

"I'm Shawn."

"Yes. I know this." I rolled my eyes and crossed my arms.

"I've seen you around. At Marsha's restaurant, Taylor's."

"Yes," I said.

"I didn't ever know your name, though."

"Glad of that," I mumbled, taking a quick sip of the vanilla chai.

"I'm sorry. Is everything alright?" He asked in that charming way he used to act back when I first met him at the bakery and he would order stuff.

"You don't remember, Shawn? I'm the girl you were very rude to in the Sunflower Room at the bakery. You told me to get out. Oh. And the girl you ran into on the street and you shoved me to the side. And let's not forget now that you and Marsha both lied to me about who you are."

"What do you mean? Lied?"

"Marsha led on that you were a woman. She said I would be meeting someone from her church today for coffee that was her friend, and she wanted me to meet her."

"She said I was a woman?" He laughed and performed a ridiculous walk right in front of the table. I hoped other people in the coffee shop weren't watching. He did the perfect imitation of a prissy girl walking down a red carpet, as if in a beauty pageant.

I held back a laugh. I wouldn't want him to think he was funny or in any way amusing. Besides, this was the guy who had been rude to me multiple times. He shouldn't get off the hook that easy, even if he did make me laugh.

"Did you know who you would be meeting today? Am I the only one who was in the dark about all this?" I said, switching to a smug look on my face.

He stopped doing his walk and sat down across from me.

"Marsha mentioned she wanted me to meet someone at a coffee shop named Missy who worked at the bakery with her and was looking for friends.

"Wow. That sounds lame. And sort of desperate. I wasn't meaning for it to." I stood.

Shawn raised his hand in the air to stop me. "I didn't think of it that way at all. All she said was that you were making a couple of changes in your life, and you wanted to find some good friends. That was all. And I was willing to come out of the kindness of my heart." He smiled over at me as he pointed to himself.

"I don't like trying to make friends with people who are rude to others. Even if it is with someone they barely know."

"I did want to apologize about the way I've been acting lately. That day in the Sunflower Room, they were about to have a meeting concerning me. I was nervous and anxious about how it was going to turn out."

"That still doesn't excuse your behavior. I was about to meet with Marsha, and I didn't know you guys needed the space."

"You're right. It didn't excuse my behavior. But I would like to share with you what's been going on lately. I mean, we are on a date, right?" He jokingly grinned. I didn't return his smile.

"Alright. Go on. I'm listening." I acted bored and plopped back down in the seat, almost toppling over.

"I just bought a piece of land and already started building on it and eventually plan to open up a business there. I was informed recently that the city has all these additional rules and codes that I need to follow before I continue construction. I've been talking to them right from the start, and they never informed me of those particular laws, even when I asked. It's going to end up costing me a ton of money that I wasn't expecting, and now I have to find a way to pay for all of it if I want to continue building where I started."

I folded my arms. Why was he telling me all this? It didn't give him the excuse to be rude those other times.

Shawn continued, his eyes showing he was genuinely sorry. "I was supposed to meet some guys who work for the city at the Sunflower Room that day. I was cranky because I had just had a rough day at work. I teach at the community college over in the next town."

I waved my hand to signal him to go on, faking my disinterest in his job.

"One of my students was angry at me for the grade he received and took it all the way up to the dean. I had this big mess I had to figure out that day, and I also had to go to that meeting afterwards in the Sunflower Room to see what extra I had to build to follow the city's codes that they failed to inform me about. I apologize for my behavior that day. I saw you sitting there, and took it out on you, when none of this was your fault."

I sat in silence for a minute, soaking in everything he had said. Unfolding my arms, I looked him in the eyes, showing surrender. "I forgive you." I simply said.

"Great! Because, honestly, it was eating me up. I thought about how I had treated you. Right after you left the room that day, I found out the meeting had been postponed. I went to look for you and apologize, but you were hanging out with Marsha in the kitchen. Sorry I didn't get a chance to apologize until now."

I decided to play it cool and let him off the hook, going against my normal character. "It's no biggie. I see you had it rough that day."

"So I'm off the hook?" He sat up straighter in his chair.

I smiled a real smile that time. "Guess so."

He went to reach for my hand for a quick handshake. "Let's do this like they do in the movies. You know how they always talk about starting over?"

"Yes, we can start over, I guess," I joked.

"I'm Shawn."

"Hi, I'm Missy," I played along.

"I teach at the local community college. I'm an avid reader and...I love Jesus."

"So I hear." I released his hand and frowned.

"Tell me about you. What do you feel is your purpose in life?"

"Ummm....my purpose?" My eyebrows went up. I may have liked it better when I was mad at him.

"Yeah. You know. Your purpose. What gets you excited? What are you passionate about? Who is Missy?" He seemed truly interested in what I had to say.

"Wow. You don't beat around the bush, do you? Just get right to it. Do you do this to all your friends?" I leaned down more in my seat. Just when I thought I was finally feeling comfortable around this guy, he threw me an awkward question about purpose and passion. How was I supposed to answer that?

"Pretty much. I like to think deeply. Sorry if I came across as being nosy. I'm just curious. Marsha had a lot of good things to say about you."

"For real?" I asked with interest. "I'm curious now what she said about me."

"Mainly that you are a good addition to her bakery and you're like family to her. She said you really are a great girl and she's enjoying getting to know you."

"Great?" I said. "I think Marsha is out of it. Maybe she's not as on top of it as she thinks she is. I mean, she is sixty years old. She had me believing you were a woman. Now she's calling me great. I think she's off her rocker."

Shawn laughed. "I don't think so. Under all those prickles, I suspect you really are a great girl."

"Prickles, huh? And just how would you know if I'm a great girl?" I challenged.

"Well, Marsha has known you longer. She said so."

"Did she also say I had prickles?"

"No. That's just an observation of mine."

"Hmmmm." I guess that was fair. I wasn't really that forgiving of him at first.

I could see then why Marsha would say I was "great." Since we were getting to know each other, I was more trusting of Marsha and open with her than anyone else I knew.

"Anyways, tell me about Missy."

I squirmed a little in my seat. Why was this guy being so pushy? Wasn't this all a big mistake? I thought I was making a new friend who was a woman. Someone I could go thrift store shopping with or talk about their dinner recipes. I wasn't expecting this.

I didn't like the way he asked questions. It was as if he wanted to really know me. I didn't want that. I felt like I didn’t even know who I was anymore. And purpose? Honestly, I'm not sure what he meant by that. Why was I still there in the coffee shop, having that conversation with him?

"You know what, Shawn? This has been nice, but I got to get home. I'm pretty tired from work today. The heat from the kitchen can really drain me."

He stood and pushed out his chair. "I made you uncomfortable. Let me make it up to you, when you're not so tired. How about lunch tomorrow? At the bakery? When is your break?"

"I'm afraid I can't. Sorry. I gotta go. Thanks for coming I guess. Sorry I thought you were going to be a woman."

I rushed out the side door of the coffee shop before he had time to respond. His questions kept replaying in my mind. Although maybe his inquiries were normal to him, it wasn't something I talked about every day with people. My purpose? My passion? It all made me feel very uncomfortable. The more I thought about it, the more angry I became. Why would he ask me that? And on the first real outing or whatever this was? If I was being honest with myself, I didn't know what my purpose was. I didn't know what I was passionate about. Who was Missy anyway? And why did this man annoy me so much?

Chapter Twenty-Five

Jesse the Midwife

I knew staying at my friend Abby's house was going to cause me to gain a ton of weight. She fed me like a queen; it was visiting a palace with exquisite cuisine. I didn't cook the same way she did, usually not allowing desserts in my house, unless it was a special occasion. Abby told me they didn't normally eat that way either, but since I was visiting, she decided to splurge. I'd have felt guilty if I refused to eat the snacks and homemade desserts she served.

"I have to tell you, Abby. These desserts are wonderful. Do you spoil your kids with them?" I shoved another giant cookie in my mouth.

"Every now and then."

"I want to try the Sunflower Restaurant and Bakery in town. I hear it's really good. One of my clients used to work there, until she had her baby. I've been told their cinnamon rolls are the best around."

I helped Abby clean up the dishes after a spaghetti dinner on the back patio. The weather had been perfect the entire time I was there. It was the best getaway.

After the dishes were washed, her kids crawled into bed. Abby and I sat on the patio and listened to the sounds of outside all around us. Their backyard was open, with only a couple of trees, which made for a breathtaking view of the stars. It was amazing how much I could see without all the extra light pollution from town.

"How is your family doing, Jesse?" Abby asked as she leaned back in her lawn chair. They were quite comfortable, with an extra pillow for cushion.

"Honestly, I wish they were a lot better," I sighed, looking up at the night sky for comfort.

"What do you mean?" Abby said.

"Well..." I stopped. I felt a twinge of guilt for talking about my kids behind their backs, but Abby and I had been friends for so long, she could be trusted not to judge or tell other people if she was told private information.

"Last weekend I was out in my backyard, taking a walk under the stars. It had been a crazy day at work, and sometimes I love to unwind in our yard, where it's quiet. I've even had a little light installed next to our picnic table and occasionally, I'll enjoy a good book there." I breathed deeply. "That night, I was praying and looking up at the stars, much like we are now. Suddenly, I heard a window opening, and turned to see it was my daughter Anne's window. I didn't think much of it at first but was interrupted again because I could see her feet lowering to the ground. She was sneaking out her back window!"

"Oh no. Teenage girls can be tough to raise sometimes," Abby said, her voice full of empathy.

"I noticed what she was wearing in the moonlight—a little summer dress that was too revealing. It wasn't awful, but something I wouldn't want her to wear in public. I'd never seen that dress before in her stuff, and I don't even know where it came from. I went after her, but before I could catch up, she was out of sight."

"Oh, Jesse. What did you do?"

"I ran inside to find my keys to the car. My husband wasn't home, as he was finishing up some last-minute things at work. I drove for what felt like hours, searching up and down every street in town. I called her cell phone, but it went directly to voicemail each time, so I had no way of reaching her. I felt desperate, and even considered calling the police. Do you think that's overreacting?"

Abby sat and listened, her head shaking. I remember sharing incidents with her in the past about when Anne had disobeyed. A couple of years before I told her she couldn't stay over at a friend's house since I didn't know the family, and I knew the girl was a bad influence. She also had a brother that was a couple years older, and I had suspected Anne really liked this boy. I told her she couldn't go, but she asked her dad the next day when I was gone, and he said she could. He didn't know all the details about this family. I came home furious, but I must remember that he didn't know she had already asked me. I think he would have backed me up, had he known.

"Anyways, Anne is not speaking to me still about the sneaking out the window thing and finding out that I tried to find her. I was so mad that night and waited for her to come home. I was about to fall asleep in the back yard when I heard her climb back through the window. I grabbed her by the arm. She was so angry, I thought for sure the neighbors were going to come over, or worse, call the police."

I could hear Abby gasp. "How embarrassing," she said.

"She told me I don't ever allow her and her sister Haley to have fun and threw a huge temper tantrum and cursed at her dad and I. Let's just say it was a very long night of tears and regrets. This was a week ago, and she's been giving me the silent treatment ever since. I don't know what to do. I never thought this parenting thing could be this hard." I folded my arms. It felt hot outside, or maybe it was just me and my emotions that were all over the place. I also told Abby about Haley, and the incident with her boyfriend coming over.

"We've had a similar thing happen with our own daughter, going back to what you said happened with Anne," Abby said. "She didn't sneak out the window, but she did out the front door one night. My husband was able to catch her, though. We found her just half a block away. She had been invited to a party too. We had let her go to one before, where we thought it was going to be okay, and there ended up being alcohol. She became drunk, and her best friend drove her home. Her friend said she'd tried to stop her, but the more she lectured her, the more she drank." I could hear Abby's voice breaking. "We were so grateful she had been there to drive her home, and very disappointed in our daughter. We were not only embarrassed but shocked she had done such a thing. Turns out she had been having a hard time at school, and she wanted to drink to get her mind off it."

"Oh no! I can't believe it." I felt bad for Abby, but at the same time was glad I wasn't the only one with teenage girls breaking the rules.

"Me either. I don't think this parenting thing gets any easier as they get older. It's just a different type of stress. When they're young, you're trying to keep them out of getting into things when they first learn to crawl and walk. When they're older, you're still trying to stop them from getting into things, just on a different scale. It's all very frustrating."

We both leaned back in our chairs for a second to watch the stars. I thought I had seen a shooting star. How beautiful it was that night. I almost didn't notice, being so wrapped up in our conversation.

"I agree with you. I just don't know what to do with Anne. I wish I knew how to connect with her." Tears stung my eyes and I wiped them away with my sleeve.

"Hmmm." Abby placed her hands behind her head. "Why don't we pray for them right now? I was reading this book the other day that talked about bringing everything to God right away, instead of using prayer as a last resort. It was about having an ongoing conversation with Him, rather than just praying to him every once and awhile. It mentioned talking to Him like we would our best friend."

"I like that idea. Let's do it." Abby led us in a prayer for our kids. She prayed for each of them by name, that they could walk in the way of the Lord. She asked for wisdom and direction in our parenting and told Him we had no idea what we were doing. I held back a laugh when she said that part. But overall, I felt so much better. Even though I still felt like I didn't solve the problem with Anne, it was good to leave it in the hands of the Lord. He knew Anne better than anyone else. He knew things that I didn't. And Abby reminded me that God is at work all around us, even when we don't see it.

Chapter Twenty-Six

Kate

My secret was out. Stupid morning sickness. At least it explained why I passed out on the old man's front lawn in the rain that day. Funny thing was, it was the first pregnancy that I'd experienced nausea and throwing up. I guess each pregnancy is different.

I always liked to find creative ways of telling people we're expecting a baby, but this time, it wasn't possible. My friends beat me to it. And yes, I'm still bitter about it. In no way did I want to steal the spotlight from Chloe and her new baby. But that's exactly what happened.

Chloe offered me her little guest place they have right by their trailer for the remainder of my stay. The arrangement would be perfect. Her husband Peter said he needed to clean it up first, then I could move all my suitcases. I was looking forward to it. I knew oftentimes Chloe felt ashamed of where they lived, but since we are such good friends, she had been quick to overlook it.

As I laid in bed in the guest area waiting to fall asleep for a nap, my phone rang.

"Kate," an older woman's raspy voice said through the receiver.

"Hey, Marge. What's up?" I yawned.

"Did I wake you?" she asked.

"No. I was just thinking about taking a nap. But you're fine. How are things going?"

"You know. Same old same old. Wanted to put in another order." Leave it to Marge to get straight to the point.

"Just so you know, I'm away in Montana, visiting a friend who just had a baby, but I should be back in California the beginning of next week."

"Okay. I don't need the order done anyways until the end of next month."

I grabbed a pen and paper, ready to take down a big order. Ever since I'd started my baking business on the side, Marge had been one of my most faithful customers.

"I'm ready," I said, pen in hand.

"Two dozen chocolate cupcakes, one small, tiered carrot cake. And use the cream cheese frosting this time, okay? That's the one we all really like. With the tiered cake, make it three tiers, with the top one a fake. I need something printed on it too. Wherever you see fit." Marge always sounded angry on the phone, although I came to learn it was just the way she was. Gruff, and to the point. Not intending to be harsh.

"Of course."

"Happy graduation, Molly. I would like that to be all in blue, right on top of that cream cheese frosting."

"You got it. No problem. Just send this all to me in an email, okay? That way I have an extra record of it when I get home too. Make sure you include the exact day you need it by, the location for delivery. You know the drill."

"Got it. Thank you, Kate. Bye."

I had been doing cakes for Marge's family for three years. I was so glad my sister had referred her to me. She was always ordering things. Sometimes, it was hard to keep the business going, what with being a mom on top of that, but I was always grateful for the help my son Brock gave me, even without me asking most of the time.

When Brock was eight, one day he came in the kitchen while I was busy doing a huge order that needed to be ready the next day for a wedding. My first thought honestly was annoyance, since what I really needed was to concentrate on what I was doing to make the order perfect.

"Mom, what are you doing?" He asked as I was measuring ingredients into a large bowl. I felt like snapping at him to leave the kitchen, but I stopped myself.

"Just measuring ingredients into the bowl. I want to make it exact, so that my special recipe turns out good for the people at this wedding."

Brock nodded his head. He just watched me. I tried to ignore it for a while and continued what I was doing. Finally, after the beginning of placing the liquid ingredients into the mix, he spoke up.

"Mom, can I help you with the order?" I stopped. It was not the first time he'd taken an interest in cooking. Many times before he had asked if he could help, and I turned him down. I was afraid he would mess up one of the orders, and I'd have to start over. That time though, I realized something. So what if he did mess up? We could always keep the batch at home and do another one. Besides, he was old enough to help, and I was standing nearby supervising him.

"Alright. I'll show you the rest of the measurements I need for this batch. You can fill up the measuring cups and dump it in, then mix it up for me." I had never seen Brock's face brighter than it was that day.

The batch turned out great. I always made a couple extra for taste testing, and I had to admit it was one of the best. I was glad Brock had asked to help me, and almost every batch since then had been made with him by my side. He even told me one day he wanted to drop out of soccer so he could help me with my baking business. At first we thought he was just saying that because he felt like I needed the help, but when I talked to his coach, he mentioned how Brock didn't seem to like soccer. Since he had just started, his dad let him drop out. Normally, dropping out would be unacceptable to him, but I think he saw how much enjoyment he had from cooking.

Back at Chloe's, my phone rang again, but this time when I answered, I could tell it was Brock. He didn't say anything at first, but just breathed into the phone.

"What's up, Brock? Everything okay?" I asked.

"Mom. You need to come home. Now." Brock whispered.

Chapter Twenty-Seven

Marsha

Missy stomped into the bakery. "Oh; you," she said to me with a frown.

"Missy! How did your time at the coffee shop go with Shawn?" I asked.

"I didn't think you were a liar, Marsha," she growled.

I stared at her, puzzled. "What do you mean, a liar?" I wiped down the counters with a damp cloth, glancing at the clock. Someone had forgotten to wipe them down good the night before. Twenty minutes till the restaurant opened for breakfast.

"Well, first you told me I'd be meeting one of your friends from church who was a woman," she sneered.

I stopped wiping down the counters and made eye contact. "I never said they were a woman. I just said it would be a friend from my church."

"I don't recall you mentioning that." Missy slammed her jacket down on a counter I had already cleaned, and it was still wet. What was her frustration all about? She wanted to meet people and I had arranged that for her. Why did it matter if it was a man or a woman?

"Missy, I think you just must have assumed," I said.

"But you said they would be wearing a purple outfit, and that made me think it would be a woman."

I chuckled. "It may be strange to some, but in Spring Mountain, not only women wear purple. It's the college's color for the outfits they wear. Also, have you ever heard of C. F. wildcats? Or Kansas State? Their color is purple too."

Missy only nodded her head, peering down at the ground I still needed to mop. Was it a look of humility I saw in her eyes this time?

"I don't really see guys going around in purple outfits too often," Missy mumbled. To my relief, she grabbed the mop nearby. It looked like the cleaning crew from the night before didn't do the best job. I was glad Missy was there to help me fix some mistakes.

"We have men wearing purple come into the shop all the time, dear. Don't you see them? Our local team is those colors. Why wouldn't they wear them? Besides, it's not a bright purple or anything. It's darker, and I actually think the men around here like to wear it."

"Anyways, I felt like I was deceived into believing it was a woman you wanted me to befriend, not the man I keep running into who's been very rude to me," Missy put a hand up on one hip after dropping the mop on the floor.

"He's been rude to you? When?"

"On several occasions. And if he's going to be that way to a stranger, then what makes you think he would make a good friend?"

In my opinion, Shawn would be a great friend for Missy. I knew she had seen him come into the shop before. He was one who would tell it like it is. Maybe he could tell Missy something she really needed to hear, and not sugar coat anything. Missy needed a friend who was a good listener, but who also would call her out. Shawn was strong. And exactly what she needed in a friend. There was no denying it, and romantic strings did not need to be attached.

"He would make a wonderful friend, Missy. Just give him a chance. You guys could start over. I think you'll find you really enjoy his company."

"Was this supposed to be like a blind date or something? Are you trying to match me up?"

Missy's eyes were on fire. I had seen her this way before, as most who worked at the restaurant had, but it still made me cringe.

"No. I simply thought you could use a friend. Now, it's up to you if you want to hang out with him or not. I'll let you two arrange what you want to do next."

"There isn't going to be a next time," Missy snapped.

I pondered what Shawn said to her as I flipped the open sign to the bakery. Did he say something to set her off or offend her? If so, it was probably something she really needed to hear. Hopefully she'd get over it sooner rather than later.

"I apologize, Missy. I really thought you two would get along. If you'd like, this time I could send over one of the women from church instead."

"No! It's too late for that. Forget I ever mentioned anything to you. I don't need any new friends anyways." Missy stomped to the kitchen, leaving me sitting at one of the booths. I felt like she just slapped me in the face.

"I'm getting too old for this," I murmured to myself. A couple people over a few booths away who just came in looked at me with pity. I just waved over at them.

"Can I get you guys any coffee?" I asked across the room.

They both shook their heads and continued with their conversation. If only Larry had been next to me to help. He would have known what to say. He agreed to work in the back that day, giving me a bit of a break and helping with cooking while I greeted customers and took orders.

The day dragged on as I worked the front counter. Most of the bakery items were all ready to go. Lots of people asked for something hot like tea or hot chocolate since it looked chilly outside.

That afternoon, Shawn came into the store and I worried that if Missy noticed him, she'd eat him alive. Thank goodness she was in the back, helping Larry with cooking and cleaning.

"Hey, Marsha!" Shawn greeted me with a high five.

"Hello, Shawn," I smiled. Part of me wished the day was already over. My eyes were drooping from being so tired.

"How is business going today?" He asked in his chipper voice.

"It's been steady today. But since there are not a lot of customers now, would you like to sit with me in the corner booth?" Sitting down sounded like heaven at that moment. My feet were aching and I was tempted to take off my shoes. It probably wouldn't be good table manners, though.

"So, Shawn. Tell me about your time with Missy the other day."

"I think it went great," he said.

"Really?" My eyebrow went up.

"Well, there was this thing I said that set her off. But I don't know if I fully understand why." He scratched his head.

"What would that be?" I asked.

“I asked her who Missy was. You know. Like what is she passionate about. Why is she here? But I talk like that all the time with people. I don't see why that would have set her off, but I'm afraid it did."

I could see why it would have turned Missy away. "Missy can hold a grudge easily at times. I hate to say that, but she does. Maybe you should go talk to her and smooth things over. Get to know her slowly. She sounds pretty upset."

"Wow. Yeah, sure. One of the reasons I came over here was to talk to her and try to figure things out. That and to get one of your cinnamon rolls, of course. And a coffee." Shawn held out a twenty dollar bill.

"There's some over there in the glass display case I can get for you." I stood up, tempted to stay seated and rub my feet until the soreness went away.

Missy came out of the kitchen. Once she made eye contact with Shawn, she turned and walked right back.

"Wait!" Shawn yelled before she could turn the corner. "I want to apologize. For what I said the other day. I didn't mean to scare you away."

"Well, you did." She turned to leave again.

"I was wondering if you'd come to dinner with me? Maybe tomorrow? Just as friends of course, but I can buy. Let it just be my way of making it up to you."

Missy's wheels were turning in her head.

"Alright. But I get to pick the place." To my surprise, she strolled closer to Shawn. I didn't think she would go for the idea at all. My mouth dropped open. What other surprises did she have up her sleeve?

"Okay. You pick. Any place you want," Shawn said.

"There's a steak house over in the next town. I want to go there," Missy pointed in that direction.

Shawn went along with her idea. "That's the best place. You'll love it. I've eaten there several times. I can even tell you some things on the menu you should try."

"Nope. Already have my mind made up. It'll be prime rib. Medium-rare. Mashed potatoes with corn mixed in. Cornbread on the side."

"Wow. I like when people know what they want," he teased.

"Oh. And there will be more. I want to be able to take leftovers home too. Expect a big bill buddy," Missy said.

Was that what these young folks around here called flirting? I scratched my head. If so, boy, things have surely changed.

Chapter Twenty-Eight

Chloe

The dinner the hospital kitchen made for Peter and I the night after the birth was delicious. I hadn't eaten like that for a long time. I ordered the steak with mashed potatoes, asparagus, and a brownie. My midwives had told me to bring my blood pressure down about a month or so before I had the baby, so I hadn't indulged since. I found it hard to cut out carbohydrates.

The day after the baby came, I didn't get any sleep. When I tried, a staff member would want to come in our room. A hospital midwife I hadn't met yet suggested we stay another night at the hospital. She said she'd seen so many new moms who would go home overwhelmed, and that the hospital staff could watch the baby while I rested. I considered what she had to say, but I was tired of all the noise coming from outside the doors and the constant hospital staff in my room every hour. How did any of the patients get rest? I decided we needed to get home that night.

Later that evening I came out of the bathroom and Peter was smiling.

"You'll never guess who our nurse was," he chuckled.

"Umm. I already give up. Who?"

"April," he said.

"April. April who?" I scratched my head, not in the mood for guessing games. Didn't he understand I'd just went through something called childbirth?

"You know. April. The one I used to go to school with?"

"Oh. That April. The one you had a crush on?" I laughed. There were many times I had wondered what it would have been like if Peter would have married April. Would they have fought about money like we often did? Maybe not with her fancy degree.

"Yep. That's the one. I knew she was going to school to be a nurse, but I had no idea she would be at this hospital." Peter placed his toothbrush into its case, preparing for check out.

"So, what did she say?"

"She was asking questions about the baby. Apparently, she just got hired about a month ago."

"Wow. That's crazy," I said, stuffing maternity clothes into my travel bag. "Good thing we're leaving now. I'd hate to see her start making googly eyes at you again." I teased, but there were some days I wondered if Peter wished he would have married her instead of me. She was pretty with her long, red braided hair. I could never get my hair to look that way. Mine was frizzy and out of control. Maybe she could at least keep her emotions under control, unlike me.

Peter brushed his arm through the air, as if sweeping my comment away. He changed the subject.

"This is the first time we've been away from the baby." Peter stared at the door with sad puppy eyes.

"Me too. I miss just holding our new baby in my arms. So warm and soft."

"At least it gives us some time to pack up our stuff. We get to check out here around 10:00. It's pretty late, but it will be nice to be in our home finally with the baby," he added.

More than anything, I wished I could communicate with Peter and share my heart with him and what was weighing me down. Finances were such a constant worry. I didn't want to repeat what my parents did. My siblings told me stories of times we didn't have much food to eat when I was little. I didn't want that for my own kids.

At last, the nurses wheeled the baby back in. 9:30 finally rolled around and April did the process for checking us out of the hospital. I looked her up and down. Slender. Short. Perfect yoga pants body. No extra rolls from pregnancy, like I had. Did Peter notice? I gulped my insecurities down with a bottle of water. Hopefully they would stay down this time. I hated having those thoughts.

Finally, all our stuff was packed and ready to go. Peter loaded the car. April checked to make sure we had everything and escorted us out the door. I was glad when she shut the car door and walked away. Finally, I could be away from the hospital.

"Wow. This seems so surreal. Is the baby really ours? I feel like we're just babysitting," I laughed as Peter drove down the road. The baby sat quietly in the car seat, eyes open.

"I know, right? Peter agreed.

"How about we get something to eat? I'm hungry. That dinner they gave us was really good, but that was hours ago."

"What do you feel like eating?"

"A hamburger would be nice." Peter drove in the direction of McDonalds, and I turned my attention back over at our new baby in the car seat. I wanted to take the baby out and hold him, but for safety, I decide against it. I'd been handed the most precious gift I could ever receive, and wasn't sure what to do.

Finally, we arrived home and I dropped my bags. It felt good to be home. Run down trailer and all.

"Well, baby. You're home. I know it isn't much, but we do have a little area for you over here."

I was zonked. Peter entertained the baby while I brushed my teeth and prepared for bed. I gazed at myself in the mirror. My hair was tangled, breath smelled like I ate a bunch of garlic, and my clothes needed to be washed. But I decided a shower could wait. I was too tired to care. I distracted myself from thinking about April again. I had just had a baby and not April. Of course she looked so perfect.

My heart sunk when I opened our bedroom door. It was full of boxes. Never ending clutter. We still weren't finished organizing everything, even after the baby was here. I knew it was a popular thing to do, but I didn't feel safe sleeping in the same bed as the baby. Our beds were too soft, and I could accidentally knock the baby on the floor if I were to try something like that. Peter decided to sleep on some blankets on the floor next to me, while the baby went on the other side in a baby box the hospital gave us.

The baby was awake, so I nursed him to sleep and laid him down in his bed. To my disappointment, his eyes opened again. I grumbled and picked him back up and nursed him again. Wow. This mothering thing was already hard. What in the world was I doing, and would I ever get to sleep? Peter was on the floor asleep, I almost wished we could switch places.

Finally, I was able to get the baby in the box, and his eyes remained shut. Dozing off, I smiled because he was asleep in his own little spot. About ten minutes later, he woke up, staring at me and whimpering. I started the process all over again, picking him back up, and nursing him to sleep. It was the third night in a row for me to not have a good night's rest. Tears rolled down my cheeks. Part of me wished these baby days away. Sleepless nights, extra flab, jealousy, and all.

Chapter Twenty-Nine

Jesse the Midwife

Abby was a good host, and I felt comfortable on the soft bed she gave me to rest on. All those long nights of being a midwife had caught up with me, and I needed the sleep.

"Jesse. Jesse! Wake up." Abby shook me awake.

"What?" Groggy, I opened one eye. Why was Abby waking me in the middle of the night? Hadn't we gone to bed late after praying for our kids together?

"I need your help. Now," Abby demanded. I had never heard her so desperate.

"Um, why?" I managed to say, sitting up in bed, rubbing my eyes. I forgot to take my mascara off the night before and was afraid it smeared all around my face and the pillowcase.

"Just come with me," Abby commanded. When I didn't pop out of bed right away, she retraced her steps, grabbed my arm, and yanked me out of bed.

"Ouch. I'm coming. Geeze," I rubbed my arm dramatically. "Just let me run to the bathroom quick."

"There's no time for that." She grabbed me by the arm again. Since I was finally awake, I felt worried.

Abby led me through the dark living room, and I stumbled over some play blocks one of her kids didn't pick up the night before.

"Ouch!" I screeched. My big toe had been jammed from a block.

"Come on." Abby pulled me off the floor. I moaned in pain. "I can walk myself," I managed to say in a not-so-nice tone. I immediately regretted the way I said it. She obviously was needing help. She was nervous and scared.

Abby let go of my arm and we walked through her front yard in the dark, where I had to avoid the sprinklers. She didn't mind the sprinkler coming right toward her, and I was able to dodge one of them as I walked around. Thank goodness she didn't notice my little detour. She probably would have pulled on my arm again to hurry up.

The moonlight bounced off the water on top of the grass, making the houses across the way less visable. Abby led me to one of the nearby houses down a dirt road. She walked into the front door without knocking. A small lamp was on in the corner of the living room. I couldn't help but notice the house looked incredibly filthy. Dishes piled everywhere on the kitchen counter with dog hairs sticking to plates and the edges of cups. Toys and dirty laundry were scattered across the floor. I peered at bits of cereal on the ground, and the floor where people came in was caked with mud. Abby plowed right through the mess, not giving it a second thought. She showed me to a back bedroom, and stopped at the doorway.

"We need your help, Jesse." Abby was shivering, most likely from the cool night air hitting her sports shorts and T-shirt after being sprayed by the sprinklers back in her yard.

"What is it?" I whispered. I could see over her shoulder in the next room there were two small children asleep on a tiny bed. I didn't want to wake them. She glanced over her shoulder, and slowly opened the door.

Across the room was a small lantern hanging in the corner. The entire space reminded me of a scene out of the 1800s. Logs made up the walls and there was a small overhang where the bed stood. I couldn't see past the mess easily and noticed a horseshoe hanging on the wall and worn out cowboy hats hanging on hooks in the corner. The bed had been propped higher up, most likely to store things underneath. Dirty clothes were scattered all around the room as well. What really caught my eye was *who* was laying on the bed. The woman was sweating, a look of worry on her face. When she saw me come in, she attempted to push herself back up on some pillows.

"Jesse," she whispered. A look of relief swept across her face.

"Ara is in labor. Her midwife couldn't make it because she's very sick. We thought about taking Ara to the hospital so she can labor there, or calling the paramedics, but since you are here..." Abby's voice trailed off.

"I'm happy to help," I said.

I could see tears on Abby's face. She nodded her thanks.

It took me a second to realize who the woman on the bed was when I had walked in. I could barely recognize her with hair messed up and her face as red as a cherry. It was the woman who I 'd been telling Abby about. The one who decided she didn't want to continue her business with the birthing center. My stomach churned. And now she was stuck with me as her midwife anyway.

Shoving my feelings aside about the choice Ara had made, I put on my professional look and shifted into midwife mode. This was what I lived for. My passion.

Please, Lord. Guide my hands tonight as I help deliver Ara's baby. Help my own personal feelings not to get in the way with her needing my help. Help me be calm and patient, just as if she were any other person in my clinic. Show me how to keep a good attitude, despite what happened before. Please help her to have a safe delivery and give her peace as this is her first child. Give her strength and energy for the night ahead of her. Amen.

I switched gears, wondering who the other children sleeping in the next room were. Ara had told me in our office this was her first child.

"It might be good if the other children are not in earshot as her labor progresses," I whispered to Abby. She nodded her head, then nudged a woman I didn't even notice before, standing in the corner. They both left the room together. It was a good thing I happened to have some supplies in my car. I always kept a set ready in case one of my clients called to tell me they were in labor, and I need to rush over to help.

Once Abby came back in the room, I sent her with my car keys to fetch the midwife kit and extra blankets while I pulled up my sleeves.

"Tell me about your labor so far, Ara." I asked between contractions. "What happened before I arrived?"

She proceeded to tell me the typical symptoms of early labor, and I listened while sitting on the edge of her bed. Once she was done talking, I gave her some space. She still had some time before the next stages.

"I don't want you to feel like I'm abandoning you. I just know when too many people are watching a woman in labor like a hawk, it can slow it down and make you uncomfortable. I'm going to be in the other room for a while. If you need anything at all, please don't hesitate to tap on this button." I handed her a button I purchased the month prior which came in handy for labors. I grabbed Abby by the arm and dragged her into the other room. Wondering where Ara's husband went, I disappeared back into the living room, welcomed by piles of laundry. The couch could not be seen.

Without saying a word, Abby picked up the clothes around her and stuffed them in a laundry basket. When she ran out of room, she hunted around the kitchen for a garbage bag, and placed the leftover laundry in it, then set it aside.

"I'm so glad you're here, Jesse. I know she really didn't want to labor in the hospital. You are a God send."

I smiled over at her. "I'm happy to help."

"You know how my kids are adopted. I've never in my life had to experience labor and seeing my friend like this scared me. She called me shortly after our prayer last night, and I rushed over to check on her. That's when I discovered her midwife couldn't come, and her cousin was thinking about taking her to the hospital. I told her how you were here visiting though, and that you're a midwife."

"What did she say?" I asked.

"She was so grateful to hear a midwife was close by. When I told her your name, she said she knew who you were." Abby peered over at me curiously. Not feeling in the mood to explain yet who she was, I simply nodded my head.

"We've seen each other here and there," I mumbled.

Thankfully, Abby didn't ask any more questions on the matter, which I was grateful for. I kept thinking how crazy the night had been. First being dragged out of bed suddenly, and discovering there's a woman in labor depending on me that made it known earlier she didn't want me delivering her baby. She was just desperate.

I considered for a moment calling in another midwife I know, but then I thought how hard it would be to call someone early in the morning. I couldn't bother them about a woman who wasn't their client, just because I was feeling self-conscience and bothered by what I heard about Ara before. I decided to stay and follow through with the labor. What were the odds that I would happen to be friends with someone who knew her?

Abby and I continued cleaning in silence. At first, I felt weird cleaning someone else's home I barely knew, especially when it was so messy. Would she mind? I peered over at Abby, who seemed like she'd known this neighbor for years. How close were they exactly, I wondered? Did they come over to each other's homes often?

"Where did you guys move the two kids who were sleeping?" I asked Abby, who was picking up the cereal one by one off the floor with her hands. There must not have been a vacuum. Either that or Abby didn't want to make so much noise.

"I walked them over to my house, where I put them in another guest room we have. They seemed so tired and didn't mind at all. They fell right back to sleep. The mom didn't want to leave them alone at first. But I woke up my husband and told him they were there and if they needed anything, he would be there with my kids too."

I assumed the children belonged to the woman who had been hiding in the corner. I nodded and continued cleaning.

"So you said it would be awhile until Ara goes into the intense part of labor? Although it sure did look intense already to me."

I smiled at Abby. Abby was a very strong woman, but I had seen her very upset over the fact that she couldn't have her own biological kids. Or could she? Abby had told me they had been trying to have a baby for three years, but nothing ever happened. They had always wanted to adopt, whether they could have kids or not, and so they put in the adoption papers and were very blessed to get their kids when they did. Many years later, they still didn't have their own.

In all the years I had been a midwife, I had noticed when a couple was very stressed out and trying to have children, it didn't seem to work. It's when they finally gave up trying and were more relaxed, they became pregnant. Not so with Abby.

I heard the ringing, interrupting my thoughts. Glancing up at the clock, I realized an hour had gone by. Time passed quickly while we were cleaning, and the living room looked much better. We could actually see the floor and had time to dust and pick up the rest of the cereal without a vacuum.

I headed back into the bedroom, Abby trailing behind me.

"How are you feeling?" I asked Ara. She looked like she just woke up.

"Fine. I think I dozed off awhile between contractions. I have never felt so tired in my life."

"I remember that feeling. Once it's time to push, though, you'll feel like you are a participant, and you'll get a second wind. It's good you're getting a little rest now."

Abby and I sat on the edge of the bed as I timed the length between each contraction. They were only a couple minutes apart. It wouldn't be long. Hopefully Abby could handle watching this part. It would help to have another set of hands.

Chapter Thirty

Kate

Lord, I think I'm ready to go home. It's been a nice visit here with Chloe in Montana, but I've been thinking a lot about my kids. And Mark. That's the challenging part, though. Since when does money and careers matter more to him than his wife and kids? Didn't he used to want to spend time with us, and care less about what his paycheck said? Yes, nice things like our house currently in L.A. is a dream. It's beautiful both inside and out, but I would much rather live in a shack and have my husband around, than to live in a big spacious house and never have him around.

After my walk down a path outside Chloe's place, I prepared dinner for her family. Working in the kitchen was always therapeutic to me.

"I have to tell you, Kate. You and Marsha are my two favorite cooks in the whole world. You should spend more time with her before you leave. You'd really like her," Chloe said, shoving another bite of casserole in her mouth.

"The times I've been able to talk with her, I have really enjoyed. She seems like a really passionate and kind woman. Everyone around town just loves her, " I said. There was no dishwasher, so I prepared the sink to wash the plates by hand.

"She's probably one of the few that have stayed here so long in this small town. She's one of the people that keep this town together. I don't know what they'd do without her," Chloe said.

"It might be good for you to get out too. You've been cooped up inside for the past couple weeks. Wouldn't you like to get out and about?" I said, grabbing Chloe's plate from the table.

"Definitely. I've felt like a hermit just hanging out here at the house. It does make it easier with the baby, having everything here, and with having to nurse him so often and everything. But you're right. It would do the soul good just to get out and see friends, or just the countryside." Chloe peered longingly out the window.

"How about this afternoon? After I call home and see how the kids are doing, do you want me to help you pack up some baby stuff and we can head over to the Sunflower bakery? I've seen part of the inside once, but would love for Marsha to give me the grand tour. You know how I am with kitchens." I opened the cabinet to look for more dish soap.

"That'd be great. You have no idea." Chloe looked excited just to get out of the house. I had to admit that when my kids were babies, I tried to take them everywhere with me. I hated being cooped up at home and was constantly trying to find excuses to get out of the house and away from the piles and piles of laundry that never ended.

I called my family to see how they were doing. They each passed the phone around so each one could say, "hi" to mom. My youngest one was having the hardest time out of all of them with me being away so long. Mark was having some of his family help out with watching the kids, and it sounded like they were keeping them busy.

"What did you do yesterday?" I asked one of the children.

"We went to the San Diego Zoo. It was amazing!" He told me about the new ape exhibit and gave me some details about their day at the zoo. I was glad that they were getting out and doing things. I felt a little bad my in-laws were paying for all of this for our kids. I talked to Mark about it and he said they had been thinking of taking them to that zoo for quite some time, and it was something they had been looking forward to. That made me feel a little better.

Afterwards I showered and went into the baby's room where Chloe stored all the clothes. The new diaper bag Chloe's sister-in-law gave them waited in the corner, so I stuffed it with baby essentials such as clean onesies, socks, hats, diapers, and wipes. I put in a nursing cover and some supplemental bottles just in case and added a few more things the baby might like such as toys and a binky and zipped it up. It was stuffed so much, it was hard at first to zip. I decided he could do without two bottles of diaper rash cream and two milk bottles and zipped it up easier the second time.

"You ready to go?" I said, diaper bag in hand.

"Ummm...almost. I just need to change his diaper and put on some nicer clothes for our outing," Chloe said.

"Oh, come on, Chloe. He's a baby. He can get away with wearing pajamas everywhere he goes."

"I know. I just want him to wear that adorable new outfit he got from the baby shower. It has foxes on it and a matching hat."

"Where's it at? I can get it for you."

"It's hanging up in his closet."

A half hour later, we finally were out the door. I drove while Chloe sat in the back seat with the baby. This seemed to really keep him calm, and he cooed all the way down the road.

"Where do I turn, again?" I glanced in Chloe's rear view mirror, hoping she could get me on the right road to the Sunflower Bakery.

"It's after this next street." She pointed ahead.

Before we knew it, we were standing in front of the restaurant. I noticed little things here that really must catch the eye of her customers. I took a few mental notes. It may have sounded a little crazy, even to myself, but one of my secret dreams was to one day run my own store or restaurant rather than from home. The decorating, the new customers I'd meet, the recipes we could create. It was something I thought about often, but didn't share with a lot of people, for fear it would never work out.

Did you put this dream in my heart, Lord? Why do I always think about having my own restaurant? At this point in my life, it sounds farfetched. Do you think it could really happen?

I turned my attention to little things the Taylors had done to the bakery. In front of the store stood a huge flower holder sitting on the sidewalk, holding beautiful sunflowers and an old-fashioned bike leaned up against it. Where had I seen that image before? It looked like something straight out of a travel magazine.

As I entered the front doors, there was quite a difference in the atmosphere than outside the restaurant. Outside made me think of a prairie, and the inside by the front entrance was themed like a scene out of the woods in Montana. Remembering how Chloe told me about Marsha's love for the state she grew up in, I could see it through her eyes. The leather sofa gave the bakery a nice rustic look, and the trees she had in the corners reminded me of the view just down the street. She had mountain pictures, and an old-fashioned map of Montana hanging on the wall.

"Wow. I like what they've done with the place," I said.

"Really? Like what?" Chloe asked while heading towards the Sunflower Room.

"Like that old map over there of Montana. And that chair over there in the corner. It looks like there's plenty of places for the customers to sit. I like it."

I followed Chloe down the hallway, as she held the baby right against her in the carrier.

"This room is my favorite," Chloe pointed over at the Sunflower Room. "I remember being so homesick when I first started working here, and I used to come in here on my breaks since it reminded me so much of home. Marsha absolutely loves flowers, and I was so glad to discover she had this room for me to explore."

"It looks absolutely wonderful," I said, turning in every direction, taking it all in. This place is like a dream." I couldn't describe how much I liked the way she'd decorated.

"Let's head into the kitchen. I think it's about that time where Marsha takes out a fresh batch of her famous cinnamon rolls. You have got to try one right out of the oven. You won't want to leave." I followed her through the hallway into the kitchen area. My eyes met the huge ovens that lined the back walls. My mouth dropped open. Jackpot!

"Chloe! You didn't tell me that Marsha had a kitchen like this." I stopped in my tracks. "It's literally the best kitchen I've ever seen in my entire life. It even beats the kitchens I have seen on my favorite cooking shows!"

Chloe shrugged her shoulders. "You didn't ask?"

To the average person who isn't into baking stuff, it would have just been a kitchen. But to me, it was a dream come true.

"Okay. I have to admit I'm totally jealous. Marsha must have so much fun with her baking. Look at those countertops. And all that space to work. Wow."

Chloe just laughed. I could tell she enjoyed watching my face light up from all the things there at the bakery.

"I can see why you liked to work here. It's amazing."

Chloe smiled. "Yes. These are very nice facilities. But that's not the only reason why I liked working here so much. It could actually be located in the slums and I wouldn't really care, as long as the Taylor's were running this place. They are the ones at the heart of it. If it weren't for them pouring their hearts into this place, it wouldn't be the haven for the town that it is."

"I can definitely see that."

Marsha came through the kitchen doors just while we took a seat in the back of the kitchen at a table hidden in the corner.

"I'm surprised you guys already looked over it and everything. Wow. And he wants me to interview for it day after tomorrow? I just can't believe how fast. I thought it would take way longer than that to even get a call back...Yes. I know. I just need to sit down and talk to Larry about it more. Okay." Marsha's voice trailed off as she walked back through the kitchen doors, into the serving area. She hadn't noticed us tucked in the back, since a part of it was covered by shelves and ingredients for baked goods. Glancing through the shelves, I saw a lot of the same items and brands I used in my cooking back home.

Chloe looked at me, her eyes wide. "You don't think Marsha would possibly...no. It can't be what I'm thinking. There's no way she would give this all up."

"What are you talking about?" I raised my eyebrows.

"Marsha. The phone call."

"Oh. I wasn't even paying attention. I try not to listen in on other people's phone conversations," I teased.

Chloe didn't smile at that one." She said something about an interview and the day after tomorrow and talking to Larry about something. What do you think is going on?"

I paused to consider it. "Maybe she's just interviewing for a part time job or something on the side. Who knows? Maybe she needs a little change in her life; that doesn't mean she's giving up the restaurant."

"I've seen the amount of hours she's spent pouring into this place. There's no way she could handle all this and a part time job on the side. I just don't see how it's possible."

"Maybe she's going to hire someone else here to help with things at the bakery so she can have more time on her hands. It could be a number of things, Chloe. And I'm sure by now she would have told you if this was something that big going on in her life. I mean, you guys are pretty close, right?"

"Yes, but I've been preoccupied with the baby and everything. Maybe she just didn't want to take away from that. I could ask one of the other workers if she's mentioned it at any of the meetings. Surely, they would be up to date. I've just been gone for quite a while since having the baby. A lot could have happened that she hasn't filled me in on yet."

"Why don't you just ask her yourself?"

"I don't want her to know I was listening in out her phone conversation. It sounds so tacky."

"I don't think it's tacky. If she's talking on the phone at work, then she should know that there's always a possibility someone could overhear her phone conversation."

"I don't know, Kate. I guess I'm just nervous. And scared. I'm afraid of the answer I'm going to get. I couldn't imagine this place without her. But I guess it shouldn't really matter to me anyways. It's not like I'm going to be working here, what with deciding to be a stay-at-home mom and all."

"That's true. You can always be a customer, though."

Chloe nodded and smiled, but I could see the sadness in her eyes.

"Guess we'll just see what's going on soon enough. It's bound to come out sooner or later."

Chapter Thirty-One

Marsha

My jaw dropped when they told me the news. I'd been offered the job to work at the Mission in Mexico, right at the end of the interview. I was the last person they were interviewing, coming highly recommended by Penny. They said out of all the candidates for the cooking position, I was the most qualified, and the one they could see mingling with their guests who came to serve with them at the mission.

I still hadn't mentioned any of the news to the staff at the bakery. Larry was offered the job too. We both told the hiring committee we wanted to continue to pray and think on it, and they agreed to hear from us in a week at the latest for what our answer would be.

I'd been walking around in a bit of a daze at work that day, just going through the motions. One customer initiated conversation, but most of it was me nodding my head and smiling, and not engaging. So much thinking to do and such a short amount of time. My whole life was wrapped up in this restaurant. It was hard to think of giving it up.

Lord, help Larry and I with this huge decision in our lives. We both are getting older, and it seems crazy to pack up our stuff and start a new life in Mexico. And yet I like the idea of having someone carry on my vision with the bakery to the next generation if we were to move. All my children have their own lives and careers, and I know they have never taken an interest in taking over the bakery. I ask for your help with it all. Show us what we should do. If we go, lead us to the right person who will take care of this place and be a good leader.

"Hey, Marsha," Chloe said, interrupting my thoughts. She came to visit often with the new baby.

"Two of my most favorite people," I said.

"I can't stay away," Chloe smiled. "And I thought I should bring Kate by and give her a tour of the place. She absolutely loves it here."

I peered at Kate. Not to be rude, but I wasn't in the mood to talk to anyone new, but I forced a cheerful tone.

"How long are you going to be staying in Montana, Kate? I've been meaning to have you guys over for dinner. Or maybe we could have dinner here?" I distracted myself by thinking about what I could make.

"I'd love that. I'm going to be here until next week. My flight takes off Tuesday evening."

I felt dizzy and lightheaded. What was going on with me?

"Please keep in touch," I said as I tumbled into the back. I sat at the kitchen table and put my head in my hands. My head was pounding. Why the sudden headache? I had a dinner to serve in the Sunflower Room, in addition to my regular baking. The room had been rented out for a wedding, and I'd been asked long before to cater the event. There was a great deal of items on the menu, some of which I already had cooking on the stove with Larry's help, and others I hadn't started yet. It was already getting late into the afternoon. How was I going to finish all that up with my head hurting so bad? I couldn't even remember the last time I had a headache. I knew it was the stress causing it.

"We're heading out in a bit, Marsha." Chloe came to the back of the kitchen where I was sitting. "Is everything okay? Are you feeling well?" Chloe's brows curved down.

"My head is hurting so bad, Chloe." I barely was able to say, my head planted in my hands. I felt like I had been hit.

"Let me get you some water," Chloe offered. She flew over to the little staff refrigerator, where I always keep waters stocked for the workers. I took it gratefully.

"Is there anything I can do?" I heard Chloe tell Kate they should take me to the emergency room.

"That won't be necessary. I just need to lie down awhile. Chloe. Is there any way you could come into work today? I really need some help with the wedding I'm catering tonight." I cringed. It hurt to talk.

"I'm afraid I don't have anyone to watch the baby for me, unless..."

Kate cut in. "I can help in the kitchen. I do my own baking and cooking at home and have my own little business. I know what it's like to have a time restraint. Let me help with the cooking and serving, Marsha."

"I had no idea you had your own baking business. That's wonderful. Just let me rest here a few minutes, and I'll show you what I'm working on. I'll ask Larry to take me home. Chloe, are you okay staying here with Kate, at least until Larry comes back? You are welcome to have the baby here with you if you want while she works, or head back home. Whatever works for you."

"I think that's a good idea, Marsha. Both Kate and I can stay here, and I can be around if she has any questions. I can have the baby here with me to nurse and help here and there if I can."

"Great." I took in a deep breath. The headache already felt a little better.

I showed Kate the recipes I started and the things that needed to be completed. I explained how Chloe knew the protocols for serving at the events, if there were any questions.

"Don't worry about a thing, Marsha. You're in good hands." Chloe reassured me.

"Thank you so much, ladies. We'll have to do that dinner soon, after I am able to get some rest."

I found Larry behind the bakery pulling up weeds and asked that he take me home. He didn't ask too many questions, but I could see the look on his face was of genuine concern. I told him of the arrangements I made with Chloe and Kate and asked if he would mind staying home with me for a bit.

At home, I went through my regular bedtime routine and snuggled between the blankets, thinking about the bakery. There had been help right when I needed it. Could it be possible this trend would continue?

Chapter Thirty-Two

Missy

Staring at the deer and elk heads on the walls of the restaurant, I savored each bite of the steak. Shawn had kept his promise of taking me out, as an apology for his rude behavior.

"How is it?" Shawn asked. I finished the bite I was on, and put my fork down to wipe my face.

"Mmmmm. So good," I said.

"So you grew up here?" Shawn asked. I didn't want to point out that he had a bit of steak sauce on the right side of his lip.

"Pretty close to here. Boring, huh? How about you? Where did you grow up?"

"All over. My dad was in the military, so we moved all over the United States."

"What brought you to this area?"

"My dad had some friends who lived about an hour from here, and we would come to visit them often. When I saw they had a job opening here after college, I decided to jump on the chance to move. I love it here."

I thought about if it weren't for the bakery and Marsha taking me in like one of her own, I'd so be out of this town. Not responding to Shawn's comment, I just sat and stared at the pictures on the wall.

"That's a pretty painting over there. It's a painting of the desert sunset. An old cowboy painting. Next to the vibrant colors is a cowboy with his rope ready to go and he's looking the other way, enjoying the sunset."

"Are you an artist?" Shawn asked while sipping his drink.

I laughed. "Not that kind of artist. I can't paint to save my life. But I appreciate good artwork, and even have some paintings I bought a long time ago at the secondhand store. They're somewhere under my bed."

"What are they?" he asked.

"One is a painting of a writer at a desk, looking out the window for inspiration. The other is of an open kitchen, a 1950s farm mother baking while the kids are playing a game in the living room. The dad is coming home from work, standing by the door," I explained. I didn't want to mention the reason I had those two paintings tucked away.

One was because of my dream to one day be an author. The other painting of the mother I bought at a local store when I was feeling down about not having a family. In a way, the painting cheered me up. The mother looked so happy baking and the children were having fun playing on the floor. I admired the looks on their faces, and every time, I felt a part of them. It was a small picture of a life I'd never have. A loving mother, her husband looking fondly at his wife and children, and the siblings on the floor playing.

"Do you know who the artist is?" Shawn asked, interrupting my thoughts.

"No clue," I murmured.

"What made you want to pick those two out?" He asked while chomping on his steak. *Here it comes.*

I pieced answers together in my head, not sure how much to tell this man. I decided to only tell him part of my story.

"I've always admired different genres of literature and their authors. That's the reason I bought the author painting looking out the window. The 1950s housewife one...let's just say I admire the 1950s." I didn't want to tell him about my family. A lot of people have felt sorry for me over the years and conversations would be awkward afterwards.

"Me too. I love the music from that era. It's so upbeat and fun," Shawn smiled. "There's a place down the street that kind of has a

1950s feel to it. We should go sometime. They have ice cream and a remake of a juke box they let people play."

"Wow. I didn't even know they had that here."

"It's a newer place." Shawn was silent for a moment. "Missy, tell me about your family. Where do they live? Do you have siblings?" he asked.

Wow. It didn't take too long to get around to that. I sighed. Another person about to feel sorry for me.

"Actually, my mom died when I was very young. It was just me and my dad for a while, and then I moved out when I was 16."

"Oh." His smile faded down to a frown. "Well tell me what you remember about them."

"I don't have too many good memories with either of them. My father was very distant. He was hardly home, and when he was, he would lock himself in his room or the garage to work on a project. He was either away drinking or working. Growing up, I mainly hung outside the home with other people from my school. It's probably a good thing I was an only child; then my family wouldn't have had to worry about another mouth to feed." I had over shared to this man. Too much too soon.

Shawn nodded his head and listened politely. "That would be so hard, Missy. I can't imagine what you've been through."

"It's okay. I managed. I got through it. Everyone has their thing they have to go through that's hard."

"Yes. But they don't have to go through it alone."

"Well, I had nobody. I gritted my teeth. I got through it. Life goes on."

His eyes got wide and he shrunk back a bit. "Whoah. Okay."

I turned it back on him. "Tell me about your family. Do you have brothers and sisters?"

"I have one sister. She lives down the road from me actually. And a brother who just got a job about an hour from here."

"Must be nice having family nearby."

"Totally." He looked down, his face kind of sad.

"My dad is going to be retiring from the military in a couple of years. He's stationed down in Florida. My mom is a high school writing teacher down there. She's done that for years, and loves her job. I guess that's where I get my passion for teaching as well. Only I chose to teach older people, and enjoy the challenge. My brother and sister and I are pretty close. They are two of my best friends." Shawn was hesitant to tell me about his family. I guessed it was because he knew my background, but I was glad he was being honest. I didn't like people feeling sorry for me.

The rest of the evening we talked a lot about teaching and the students he'd had, which I took great interest in. I hadn't met anyone who enjoyed their job as much as he did. We went for a walk at the park around sunset, my favorite time of day. Climbing a hill that overlooked the sunset, we sat at the top. There was not a tree in sight on top of this hill, and I liked how open it was all around us. He told me how he and his siblings liked to go there in the wintertime and sled down this hill every New Year's Eve. It was a tradition they'd done since they were little, he said. I would love to be a part of something like that but didn't mention it to Shawn. Later in the evening, though, he invited me to come along with them, which I greatly appreciated.

There was something Shawn said on the hill that night I couldn't stop thinking about. We were talking about the colors of the sunset and where it met the field, then he said, "You know, you do have a Father. And he cares about you very much." That's really one of the last things he said to me before we walked down the hill and I hopped in my car and drove away.

It took me awhile to realize what he really meant. He wasn't talking about my biological father that had been distant to me. He was talking about the Father in Heaven he believes in. I remember

Marsha saying that exact same thing to me one day when I opened up to her a little about my family and past. I didn't think much of it then, but now it's clear what she meant. I thought about this concept, trying to sleep. It might sound silly to some, but I reached my arms up in the air for a little while, while lying in my bed, as if to give this Heavenly Father a hug. That's one thing I don't remember my earthly father ever giving me. A real hug.

Chapter Thirty-Three

Jesse the Midwife

Ara had been in labor for quite some time. Secretly, I was beginning to worry, although I didn't allow myself to show it. After all the years of being a midwife, I tried my best to stay as professional as possible- calm and constant. I thought about how transporting her to the hospital would be the best solution, if she didn't progress within that next hour. She was dehydrated, despite Abby's efforts of getting her to drink some of the electrolytes she found at a natural food store. It was similar to Gatorade but had less sugar and no dyes. I wished at that moment I could administer an IV on my own. It's Montana state law a midwife outside of the hospital must have a nurse give the IV.

"Ara, I know you must be the most exhausted you have ever been in your entire life. But I really need you to focus. I want to get the baby out soon, otherwise we'll need to transport you to the hospital so you can be monitored and get an IV. You're getting very dehydrated."

Ara sighed. At that point the poor exhausted mother didn't even care. She was ready to fall asleep. I took a different approach, one I use now and again when patients are having a hard time progressing.

"Okay, Ara. I want you to think of something to motivate you. Something you can do for yourself, or we can give you after you get through this part of labor. What could be your reward after really focusing and pushing?" I grabbed a cloth from the nightstand to wipe the sweat off her face.

Ara blinked a couple times and said, "Sleep. That's what my motivation is. If I can get through this part, afterwards I can sleep."

I hold back a laugh. Memories flooded me from when I had my girls. "That's a good motivator. Yes. Go with that one. After this part, you can nurse the baby and then Abby and I can take him while you get some rest."

She nodded and something in her switched. Ara focused more on the pushing and breathing as I coached her through. She did a phenomenal job. This had worked with Chloe, and I knew it would work with her. It wouldn't be long before she was holding her beautiful baby in her arms.

I could finally see the baby's head. Abby grabbed a mirror so Ara could see how she was progressing, and this motivated her even more. Before we knew it, we had a baby boy! I felt overjoyed, as Ara did too. The baby latched on to her right away, and I fetched a baby blanket to keep him warm. The room was full of smiling faces. Those moments as a midwife never get old. I wished I could live that part of it every moment of my life.

Chapter Thirty-Four

Kate

Soft music played in the background as each table took turns at the buffet with the delicious food Marsha had started. She had most of the food ready to go. I'd only had to take over a couple recipes and felt grateful they were dishes I'd made before. The stuffed mushroom recipe called for more cream cheese than in my own recipe at home. While preparing them, I couldn't help but take more than just a sample taste. I loved each of the ingredients, and even had to ask Chloe to get them away from me and onto the serving table, or there would not be enough for the guests.

Once the food was placed in the serving area, I checked around the room to see if all the guests were seated and ready to eat. It was time to make my rounds and have some fun.

I had time to run back to Chloe's house and grab the Cinderella costume I had brought all the way from California. I packed it to surprise her after her baby came, knowing that Cinderella was one of her favorites. Since all the commotion with everyone finding out I was pregnant, it had been forgotten. I had a few minutes to chat with one of the others helping to wait tables, and they told me how they personally knew the couple. They explained to me the theme of their wedding, and we knew the costume would be perfect to bring out for the reception. It would be my little present to the newlyweds.

Changing into the Cinderella gown, I laughed to myself how this reminded me of when I was a little girl. My mother would buy me dress up clothes and I'd pretend to be a real princess in the back yard. We had huge planters on our back patio we hardly ever used for planting, and I would act like it was a wishing well and sing into it like Snow White.

Feeling the silk gown beneath my fingers, I smiled in the mirror, like a real princess. When I stepped out of the bathroom, I watched an older couple do a double take. They both dropped their forks in the middle of the meal and stared at my silky blue costume. Both of their eyes lit up. I continued my job, moving from table to table, asking to fill water glasses, offering to replenish the bread, and adding more butter to the fancy dishes.

Halfway through making my way around the tables, I heard the DJ play one of Cinderella's songs from the Disney version. He grinned at me, and I waved back. The dim lights created the right atmosphere in the dining room, and everything was decorated to fit the Cinderella theme. Marsha had displayed the decorations perfectly.

The first time the bride and groom noticed me, they both were turned the other direction, talking to someone at one of the tables across the room, and whoever they were talking to pointed in my direction. The couple turned around, their faces lighting up. The bride stood to walk toward me and gave me a big hug. She asked me who had arranged this special surprise, and I just laughed. She requested the DJ play another Cinderella song so the new married couple could dance together. How magical to watch them dance beneath the white canopies, holding hands and laughing.

Unexpectedly, I felt that familiar, stab of jealousy. I wanted what they had. Oh, what it would feel like to be newly married again. I remembered having a hard first couple years of marriage, but I'd never forget that initial feeling after the wedding and honeymoon. Before we had ever lived together long enough to get on each other's nerves. Before the awful job he had that took him away from his family. Attempting to shake off that familiar feeling, I told myself to get my head in the game. Forcing myself back into character, I noticed a man brush shoulders with me.

"You look so beautiful," he said. "I just love the way you mingled with the guests. Everyone enjoyed having you here. You're a natural at this." Before I could respond, the man reached into his pocket and grabbed out a card, handing it over to me. At the top, his name and a construction company showed in big, bold letters, as well as two phone numbers and an email address.

"Give me a call sometime if you'd like to go out to dinner. I happen to know a wonderful Italian place if you'd like to go. Perfect spot for a first date." Did I imagine it or did this man wink at me? He couldn't see my wedding ring, as I had been wearing gloves with the Cinderella costume.

Just as fast as the man had appeared, he was gone. I tucked his card into my Cinderella pocket, not knowing where else to place it. Shrugging off this man's gesture, I slid across the dance floor to get to another table across the room, where some younger people were seated. They appeared to be sitting in pairs. They smiled and waved as I came by to ask if they'd like more bread for their table. A few said no, and others begged for more. I'd tasted a little slice of bread while it was hot out of the oven. Delicious.

One of the teenage girls asked me where the costume was from, and I explained about an online store I found it on many years before. She complimented me and commented on how much she loved the sparkles and the shade of blue.

"It looks like it could be Cinderella's real gown," she said.

"Thank you. I'm glad you like it."

The evening went by smooth as I mingled with the dinner guests, then the music started for the dance. The bride invited me to join them on the dance floor, and I kindly declined.

"I do have a lot to do back in the kitchen. I need to help clean up."

"In that lovely dress? You'll get it dirty!" The tone of her voice made me chuckle.

"I'll be sure to change."

"Well, if you have time afterwards, I'm sure there will still be people out here dancing. And we would love for you to join us, whether in or out of costume."

"You're so kind. Thank you. If I have time, I might just do that."

The bride gave me one more hug and stood beside her beloved husband. He stuck his arm out as she wrapped her arm around his. Her dress had a classy look to it, almost like Audrey Hepburn. She had the strapless dress and long white gloves that made her whole dress look elegant. There was a shawl around her shoulders as well. The couple made their way over to the dance floor.

The DJ played an upbeat song where you had to follow what he said to the beat. Slightly disappointed to miss that part of the dance, I slipped away to change back into my regular clothes. Remembering the card tucked away in my pocket, I stared at it for a moment.

For a minute in time, the possibilities were considered. My husband would never have to know. Just one or two dates, get a little attention, then dump the guy. Besides, how long had it been since my own husband had told me I was beautiful? Or even took me out on a real date? The thoughts overwhelmed me, and to my shame, I opened the cell phone, and was just about to dial the number.

Something stopped me. Shoving the thoughts aside, I tossed the business card into the garbage. This man had been very charming and warm, and his complements had captured my attention. Deep down, I knew it could lead down a dark path if pursued. Perhaps I could talk myself into thinking he would "just be a friend."

A teaching I'd heard months before came to mind. It was about compromising in the little things, and how they can grow into big things, and how sin spreads easily. Glad about my decision to throw away this man's card, I hung up my Cinderella dress, fixed my hair, and headed out the bathroom door.

Chloe stood by the kitchen sink with the baby trying to prepare the dishes for the dishwasher over in the corner. The baby was in a carrier, in the front. I laughed and watched her lean over to put dishes in while maneuvering the baby.

"I'll take over this part, Chloe. You take a break."

Chloe breathed a sigh of relief. "Thank you. I think he's overdue for his nursing time, and I could see he was getting a little fussy. We'll be right back."

"Take your time. I know babies can't be rushed with these things."

I rinsed some of the dishes and placed them in the dishwasher and wrapped up the leftovers. To my surprise, plenty of food had been untouched. My thought was maybe the guests would have eaten it all, but I figured Marsha was an expert now on exactly how much to make just in case. Better to have way over the amount, then to not have enough. That's also something I had to learn with my own baking business.

I was just about ready to lock up and turn off the lights when Chloe came around the corner.

"Sorry about that. It always takes longer than I think."

"No problem at all. I actually enjoy cleaning up after a big party."

Chloe blinked at me like I was crazy. I put my hands up.

"Hey! It's all part of the experience."

"This is so your thing. Marsha couldn't have picked a better helper tonight. You totally killed it. And that Cinderella outfit? You have no idea how much that meant to the bride. She mentioned it to me when I went to mingle with the guests a little bit at dinner."

"It was no problem at all. I enjoyed every moment of it. Maybe Marsha will need more help in her kitchen before I leave for California."

"Maybe. And even if she doesn't, I'm sure she would love to share some of her recipes with you and give you a few to take back home with you to make for the kids."

"That would be so great. I love her cooking." I glanced around the kitchen and prepared to lock up and turn off the lights, wishing for more magical times like this in a beautiful restaurant.

Chapter Thirty-Five

Marsha

I wasn't used to getting phone calls early in the morning. "Marsha. Did I wake you? You sound tired. Just thought I would call you to tell you how you did a phenomenal job last night at the wedding. Nice touch with the gown too. Everyone loved her!"

"Gown? Um...."

"The food was amazing as usual; the decorations were the best I've seen at a wedding...and the service. You did it again!"

"Thank you, Claire. But what do you mean..."

"Sorry to cut you off so soon, but I have to go. One of my grandkids is getting into the kitchen stuff. Gotta go."

Seconds after that phone call, it rang again.

"It's Mylee. How's it going?"

"Okay, I guess. I was sick yesterday, but I'm feeling so much better after a good night's sleep."

"Just wanted to let you know that my niece loved the wedding so much, she wants you to cater her wedding too. And make sure to bring Cinderella. That was her favorite part."

I didn't know what she meant by bringing Cinderella, but I didn't feel awake enough to ask her.

"I would be glad to do your niece's wedding. Have her stop by the restaurant when she has a chance, and we can go over what she would like."

"Let her get whatever she wants. Her uncle and I are paying for her wedding. What with her parents divorced and everything, and both going through financial difficulties, we decided we would take it on. She's been through so much. I just want her to have the very best."

"That's so kind of you, Mylee. What a wonderful aunt."

"Well, let's chat some more later, Marsha. Okay? Maybe I'll see you tomorrow when I bring my nephew to the restaurant tomorrow. He just adores having breakfast at your place."

I finally dragged out of bed, and felt relieved to find I felt so much better compared to the night before. Glad for the energy, I prepared my favorite biscuits with butter and strawberry jam on top, and grabbed my outfit for work.

When I approached the front door of the bakery, Chloe walked to the front door as well with the baby in her arms.

"How are you feeling today? Were you able to get some good rest?" Chloe said.

"Oh, yes. It was so nice. You have no idea how grateful I am for you two wonderful women stepping in and helping me out last minute."

"Kate was exceptional. She had this idea to bring in her Cinderella costume that she brought with her originally to surprise me with. She dressed in the outfit and went from table to table greeting and serving people. It was a hit. The bride and groom absolutely loved it. I have never heard so many compliments before and they were all because of you and Kate."

"That explains a lot. I got a couple calls this morning and one of them mentioned Cinderella, and I had no idea what they were talking about!"

Chloe laughed and bounced the baby in her arms, and he smiled.

"She finished the recipes, and they turned out so good, and I cleaned. I think she's a natural at this."

"You don't know how glad I am to hear you say that. I was worried to leave at first, not because I didn't trust you guys to take care of everything, but because I feel sometimes like everything is my responsibility. I need to learn to delegate more, even while I'm here at work. My goal is to also show more how much I appreciate my workers.

"I don't think you need to worry so much about that part. There wasn't a moment when I worked here I didn't feel loved and appreciated. You have a true gift of making everyone feel welcome."

"Thank you, dear. That means a lot to me. It's what I love doing."

"I stopped by today to make sure you're feeling okay, and see if you needed any extra hands. I can usually do a lot when the baby is in the carrier, and sometimes he just sleeps."

"You are so thoughtful, Chloe. To be honest, I would appreciate the help. Would you mind helping to set up for the staff meeting today? I have some memory verse cards I'd like to set out on these placemats I found at home. And you are always welcome here, Chloe. Remember that. Even though you may not officially work here anymore, you're still welcome to come to the meetings and just hang out with us. I love having you around."

Chloe's eyes teared up. "Thank you so much, Marsha. You're so kind. And I love helping wherever I can."

I handed Chloe the memory verse cards made the week before and walked around near the display case up front. Thank-you cards had been placed on the counter. The first one was a note from the bride and groom of the last wedding. Another was a thank-you card from the bride and groom's parents. Each of them mentioned Kate and the service she provided. The groom's parents said they hoped she would be at the next wedding they attend here, and how I really know how to pick good staff members. It was unfortunate Kate lived in California.

In the kitchen everything looked so organized and clean. To my surprise, some of the things on my white board to-do list were crossed off. One of the things listed was organizing my recipes by category and in alphabetical order, to be able to find them easier. Many of them are memorized, but I always loved to pull an old one out on occasion and tweak it. Some of the recipes were handed down to me from my mother and grandmother, and my desire was to hand those recipes down to my kids. Someone had organized every recipe.

"I see you found your to do list," Chloe said. "I tried to convince her she needed to come to my place and get some rest, but she insisted on coming back and getting some things crossed off your list."

"You mean Kate did this too?" I asked. This girl is amazing.

"Yep. I think she wanted to get more done off your list, but she stayed up half the night just sorting the recipes. She said once she started, it was hard to stop. She read through some of the recipes, and will probably be asking you for copies."

"And I'd be happy to give her some."

Just as Chloe turned to leave, I stopped her.

"Would you and Kate want to have dinner with me in the Sunflower Room tonight? It's Saturday, so we close a little early today. I would love to have you guys over. You could bring your husband and the baby of course."

"Peter has to study tonight for a big test, but I'd love to come. I'm sure Kate would to, but I'll run it by her."

"Perfect. I'll prepare the menu."

"You have no idea how much I appreciate it. It's been hard to want to cook what with my new baby and all. He just takes so much out of me."

"I can remember those days. Several people brought me homemade lasagna and casseroles shortly after my first child. They lasted about a week, but it was a huge blessing to not have to worry about cooking while adjusting to a new baby. Sure is nice when folks step up and help like that. One lady told me to ask her if I needed anything, and I have to tell you that sometimes it's best to just do. Don't even ask. Just do. Lots of people don't want to ask for the things they need, but new mothers could always use meals and diapers.

"Well, I sure am looking forward to dinner. Thank you so much for the invitation."

"And you can always take home plenty of leftovers to Peter."

"He's always loved your cooking. If you need anything, Marsha, I'll be in the back nursing the baby for a bit. After, I'll head home and see if I can squeeze in a nap. Hopefully the baby will sleep too. I'm trying to get him on a little schedule but basing it on his natural sleeping and eating times, of course."

"Thank you, Chloe." Distracted, I whipped up the first batch of cinnamon rolls. It was nerve-wracking to be alone with my thoughts, and I didn't want them to come, but they did.

Lord, after all these years of building up this business, it may finally be time to move on. But I don't want to shut it down. I want this restaurant and bakery to continue serving this community. Would you bring the right person to me? I need someone we can trust to help. Please show me the way, if you put this dream of Mexico in my heart.

After it was finally time to place the cinnamon rolls in the oven, I set the timer and backed up, watching the oven do its magic. My arm hit something. Or someone. Startled, I jumped back with surprise, hitting the outside of one of the ovens.

"Hey, mom," my son Gordon said. "Sorry I startled you. Thought I'd come for a visit with Maggie." He gave me a hug. My prodigal son had finally come back.

Chapter Thirty-Six

Missy

One of my favorite things to do on my days off from the restaurant were to hang out at the library, browsing the books. I couldn't get enough of it. On the second floor, grateful for the quiet, I discovered a table next to a window. Staring out, it was interesting watching people come in and out of the back library door downstairs. Thankfully, the table fit only one person.

My mind kept taking me back to what Shawn said about me having a good Father. I couldn't wrap my mind around it. My biological father was distant to me when I was a kid, in so many ways, and still was. Whenever a memory of him surfaced, I'd block it out as best as I could. There were not many good memories with him. The concept of Shawn talking about a father who cares about me just blew my mind. Was this guy a lunatic?

I vaguely remember the one or two times I attended church as a child. They mentioned some guy named Jesus who was sent to die so we could live in Heaven or something like that. It was confusing. Was that what Shawn had been referring to?

The teacher said we each have done bad things and Jesus was sent to pay for our sins. She said this was the only way we could have a relationship with God, and that was to believe in Jesus and what he did for us. She talked about how he proved that he was from God because he rose from the dead, which is the greatest miracle ever recorded in history.

"But how do we know that really happened?" A little boy asked the teacher. "I wasn't there. And I don't know anybody that was. How can we know this is all for real?"

"Well, just like your history books you've read at school. How do you know those things really happened? The witnesses around at that time saw what happened and wrote it down. Just like the Bible. There were over five hundred people who saw Jesus after he rose from the dead. Also, his friends that hung out with him before he died knew him pretty well, and tell the stories of what happened with Jesus. They didn't fully understand what was going to happen to him, but after he died and rose again, they were willing to die for talking about what they saw."

I hadn't thought about this memory in a very long time. Never taking much of an interest in spiritual things, recently I found myself thinking more and more about it. Must have been since working at the bakery, with Marsha mentioning things here and there. And now Shawn.

I'd heard of this group of people back in the day who were brainwashed into believing what some guy thought, and they drank a Kool-Aid drink and all died. What if this was something like that? Were they trying to brainwash me into believing something that was totally a lie? Somehow, I didn't think this was the same thing.

Turning my attention back out the window, I recognized somebody. Where had I seen that wide grin before? Sure enough, a few minutes later, a hand grabs a nearby chair and pulls it up next to mine.

"Why, what a coincidence. It happens to my day off too," Shawn grinned. I roll my eyes. Was he there to terrorize me?

"Whatcha reading?" He grabbed one of the books I had piled on the table before I'm able to protest.

"Jesus Among Other Gods," he reads. His eyebrows shot up. I shrugged.

"Just saw it displayed and thought it might be interesting."

"Case for Christ," he says, grabbing the next book underneath it.

Embarrassed, I grabbed the stack of books and moved them to the far side of the table, out of his reach. "I didn't come here for someone to snoop at what I was reading. I came here to be alone."

I clear my throat. "So if you'll excuse me, I'd like my table back. Looks like there's a free one on the other side of the computers." I laid the stack of books down and pointed to the north side of the room. Shawn didn't move an inch. He grabbed a giant book out of his backpack instead and opened it up to reveal tons of highlighted words.

"It's okay to have questions," he said. "I did too." He scooted his chair close enough to me, I could feel his breath. He gently grabbed my hand and guided it to the book in front of him, moving it down the page. I'm surprised by a sudden feeling in my stomach from being close to this man. Was that butterflies?

Chapter Thirty-Seven

Chloe

"What do you think I should wear tonight for our dinner with Marsha?" I asked Kate, holding up two options for outfits. Kate's always honest, but in a sweet way.

"I totally love the sunflower pattern on that skirt you have with the yellow dress shirt to match. It would match the theme in the Sunflower Room. But the dark blue dress with the flowers is also very becoming on you. Hmm. I would go with the Sunflower skirt."

"Definitely. I agree and was hoping you'd say that. How about you? What are you wearing? Your Cinderella dress?" I joked.

She laughed. "No. I'm so glad how everyone appreciated the costume. It was a last- minute thought for me, but I thought it would be perfect, what with the theme and all for their wedding."

"You looked absolutely stunning. I wish we could start our own business where people could hire us to dress up like princesses for birthday parties and such for kids. It would be so much fun!"

"That does sound like a blast," Kate said.

We hopped in the car to head to the restaurant. It felt nice to have the whole place to ourselves. When we arrived, Marsha had the table set for us, and had placed her famous fried chicken hot fresh from the oven on top of a flat oven mitt on the table. Each place she had set, included a handwritten note next to the plates.

My note mentioned how I have a gift for making people feel comfortable and about being kind and gentle.

"Ask my husband about that," I mumbled under my breath to no one in particular.

Kate's note said how talented she is with a crowd as well as the culinary arts and a very strong woman.

Sitting down to eat, I make a mental note to pick up a thank you card for Marsha for this wonderful evening.

"Let's dig in," Marsha announces after she places the creamy mashed potatoes next to the lemonade on the table.

"There's plenty to eat, so don't be shy. I also have lots of corn on the cob that you guys can take home with you." I knew she wouldn't take no for an answer when it came to taking leftovers home, so I nodded.

During dinner, we chatted about everything from California to Larry's favorite dessert recipes.

Finally, the dessert timer went off. Marsha grabbed her peach cobbler and ice cream. After she served up the cobbler, she leaned back in her chair.

"I'm so glad you both came today. I always enjoy your company. But I must tell you, I also have another reason for bringing you guys here," Marsha said. "Let me just start at the beginning. There's something I haven't been telling you guys, "she said, pushing her finished dessert plate to the side.

"Ever since I went on a mission trip to Mexico many years ago with my friend, I fell in love with the people and the ministry they've been doing. They build houses for poor people, and there's a camp for teams to stay in their bunkhouses and help with building projects. Their whole camp houses families that are on staff full time. My friend Penny told me she's moving away to be closer to her granddaughter, and how they're hiring now for a full time cook and maintenance worker. This job is perfect for a married couple, and I prayed about it and talked to Larry."

Kate and I stopped eating our dessert and looked at each other.

"So you and Larry are moving to Mexico?" I asked.

My jaw dropped. I knew from overhearing her phone conversation the other day something was up. I'd never dreamed it would be a job so far away.

"I think so. There's still some loose ends I'd need to tie up. It was hard for me to even put in my application. We just have so much we've poured into this place over the years."

It was hard to mask my disappointment and anger. "How come you never mentioned this to us before? That you were thinking about applying other places?" I asked. My throat sounded froggy, as my little nephew used to say.

"I wasn't sure about it and didn't see the point in telling people unless we were really serious. This all happened so fast. One day I got a call from my friend Penny about the job opening, and the next they offer me the job before I even have time to think about it."

I peered over at Kate. This didn't even affect her, since she lived in California. What would she care?

I pretend excitement. "I think that's great Marsha. I know how you've had this place a big part of your life years, but to get a job offer in Mexico? Wow. You get to travel a whole different country and meet tons of new people. They'd be so lucky to have you there on staff with them. What's the name of the ministry hiring you?"

"It's called Emmanuel's Mission. Their main focus is to build homes for the locals there, but they do other things such as bring meals and clean water and offer classes. My job would be to make the meals for the teams that come in and work on the projects, as well as for the full- time staff. Larry would be in charge of maintaining the place and helping with the building projects."

"I have actually heard of this place before, and amazing things about them. Peter has a friend who has been on a short-term mission trip with them back when he was in college. He loved it so much and said the staff there was so loving and welcoming. This is a great opportunity for you guys." I frowned. "Selfishly, I would like you to stay here. Working here was one of the best things that's ever happened to me."

"I'm going to miss you guys so much, and the bakery here too. You can't imagine how hard this decision was for me. This place is my whole life."

"What are you going to do with the bakery? This town would die without you," I said.

Marsha laughed. "It wouldn't die. But I'm not shutting it down. Larry and I have prayed long and hard about this and decided we're not going to sell it, but we're going to hire someone to oversee and run it and keep the bakery the way it is now. We'll give them permission to make some changes, but we'll still own the building. We're willing to train someone, but we would prefer someone who has plenty of experience, of course.

"Your son's here in town, right? Is he going to take over it?" Kate chimed in.

Marsha looked down at her hands, a sad look on her face. "No. He showed up here yesterday unexpectedly. I have a feeling he's going through a very hard time. He's breaking up his marriage, and it's tearing me apart. But that's a different story. I have someone else in mind," Marsha looked up and smiled.

"Wow," I said. "Who is it?"

Marsha reached over the table and gently grabbed Kate's hand.

"Kate. You have an obvious gift. Not only for cooking, but also for being a leader and working with people. Larry and I would like to make your family an offer. I know it would be a huge change both to you and your family, but I think you will find that..oh, how do they say it these days? This place will rock your socks off!" She let go of Kate's hand, and we turn to each other and laugh.

"I have to tell you, Marsha. I didn't even see this one coming. This is such a surprise. Not to mention, a very sweet offer. I just don't think it will work out, you know, with Mark moving over here with the kids and everything. I appreciate your offer though."

"I want to go more in-depth with my offer to you. There's just so much more to it. I know you and your family are really planted in L.A. But Larry and I have an offer for your husband as well, and would really like to sit down with him and talk more about this. I know he's all the way in California, but they have those video calls where you can see the person, right? We could have one tomorrow and.."

"I don't know if this will work out, Marsha. My husband, you see, is married to his work. Honestly, he wouldn't even consider moving." One tear fell down Kate's cheek.

"I understand he has a great job over there. That's another thing I wanted to mention. I know his expertise is in marketing and other things, and Larry informed me his best friend is looking for someone to hire over in the next town. When he told me the job qualifications, your husband fits the description perfectly. The hours are also great. It may be a little cut in pay, but between what you guys will be making here at the restaurant, and also this job, I think you will find that there is plenty."

"Better hours would be such a blessing. I've really been praying for something like this to come for quite some time now. I just wonder if this could be the answer," Kate cried. I wondered if her marriage problems were even bigger than I'd imagined. Living in L.A. was also such a fast-paced life, and being in Montana, they could walk out their back door and be in a country setting.

"There are so many details that I would want to go over with you. I know it may seem last minute, but if I could just talk to your husband tomorrow through a video chat, I think he would come to see this is the deal of a life time. Larry and I would also like to have you and your family come live in our house. No charge, of course. It's paid off in full."

"This is such a generous offer. I don't know what to say," Kate said, as I handed her the tissue box. Must be the hormones with her pregnancy. How could she manage a new restaurant with a baby on the way?

Chapter Thirty-Eight

Jesse

After the vacation at Abby's house, I crashed in my bed for about two days and slept and slept. Those long nights as a midwife and from staying up late and chatting into the night had finally caught up with me.

At least one of my kids seemed to miss me. But not Haley. She still held a bit of a grudge, but at least she said, "hey" to me when I walked in the door and offered for her to make a sandwich for me, since she was making one for herself anyways. Geez. I guess I'll take what I can get. I swear two of the most challenging things in my life have been the pain of childbirth and then dealing with teenage girls. It must be God's way of teaching me so many different lessons- from patience to anger management to tons of other things.

"Mom!" I heard a piercing scream come from the bottom of the stairs. I jumped up from my bed, where I was laying down and run down the stairs in my pajama pants and cartoon pajama top. Why did I all of the sudden feel like I was the teenager and the roles had been reversed?

"What is it, sweetie?" I said, grabbing my sweater off the couch.

"You read my diary?! Haley shouted right in my face. I held back the temptation to cover my ears.

"Um, no, sweetie. I didn't. What makes you say I did?" I said, smoothing out my hair. It felt gross and greasy. I made a mental note to hop in the shower right after her episode of teenage drama queen. This time, maybe I'm playing the teenager who needs to shower, and my daughter is playing the role of the mother.

"Then why is it out and open on my bed? You're the only other one here. It wasn't like that when I left for Mandy's!"

"Are you sure you didn't accidentally leave it there, sweetie?"

"Stop calling me sweetie! And no, I never leave it out because I don't want to give people an invitation to sneak around and read my private stuff. But I guess it doesn't matter either way, because you found it anyways and read it. It's none of your business!" Then a horrible thing happened. All these terrible words came pouring out of my teenage daughter's mouth I've never heard her say before. I stood there in shock.

"Are you done?" I asked after there is finally silence in the room.

She sighed and I can see her anger turn down a couple notches. She looked like she was about to cry. After cooling down a bit, I planned on punishing her for the unnecessary outburst.

"That was supposed to be a gift from you, to write down my thoughts. No one else was aloud to read it." She sounded more calm, but her voice still a little shaky.

"I promise you. I've never touched that diary since I gave it to you. I don't know what happened, but you can be sure it wasn't me. I wouldn't lie to you about something like this."

"How do I know that? After the way you've been acting, how would I know if you were making that whole thing up? You probably read it and then went out and told everybody." I saw tears forming in her eyes. Before I could say anything, she stomped to her room and slammed the door. Classic teenager. Even though I didn't read her diary at all, part of me was very tempted to do that, since she obviously was very embarrassed by whatever she had written. I worried again.

"There you are!" My younger child walks through my bedroom door, unannounced. She seemed annoyed. "Why didn't you wash my basketball shirt? I was looking all over for it when I came home earlier today!"

Relief washed over me. "You mean you were here? In the house earlier?" Finally someone else who could testify I wasn't the one that dragged out the diary.

"Yes! I looked all over Haley's room for it too, and it wasn't there. I know sometimes you put things in our folded laundry piles that aren't ours, so I thought I'd look through all the drawers in the house."

"I think I know where it is. Hey, you didn't happen to notice that you brought out Haley's diary, did you?"

She shrugged her shoulders. "I was in a hurry. I think I saw some notebook thing fall of out of one the drawers. So what?"

"Great!" I yelled and grabbed her hand and led her over to Haley's room. I tapped on the door.

"What do you want? Leave me alone," Haley growled.

"Your sister is here and would like to tell you something. It's about your diary."

She opened the door dramatically and gave us both a frown. "What?"

"Your stupid diary must have fallen out when I was looking for my basketball shirt that was supposed to be washed. So what's the big deal?"

Haley gazed at me with sad, apologetic eyes. She finally whispered, "I'm sorry, mom. I didn't know she came home today and was looking through the drawers." She turned to her sister. "You didn't read anything, did you, you little demon?"

She rolled her eyes back to her. "No. Why would I want to read your stupid diary? I have better things to do then to read about your boring life."

Haley rolled her eyes back, but surprisingly, she gave her sister a big hug. Must be because she's relieved no one read it. Really? She believes her sister, but she wouldn't believe her own mother. I shrugged it off, relieved at least her sister came home and confessed, and mom was off the hook. This called for a celebration, so I decide on The Sunflower Bakery. The girls would be lucky if I'd brought something back for them.

Entering the bakery, Chloe came out at the same time.

"Oh my goodness! How are you? He's getting so big!" I said.

Chloe beamed. "It's so good to see you. I was hoping we'd run into each other so you could see him. I miss seeing you guys for our appointments and chats."

"I do too. Want to sit with me and have a cinnamon roll?"

"That sounds good, but I got to get the baby down for a nap. I hope to see you around soon, though." Chloe gave me a big side hug.

I had a little pity party while ordering my cinnamon roll. It would have been nice to have Chloe's company, but I vaguely remember those days. It was important that the baby gets his nap.

A woman I've never seen at the restaurant before takes my cash and serves the cinnamon roll to me in a pretty basket, since I told her I'd be eating there.

"You hear about Marsha?" Someone from the back asked softly to the woman as I found a table. I overheard them call her Missy.

Missy looked down, a frown on her face. "Yeah. About her taking that job in Mexico? I just don't know what's going to happen to this bakery. All her hard work is going down the toilet. She's making a big mistake if you ask me. And to top it off, I hear she's asking one of *Chloe's* friends to take over. Out of all the people. I give it a year tops this place will last."

My ears perked up at Chloe's name. Hadn't she told me she used to work here before the baby came? Sounded like this young woman had something against Chloe, by the way she said her name. Was it jealousy? If there's one thing I've learned about other people and their attitudes, sometimes they speak the way they do when they're feeling insecure or jealous. And this lady definitely had something brewing just beneath the surface.

Chapter Thirty-Nine

Kate

It was time for a pep talk. *You can do this, Kate. You'll never know unless you ask.* Shaking, I picked up my cell phone to call Mark. He picked up on the second ring.

"Hey, I'm glad I caught you. Are you on break or something?"

"Yep. Just started." Something in his voice sounded sad and tired.

"You're not going to believe this. You know that bakery and restaurant Chloe worked at before she had her baby?"

"Yeah."

"Um, the owner just made our family this terrific offer, but I want you to hear it from her. She'd be able to explain all the details better than I could. She wants to do a video chat with you tonight. I know it sounds last minute and everything, and you're probably busy."

"Sounds great. I'd love to hear what she has to say." Did I hear excitement in his voice? What was going on with him? No fighting?

Not knowing what to say, I whispered a prayer of thankfulness. "Okay. I'm going to be home the day after tomorrow and we can talk more about the video call then. I just wanted to check and see if tonight works for you."

"Tonight I have nothing going on. Perfect," Mark said. What was wrong and what had this man done with my husband?

"Great. How are the kids? Are they enjoying your parent's place?" I said.

"Oh yeah. Every time I stop over there, they have a blast. They've asked me to stay the past few nights, and I took them up on the offer."

"Wow. Really? You haven't been needing to work late?"

"I have tons and tons to do, and I probably should be working late, but honestly I've needed this break. It's actually been really nice to hang out over at their house."

"Did you guys run out of those frozen dinners I made for you?" I teased. "Is that why you're going over to your mom's house? To get a nice home cooked meal?" I laughed.

"That is a plus. She's a great cook. But no. I've been needing to spend time with family. I really wish you were here with us."

"I'll be home soon."

"Love you, Kate," he said. Now when was the last time I'd heard him say that?

"Love you too. I gotta go. Bye."

I was beyond surprised he agreed to the video chat that night. Maybe the distance had been good for our marriage? Secretly, divorce had crossed my mind several times since he got his new job. I'd tried to be understanding, but he was spending so much time working, when he could have been spending it with us. I knew many of those nights he really didn't have to be out there working overtime. I had resented him for it, and prayed God would change his heart and turn him back into the family man I'd fallen in love with.

After a cinnamon roll and relaxing at the bakery, I drove to Chloe's, where she was preparing lunch.

"You need any help?" I asked.

"Nope. I'm just about done. Just making sandwiches again. What did Mark say about the video chat tonight?"

"You won't believe it but, he's on board with it. Sounds like he's taking some time in the evenings to relax lately, so he was open to what I had to say, no questions asked and I didn't give him much detail. I just told him the owner of the bakery you worked at is making our family an amazing offer. Maybe he thinks we won something like a life-time supply of donuts. I can't imagine why he would agree to this. This is so not like him."

"Maybe he's realizing how great he has it at home, and he just wants to spend more time with the kids and he's missing you. You've been gone quite a while, Kate. Who wouldn't have missed you?" Chloe spread more mayonnaise on the bread.

"I see what you're saying. It just caught me off guard, that's all. Anyways, I'm going to pick out something to wear for the video chat tonight. Marsha invited me to come and sit in on the conversation. It may just be over the computer, but I want to look my best. For him." I blushed.

"I'm proud of you, Kate. Even though things haven't been the easiest for you back home, you still are trying to dress up for your husband, even it being a video chat. They appreciate when their woman does that. I need to do that more for my husband. You've inspired me. Even though I've been super busy and tired with the baby and everything, I still need to put in the effort of looking nice for Peter. Maybe you could help me find something today at one of the thrift stores?"

"That sounds fun. Maybe I'll get a new summer dress with you to take back to California. I could surprise Mark and wear it when I get off the plane," Kate said.

"I've always saw myself as more of a tom boy. A lot of women I meet like to dress up in dresses and high heels or other dress-up clothes, and I'm over here just in my T-shirt and jeans."

"You still look nice in T-shirts and jeans, though."

"I don't feel like it, honestly. A lot of the time I feel like a slob compared to those other people, but I guess it's mainly because I like to feel comfortable. I'm on the floor all the time playing with kids, and I don't want to wear something that I'm going to have to keep adjusting or having to worry about being all lady-like in."

"That makes sense. For me, I get in these random moods where I feel like dressing up. I just feel like I hardly buy new clothes. Thrift stores will suffice. Why buy new when I can pay way less?"

Chloe and I head to a thrift store where everything is half off once a week, and I'm glad it happened to be that day. I expected to just buy one summer dress but found three that were modest. One was a light blue, the other reminded me of a Fourth of July outfit, and the other a peach dress with spaghetti straps. I don't normally wear spaghetti straps, but I decided to just wear it around the house or find a short-sleeve pullover to cover up.

For the video chat with Mark, I picked a light blue dress. It was very fitting, but I loved it because it had short sleeves, and went up high by my neck. It was modest, yet beautiful. I really hoped Mark would like it. Or would he even notice?

That evening, while Marsha and Larry set everything up for the video chat with Mark, I said a quiet prayer and bit my nails. It had been a long time since I'd destroyed my nails.

Mark mainly listened and nodded his head a lot as Marsha presented everything during the video chat. She discussed the offer made to her in Mexico to replace her friend, the bakery business and how well it was going, and took a large chunk of time to explain how qualified I would be for the job and how he would fit in as well. They explained how Larry's good friend had a job opening nearby that would be a good fit for Mark, if he wanted to continue in his regular line of work.

She explained profits to Mark and he wrote down some of the things Marsha said, and he actually looked happy. The more she talked, the more he Mark wanted to hear. It made me hopeful, yet surprised. He seemed interested in all she had to say. Who was this guy and what did he do with my husband? Seriously, where did this all come from?

Before I met Mark, he helped to run his family business. His mom owned a coffee shop, and he was the manager and groundskeeper. Marsha picked the right family, if you asked me. But I didn't want to get my hopes up yet.

Lost in my own thoughts while they talked details, Mark took his turn asking questions. They weren't about salary, but about what he would be doing, and how much time he would have for family. Near the end of the video chat, he asked her a question about family activities to do in the area. I was absolutely shocked.

Marsha happily answered all his questions, and told him she hopes he considers her offer. With the way Mark was acting, I wouldn't be surprised if he took the offer right then and there. Instead he says, "I'm so grateful you thought of Kate and I for this position. Can I be honest with you, Marsha? This all has been an answer to my prayers lately. Everything you've described to me would fit perfectly with what our family needs. However, I would like to talk it over more with Kate and possibly mention it to the kids. There's some things we need to consider, but would it be okay if we give you our answer by this next Friday at the latest?"

Marsha smiled and nodded her head. "Of course. That's perfect. Thank you for listening to me and for considering your options. Let me tell you, there is not a better family I'd ask to be on board with us. I hope you will prayerfully consider this, and that you have a good evening."

Mark seemed to be doing a happy dance as he said "goodbye."

"What was that?" I said to Marsha after the video chat ended. "I hate to say this, but that guy is not my husband. Mark is usually not that cheerful and agreeable. He seemed like he wanted to take the job right on the spot. I don't know what's been up with him lately."

Marsha laughed. "Sounds like you should be praising God right now!"

"I just don't know what's going on. His attitude has completely changed. This is very personal, but this trip, I've really been struggling. I pined for the old days, when Mark and I were closer, and he cared."

Marsha gave me a big hug. I hadn't told her the details of our marriage, and she didn't ask questions, but just held me. I let the tears come and told Marsha everything. How I felt like Mark had been putting his work above family. I explained how I'd imagined divorce so many times this last year, and that Mark often had outbursts of anger at home. I vented how I felt trapped in a prison called L.A. and how I was sick of it there and wanted to get out of the city. She listened to me pour my heart out about how Mark led our household and hadn't been interested in anything to do with God the past couple years. Yet today he'd mentioned prayer.

Marsha didn't mind me crying all over her nice business outfit she'd chosen for the video call. I think the hormones from the baby were also a factor in all of this. I'd almost forgotten about the baby. In the midst of all of the marriage drama, a new baby was coming, as a result of some random night together with Mark that rarely happened any more.

Once the tears slowed down to a sniffle, Marsha reached for another tissue for me to wipe my nose. We sat in silence for a while, listening to the lull of the dishwasher in the distance.

"I'm so sorry, Marsha. I didn't mean for all this to spill out to you. I'm a horrible wife. I've heard it said somewhere that you shouldn't share your marriage troubles with other people. That it has to stay between you and your husband."

"I have heard that too. It's probably a case-by-case thing. But right now, you just need someone to pray for you and encourage you."

"Thank you, Marsha."

"I forgot about this for a while, but there was a time early on in my own marriage where something similar happened."

"Really? A similar thing happened to you?"

"Yes, I can remember a time where Larry and I were having some struggles. It was around the second or third year of marriage We barely had any money to start with and we were struggling to make ends meet. He had two choices at the time that we could see. One was to take a job as a logger, and the other was to go and help out on his uncle's farm. He chose his uncle's farm. It didn't last too long, though," Marsha said.

"We slept in the barn most nights in the hay loft. Larry would help with the cattle and crops as much as he could. His uncle assured us this arrangement was a good idea. He told us it would be warm up in that old hayloft, but I was freezing every night. That cold mountain air came through, and even though I'd pile those blankets up mighty high, I still felt so cold many nights, even in summertime. I'd do what I could around the farm to help, but it was so hard. I'd wanted to take over the cooking and cleaning since his wife had passed away, but he wouldn't have it. He was trying to be nice, by not having me cook the meals, but it really bothered me he wouldn't allow me to help out the best way I knew how. He said we were too broke and couldn't afford to even buy the ingredients for the meals. That really bothered me when he said that," Marsha said, standing to straighten things up in the room.

"I'd find other ways to help out around the farm, but his uncle had a mighty strong temper. It seemed everything made him angry when we would work with him. He was such a perfectionist. Anyways, this took a toll on our marriage. I felt trapped there and I hated being there so much, so I told Larry."

"I bet that was really hard for you," I said.

"It sure was. It was hard for Larry because his uncle was kin, and I was his wife. He felt caught between us. To me, it felt like I was in prison, and he felt like we needed to stay. But I fought it. I searched for other places to stay, complaining every day, until finally I gave up. I decided if it was time to leave, then it would have to be his decision. The crazy thing is, once I'd made my mind up to give up and just put up with all of it, Larry and his uncle got into this huge fight."

"Living with extended family can be difficult," I said.

"Yes. Larry finally decided it was time to move, and I was relieved. We kissed that place goodbye, packed up all our stuff into the back of our old rundown pick up, and high tailed it out of there."

"I would have been so relieved to leave. I bet that was hard not having a warm place to stay and feeling like you couldn't do what you enjoy most-cooking."

"It was mighty hard. I realized though I should have been more grateful and more appreciative to his uncle. He was only trying to help us, and that whole time I was there I should have been looking for the blessings, and not focusing so much on the tough stuff. His uncle was truly a wonderful and thoughtful man. He was just probably so stressed out with everything that needed to get done around the farm."

"Did the uncle ever apologize?"

"Later on, yes he did. But as far as my marriage went, I learned sometimes we have to let go. We may want so much to control the situation, but there are times we just have to wait it out and let the Lord lead the way. I'm not saying you shouldn't share your opinions, but that wives should react to situations out of a beautiful heart that appreciates everything they have. There are ways to share your hopes kindly, and not try to force your own way, causing strife and dissension. I realized God designed husbands to be the leader of the household, and while we are still a team, the only thing I should be doing for my husband is to pray constantly for him, rather than try and manipulate him into doing something I want. One of my good friends always told me to do that, and it made such a difference in our marriage."

"That's what I should have been doing all along in our marriage. I just got so discouraged," I said.

"Later on in our marriage, instead of fighting with Larry about what I wanted to do and when, I'd shut up, go to a quiet place in the house, and just pray for him. My prayers were that the Lord would show him the way as the leader of our family. I'd pray the Lord would strengthen him and help him make decisions that were good for our family. I'd surrender myself over, rather than fight like I would have in the past. After that, peace came over our household."

"I gotta be honest with you, the first thing I want to do when my husband gets me upset somehow is to just jump right back at him. That's one thing I've been confused about, though. My aunt told me how it's important a wife stands up for themselves. How should I really respond to my husband? Is it about being true to myself and just sharing all of my feelings, yelling back at him, and causing even more of a conflict?" I asked.

"That's the hard part about it all. If a husband is ever physically abusive, that's an entirely different story. But with just arguing, what our flesh wants to do and what we should do are sometimes entirely different things. The human part of us wants to stand up for ourselves, and lash right back at them when they become angry at us. I could tell you many stories about early on in our marriage how often I would snap back. We would get in so many fights. People would tell me this was the norm for a marriage, that this is what marriage was like, and that I better get used to it. But, I felt like my marriage was going to dissolve if I continued that way. We'd be on the brink of divorce if I kept fighting back with him. We'd never get anywhere, and it was an exhausting game of back and forth, back and forth. I decided to dig in deep and study what God's word said about our character, and how we should respond to others, even when we feel like they really hurt us."

"This is something I needed to hear. I wish you lived close to us so we could have these talks all the time."

Marsha smiled back at me and reached for another hug.

"I do too, Kate," she said.

The tears came again. I felt so grateful to have her as my new friend. I knew about prayer and prayed often, but I didn't realize how much of my thinking time was dedicated to worrying, and not praying. I wanted God to become the center of my thought life, and not my negative thinking. It also felt so good to finally share with Marsha what I'd been struggling with for so long. *Thank you for good friends that care, Lord.*

Chapter Forty

Marsha

The next morning after the chat with Kate, I woke up with an awful pain in my back. Not sure at the time what it was, but I made the decision to go to work, hoping it would get my mind off it. I thought about a new recipe Kate had suggested to me. It was a type of oven fried chicken, and much healthier than regular deep fried. With the keto diet's growing popularity, I wondered if it would be good for business to advertise an additional Keto-friendly menu, starting with Kate's version of oven fried chicken, using a different kind of flour. And of course, I wouldn't let my regular customers down and take off gold ol' regular southern friend chicken. I may have not been from the south, but have been told many times I can make a good fried chicken. Larry says Montana is known for bland food, but I'd like to prove them wrong when they taste the food at our restaurant.

"Good morning, Marsha." The new waitress we hired the week before, started that day. I was distracted with many other things, and almost forgot.

"Hey, Shana. I'll help you get started with taking these orders, then I'll show you a few things that need to be cleaned in the back. When you're done, I'll go over more what today will look like."

"Sounds perfect," Shana said.

I peered down at her feet. She wore high heels that didn't seem to match her personality. Missy had recommended Shana to us, announcing how she had a lot of money she owed people and how she could use the job. Shana would have been the youngest person we'd ever hired before.

I spent some time hoping it would work out with our new employee, and that she could learn fast. As much as I hated to admit it, I wasn't sure how much patience I'd have. The pain in my back seemed to only be getting worse the more I walked around.

"Hopefully they can read my chicken scratching," Shana said, handing me an order that came from table seven.

I glanced at what she wrote. "We've had a lot of practice. Don't worry about it. If we have any questions, I'll send some of the helper cooks to ask you." I clipped the note up for one of the other employees to take a look at, while I prepared some things in the kitchen and showed Shana what she'd be working on.

"Let's step in the pantry where we can chat a bit," I said, grabbing my apron from one of the new hooks Larry added in the back.

"You'll find your apron hanging on the sixth hook, Shana. It has your name on it."

Shana grabbed her apron off the hook, and with her other hand, felt her name embroidered on the front in a light pink.

"Oh, my goodness. Did you make this?" Shana said.

"I did," I smiled. "Welcome to our team."

Her eyes teared up. "Wow. This is so beautiful. Thank you."

"It's yours to keep forever."

Her eyes lit up even brighter as she tried on the apron. "It's perfect."

I showed her around the back where we stocked ingredients, cleaning supplies, and then the location of the Sunflower room. Taking inventory, I made a mental note to pick up almond flour for our new recipes inspired by Kate.

I jotted down a schedule for Shana in my best handwriting and went over the details with her.

"If you have any questions, you'll most likely find me in the kitchen today. Your schedule is straight forward, but each day will be slightly different. In the mornings this week when you come in, you'll find a note from me with your schedule written out. I'll keep doing this till you feel comfortable. I think you'll catch on in no time."

Priding myself on being different from other restaurants, it's a job I look forward to doing every day. Any questions?" I asked Shana, tucking my pencil into my apron.

"Not that I can think of. I'll let you know if I do," Shana said.

I left Shana to check on things the other workers started that morning in the kitchen. They had prepared the mix for the muffins and had the oven going for me. Ready to start the next batch, I whispered a prayer for the day, working on putting the batter into muffin tins.

Lord, you know how much my back has been bothering me this morning. Please help me get through this day without further problems. Help Shana as she adjusts to her new job.

An hour later, I grabbed more ingredients from the pantry and was startled when I saw Shana sitting down in the back corner on one of the chairs, looking at her phone. She looked upset.

"Hey, Shana." I glanced up at the clock. It had been her turn for about ten minutes to be on the floor, taking breakfast orders.

"Hi," Shana said, not even looking up at me. I thought about the disgruntled customers who were probably wondering when they'd get their order taken.

"It's past the time for you to be out taking orders. Is everything alright?"

"Oh. My friend suspects her boyfriend is about to break up with her, and she's having a hard time with it. I'm just texting her to know it's all going to be okay. He wasn't the best boyfriend to her anyways," Shana said.

In all the years I've run this bakery, never once had I seen a worker do something like that. I remembered it was her first day, and that she's a teenager. Did I make the wrong decision in hiring her?

"I think it's great you're comforting your friend. That's very thoughtful and kind of you," I said.

She smiled and nodded in agreement.

"But I gave you a list of tasks for the day and while you're at work, I want to remind you one of the things listed in the handbook is workers should'nt be on their phones unless they're on a break or their shift has just ended. Remember that hook I showed you with the aprons?"

Shana looked up at me and nodded her head, not seeming bothered by any of this.

"That's where you store your phone until break time. Put away in your bag. Everyone does that, so they're not tempted to look at their phone."

"Wow. I don't know how you guys do that," Shana said. She doesn't seem to be getting the fact that she needs to put away the phone right away and get to work.

"Shana. Go put away your phone right now and start taking the breakfast orders. I need to work in the kitchen and no other waitress is coming at least for another hour," I said in the firmest voice I could. I hadn't talked like that since my kids were teenagers.

"Just let me finish this conversation real quick. I'll be right there." Shana continued texting.

What was Missy thinking in suggesting Shana to work here? I walked away, taking some deep breaths. Although this normally would not be a day I'd be taking orders, I make my way up front until Shana finally gets off her phone. Halfway tempted to march back in there and take the phone out of her hands, I stop myself. How could she be so irresponsible? Wasn't she ever taught to work hard?

There was a long line up front, and I greet some of the regulars and apologize for the wait, letting them know there was training going on in the back with some new employees. The men I take the orders from don't seem to mind. They were wrapped up in their conversations about some game and guessing what the next season would be like. The next customer in line didn't seem as forgiving. I'd never seen this woman before.

"I'm sorry for the wait. What can I get for you?" I greeted her with a smile. She sat in a wheelchair, studying the menu.

"If I don't eat within a certain amount of time, I start to get all shaky and feel like I'm going to pass out. Do you realize that I've been waiting over 15 minutes? What did you do? Forget about us?"

"I apologize for the inconvenience. I'm training a new employee and we lost track of the time."

The woman frowned. "Still doesn't stop the fact I feel like I might need to go to the hospital," she grumbled. The woman's dentures looked like they were about to fall out. So far, it had been the highlight of my day, even though I hate seeing customers upset. Her outburst was comical to me.

Finally, I spotted Shana at the corner of my eye dragging towards the counter where I was taking the order. Part of me hoped she saw how upset the customer had been, so she could take her job more seriously, putting her drama with her friend away for now. She didn't appear to be too worried. She stepped up to the counter and asked, "What can I get for you today?"

The old lady stopped mid-sentence and stared at Shana. She looked from me to her, then back at me again.

"Ahh. Must be the newbie you were talking about. Can't you see she's already taking my order?" she barked. "You're too late. Pay better attention next time to your job," she said.

"Well excuse me, lady." Shana snapped. "I happen to have a life too. You have no right to treat me this way! Why don't you get off your high horse and go home?"

I stood nearby, speechless. I'd never witnessed any worker at my restaurant treat a customer that way. Reminding myself it wasn't professional to scold in front of the customers, I led Shana to the back, where she could sit down while I finished taking orders.

I headed over to the front counter again, ready to apologize, but noticed the old lady with her helper heading out the front door.

"See if I ever come here again." The woman raised her fist in the air as she wheeled out the door.

"I've never been treated that way before. I'll tell my friends about it, too." She gave an angry glare over her shoulder. Not sure what to say, I stared out the front door, waiting for the pain in my back to subside. It was getting worse.

Chapter Fourty-One

Jesse

There's something about teenage daughters that feels like I'm on a crazy new ride at an amusement park. One that is smooth sailing at first, then all the sudden, it drops into complete darkness. I can't see anything around me for a long time, and finally a dim light shows up. That had been life lately with my girls. It seemed everything was going okay and then, "WHACK!" I get hit with news that one of my girls did something bad or had something bad done to her. Today was one of those days.

"We haven't talked in a while. How is school going for you, Zoe? Are you liking your freshman year?"

She shrugged her shoulders. "Ehh. Oh, before I forget, Macy's mom wanted me to ask if you'd be willing to make desserts for the fundraiser they're having this weekend to buy new jerseys for next year."

"Another fundraiser?" I moaned.

Zoe looked at me, her eyes pleading.

"Alright. Of course. How much do you need?"

"A few dozen should be fine," Zoe said.

"Great. I'll have you help me bake them today after school."

"Sweet. Thanks, mom." She grabbed the keys off the counter so Haley could drive her to school. It's amazing to think how she could drive. Whenever I looked at her, I still saw a little toddler girl looking up and smiling at me.

I thought the same about Zoe, picturing this cute little girl with her brown hair in braids. My girls are about three years apart. Like most siblings, they fight at times, but overall, they get along okay. I wouldn't say they're super close like best friends, but they're definitely friends, which I'm so glad about. I've heard of other families where the kids hardly speak to one another and just go about their daily activities by themselves, and I guess part of the reason mine are friends is that I push Haley to drive around Zoe a lot. I told her that with getting her license last year, it also came with quite a bit of responsibility, which included driving her sister around and helping maintain the car.

After school and a few appointments with new moms at the birthing center, Zoe burst through the door with a hand full of groceries. I'd asked her and Haley to pick up the ingredients for the cookies she wanted me to make for the fundraiser. She appeared to be in high spirits.

"Mom. I found this recipe on my phone for chocolate chip cookies that we can try. It has a twist to it. The recipe says it has coconut, and I think it would be great to put a little spin on it, rather than just have regular chocolate chip cookies."

"Sounds really good. Wish I could sit down and eat them now." I grabbed out the glass dish, mixing bowls, the mixer, and some other ingredients we already had for cookies.

"How was your day at the birthing center?" Zoe asked, taking the ingredients out of the grocery bags. I can remember Zoe always being very kind and thoughtful, since she was a little girl.

Zoe and I were overdue for some quality mother and daughter time. Although I'd tried it before with Haley, it always ended with her having an attitude and wanting to get back on her phone and text her friends or some boy.

It had been my rule to have them leave their phones upstairs when we were hanging out together as a family, and Haley absolutely hated it. During those times, she would have withdrawals, and I regretted ever buying her a phone. I'd been tempted one day to join an Amish community so we wouldn't have any of the new technology.

Zoe, on the other hand, would rather be reading a book or outside playing a sport, which I'm grateful for. Both my girls were so different.

"Do you have the salt?" Zoe asked as she mixed ingredients. "It's amazing, you know? I've heard if you don't add the right amount of salt to cookies, they don't turn out right. You wouldn't think this sweet of a treat would have any salt at all."

We chatted a little about the birthing center and some of her classes at school as we made several batches of cookies.

"My favorite class so far is English with Mrs. Cupp. She lets us listen to classical music while we write in our journals, and I love how much she cares about us. It's like she wants to get to know each of us personally."

"Sounds like a wonderful teacher." I mixed up the next batch and poured in the chocolate chips. Zoe grabbed a couple from the top to snack on. She decided to make half the cookies regular chocolate chip, and the others she wanted to add coconut.

"Hey mom. Could you read off my phone what it says about the coconut? I've never made that version before and want to make sure we're doing it right.

I grabbed her phone off the counter. She didn't notice, but I heard it vibrate a bit; a text had been delivered. I didn't want to look at her personal texts, but there it was, right in front of me. It blocked the recipe. I clicked on it to read the whole thing. Maybe I should have won the worst mom of the year award for invading my teenage daughter's privacy.

"You are such a stuck-up jerk. You think you're better than everybody, don't you? And by the way, I think you looked hideous today. You look like a freaking boy and can't even manage to dress up or wear any make up. Stupid tomboy."

My heart sank. Wow. Who talked like that? And to my own daughter out of all people? Zoe is the sweetest kid you could ever meet. Maybe not to her sister sometimes, but overall, she's a good kid. I wonder what Zoe said, causing this person to text her that.

"What does it say?"

"Oh," I said, clicking out of the text as fast as I could. "Right. The coconut. It says to get..." I prayed she didn't notice I was reading her texts. Thankfully, she didn't.

Partway through baking, Zoe picked up her phone and clicked into another window. She froze for a minute, reading something I couldn't see, but from the reaction on her face, I knew she had seen the text. Tears came to her eyes, and it took everything in me to stop myself from pulling her close and let her cry on my shoulder. Instead, I continued with the batch of cookies, not wanting to give her any indication I had invaded her privacy. If she wanted to tell me about it, she could come to me first.

I wished I'd deleted the text before she saw it. I couldn't imagine why anyone would want to call Zoe mean names. Although she may not wear any make up and usually only dresses up for special occasions, she's still so beautiful inside and out.

To my disappointment, Zoe didn't say anything about the text conversation. She wiped her eyes with the back of her hand and continued baking. She was silent the rest of the time in the kitchen, nodding occasionally while I distracted her with talking about her and Haley when they were little and how we'd all cook together. I told her about the time we made taffy together but forgot to add enough water. Normally, Zoe would have laughed, but instead she just nodded. Sometimes, I really do forget what it's like to be a teenager. Then there's days when a few little memories come back.

Chapter Forty-Two

Kate

The plane ride home felt relaxing for me. It can be a pain to ask the person next to me to move if I need to get up, but I admit my favorite part is looking out the window. I think a lot about how the plains below look like little patch work quilts neatly sewn together. With little roads in between them, of course. I also like looking above the clouds and up at the sky.

I wore my new outfit from when I went shopping with Chloe. It's a solid turquoise dress from the waist up, and the rest has a colorful zig-zag pattern with white weaved into the blues. I love how soft it feels, and smooth out my dress, thinking about what Mark will think about my new attire.

Why had he been so interested in this job offer that just came out of nowhere from Marsha? Or maybe he was only pretending to be interested for my sake.

I rehearsed what was I going to say when I stepped off the plane, then turned my attention to a mother who was a couple aisles up ahead and to the corner. She was sitting next to her four-year-old and also holding a crying baby at the same time. She looked overwhelmed and wanted to get the baby to stop crying. I thought back to those days and how much I missed holding a little baby in my arms. It wouldn't be long.

The news while at Chloe's took me so much by surprise, and with it being pretty new, sometimes I forgot I was expecting a baby. I wasn't showing yet, but I think about when I will start to show, along with all the side effects of being pregnant again. With each of my kids, I always had bad swollen ankles and had to wear support hose.

"From the cabin. I hope you're enjoying your flight. Should be down on the ground in about 15 minutes or so. Weather in L.A. Is

68 degrees, partly cloudy. Should be pulling into the gate a little early today. Glad you got to join us for your flight," the pilot said.

I missed home, but also already missed Chloe and the gang back in Montana. Staying seated, the crowd in front of me grabbed their things from the overhead bins and waited to come off the plane.

I heard once of a mom who would make packages full of goodies and hand them out to the passengers on the airplane near her. Inside, she would put a little note that said, "You deserve a treat. Sorry for the noise." Apologize for a baby crying by giving out treats? In my opinion, it was absurd. People should learn it's just a part of life, and sometimes babies cry and can be hard to console. I don't think it's anything mothers should apologize for.

Finally, my turn came to hop in the aisle and grab my bag from the overhead bin. The gentlemen next to me asked which one was mine and brought it down for me. What a nice elderly man. He handed me my blue duffle bag and told me to have a nice day. I smiled back at him and prepared to see Mark by running my hands down my dress to get the wrinkles out from sitting so long.

To my delight, Mark waited right outside the doors, as I carried my bag out. He held a bouquet of Gerber daisies and a small stuffed bear.

"Wow," I marveled. "Is it Valentine's Day and I forgot?" I said with a hint of being flirtatious.

Mark looked straight into my eyes and planted a nice, long kiss. That surprised me since in all the time we'd been married, he'd never been a fan of showing affection in public. He said it drew attention and how people just stare. But there at the airport, he didn't seem to mind at all. I take it all in. Before I knew it, he reached down to touch my belly whispered in my ear how excited he is to have another baby with me.

When I turned around, some women my age that were sitting nearby me on the plane turned and whispered to one another.

"I wish my husband would do stuff like that," one of the ladies said and then pointed my direction. If they only knew this wasn't a normal thing. My thoughts take over as Mark backs away and takes my hand to walk with me to the car. Where is my husband and what did this guy do with him?

Mark opened the passenger side door for me first and deposited the duffle bag and other luggage into the back. As he drove, I stayed silent most of the way. He seemed content just driving and holding my hand. He squeezed it a few times. I almost didn't want the moment to end, but I break the silence.

"Where are the kids?" I said.

He chuckled. "My parents agreed to stay with them an extra day. I told them your flight was coming in and I wanted to just spend time with you. They were so excited when I mentioned it and were all for keeping them an extra day."

"Wow. That's great. I do miss them though, and I'm really excited to tell the news about the baby."

"So am I, but I did make a reservation at our favorite hotel. It's only about a ten-minute drive from here. We could get something to eat first if you'd like. I'll take you wherever you want to go."

"You made a reservation?"

"If you want, I can cancel."

"Oh no. I wouldn't want to do that. I like the idea of a little getaway. It's just that I wasn't expecting you to do anything like this. I know how busy you've been at work and everything, and I hope this doesn't set you back or anything."

"That's exactly what I wanted to talk to you about. I was going to wait until we settled down a bit, but now that we're on the subject." He stopped and I let him gather his thoughts a bit.

"I've been doing a lot of praying, Kate. While you were gone and the kids were with my parents, I was able to pray so much more than I have the entire time I've worked here. I prayed for a new direction in my life, and saw how this job was taking a toll on my family. I love how much I make and how we're able to save a lot of money, but I knew I couldn't go on living this way. It's not worth losing my family over."

He took a deep breath and glanced out the window. "My boss doesn't care if his employees have to sacrifice family time. He just wants what he wants, no matter the cost. He would ask me to do these projects I wasn't even getting paid for, and I tried to talk to someone about it. They said if I wanted to move my way up, this guy was the one to please and I better just shut my mouth and do whatever he tells me to do. I went along with it, wanting nothing more than just more money and to please my boss. That's when realized this wasn't right, and I began to pray."

"I prayed for an opportunity to still provide well for my family, yet still be able to spend an adequate amount of time with them. Our kids our getting older, Kate. I don't want them to come in and out of here and think how they never got to see their daddy around much."

I stared out the window at the L.A. traffic. Even though there was so much congestion this time of day, I still appreciated the way the sun shone through the clouds. Mark and I sit in silence for a while again as he collected his thoughts.

"The other day, when Marsha presented me with this offer, I couldn't help but think it was God's answer to my prayers. He knows how much I've been stressing at work and how it's taking a toll on us. I feel like the timing was only something God could do. I think this is something we should do, Kate. But I also wanted to hear your side of things, too. What are your thoughts on this job in Montana?"

Was he for real? Of course I wanted to take up that offer with Marsha! It would be my dream to help run her restaurant and move to a new place and be near Chloe and her family. I had so many ideas for the place I wouldn't even know where to begin.

"Of course, I want to continue praying about this opportunity that Marsha told me on this job that is available nearby them. I want to be there to help you run the restaurant, but she told me there would be other people in place to do that if I decided to try for that job. Either way, I could help you of course. Just not full time if I took on this other job."

My head spun with the endless possibilities. One moment, we're here in L.A. living our lives, and the next, I'm expecting another baby and am presented with one of the most amazing opportunities of my life.

Then something hit me. The baby. Maybe the plan was too good to be true. Why would Marsha offer us this when she knew we were expecting a baby?

Chapter Forty-Three

Marsha

The smell of the clinic with the chemicals they used to clean made my stomach churn. It wasn't too often I went to a doctor.

"You have a kidney stone," the nurse practitioner said, setting his coffee thermos on the counter. Larry and I decided it would be a good idea if I went to the walk-in clinic just to see what the cause of all my back pain was, as well as the vomiting that had started after work.

"That explains the throwing up and the really bad back pain. I had a friend who had kidney stones, and I remember now her talking about how much it hurt."

"We're giving you a pain med for the time being, as well as medicine that will help with the nausea. As far as the kidney stone goes, we would think it would be best if you passed it naturally, and if nothing happens in two weeks, we'll re-evaluate where you're at and what we can do next."

"Two weeks?" I said, cringing. I had so much to do around the restaurant and thinking about the trip to Mexico, if it all worked out. The nurse practitioner handed me a net looking thing and explained what to do. Hoping Larry was taking notes, I had trouble focusing on all he said, wishing I was in my bed at that moment, falling asleep.

I dragged out of the clinic, ready to collapse. "I can't do this right now, Larry. There's just so much that needs to be done in the next couple weeks. We have arrangements for Mexico, getting our house ready, and not to mention the restaurant. I don't even know what's going to happen with it."

"Don't worry, Marsha. There's still time. And you won't be doing it alone. I'm here to take care of stuff, and I want you to focus on feeling better. When you get some rest and feel up to it, you can join me. In the meantime, I need you to eat, lie down and take your medicine. You've been losing a lot of sleep lately from the pain and you need to catch up."

I decided not to argue with him and plopped down on the seat in our Ford pickup. That truck had been with us through a lot, including hitting a few deer, being rear-ended, and the back window shattering. And yet it still ran. Larry took good care of it, even though it was an older truck.

Larry suggested I take some of the medicine, but I insisted on waiting till we arrived home and I could re-heat some of the soup from yesterday's dinner. My appetite seemed to have come back, even after a long bout of nausea on the way over. I'm relieved they figured out what was wrong. Sometimes the fear of the unknown can be scary, but one thing I've learned in my older age is to always lean on the Lord, and not waste time with worrying about things I couldn't control.

Larry pulled our pick-up into the driveway and I headed to the kitchen to warm up the soup, slip into pajamas, and measure out the medicine.

The pain medicine worked a little, but only for a couple hours. I've never really been one to take medicine, so when it's time for my next dose, I decided to just endure the pain. As early evening the next day rolled around, Larry came in again to check on me.

"You wanting to go to small group, or are you still not feeling good?" Larry and I had been a part of a church small group since the beginning of our marriage. We've found it very refreshing, being a part of a group that meets once a week, talked about the sermon we heard on Sunday, and to fellowship with other believers. They also started serving dinner. As much as I wish I was feeling well enough to go, I decided it best to get some rest. My back still had pain, but when I rolled over to one side and laid in this weird position, it helped alleviate the pain a bit.

"You better go without me," I groaned.

The next hour before he leaves, Larry forced me to drink tons of water.

"Come on, Marsha. The doctor said to be sure to drink lots of water. It will help you feel better." The last thing I wanted to do was to drink a ton of water.

"It's hard to drink that much all at once." Larry persisted, so I gulped as much as I could. He stood at the side of the bed, pushing me to drink more.

"Uhgg!" I cried out.

"You just have half the water bottle to go, then you can take a break. While I refill it, you can breathe a little bit."

I sighed. "Oh, all right." I took another drink, feeling a bit waterlogged. I'd probably have to go to the bathroom every ten seconds.

After the torture was over, Larry refilled my water bottle and I finally get a breather. He persuaded me to drink half the bottle, then glanced at the clock on the wall.

"I guess it's time for small group. Want me to bring you back some food?"

"If they offer, that would be wonderful. I feel so bad I haven't been cooking lately." Those past two days I'd made quick stuff like soup from a can or threw together some sandwiches. Poor Larry probably felt deprived, but he's a pretty understanding guy. He'd been pretty busy himself, otherwise I'm sure he would have offered to make meals for us.

"Don't worry about it at all. You need the break. Get some rest. I love you, Marsha."

I smiled. "Love you, too Larry."

How blessed to have him as my husband. He's stuck by me all these years and has even seen me at my worst. What a wonderful man.

After Larry left, I attempted to distract myself and picked up the novel I'd been reading where I kept it on my nightstand. Reading a couple pages, I dozed off. I laid on my left side and shut off the light. Waking up an hour or so later, I see an hour had passed. The pain was completely gone!

I whispered a quick prayer to the Lord for helping me feel better and laid back down to fall asleep before Larry pulled in the driveway. He liked to stay there later than everybody, since he loved to socialize and talk with the leaders. Maybe since I wasn't there, he'd be home earlier, but who knew.

The next morning the stone passed; thanks be to God. It felt good to think I wouldn't have to go back to the hospital and talk to any more doctors about it. They might want to do a follow-up though. Maybe they'd still have me come in for an exam, to check on my kidneys and make sure they were still functioning normal.

I showed up late to work, after Larry covered for me with some of the tasks in the restaurant kitchen. Trusting he knew exactly what I wanted that time of day and with the customers, it was nice to be able to take my time getting ready.

Walking to the back of our restaurant and putting on my apron, I breathed in the fresh scent of cinnamon rolls Larry had started for me. Boy, did I miss that smell. And I wasn't even gone that long. I was really going to miss the place. A sudden, deep, inner ache carried right to the core of me. I'd be leaving all this behind for a totally new life. Was I ready for it?

Chapter Forty-Four

Missy

"When does your shift end?" Shawn asked as I held a plate of steaming hot pancakes and sausage in my right hand, and an orange juice glass in my left.

"Here in about five minutes," I said, handing a customer his order.

"Just let me wipe down these counters, and I'll be right out." Shawn picked a table and say down.

Deciding to make a bathroom run to freshen up, my thoughts turned to Shawn. Why did I turn to mush around this guy? We were just friends. The whole thing started because Marsha was trying to find me some better friends that weren't just drinking buddies. Shawn's just probably wanting to hang out with me a lot for Marsha's sake. There's no way he could be taking an interest in me. I brushed the thoughts aside so I could focus on getting ready.

I pulled a brush out of my bag kept in the restroom cabinet, as well as my mascara and light lip gloss. I've never really been one to wear much make-up, but I felt in the mood to wear extra. I wished for my hair straightener, only having time that morning to throw my hair in a messy bun, since the snooze button had been hit a couple times. I always had the intention of getting up early and doing my hair, then decided I preferred to sleep at the time when I heard my alarm clock go off.

I decided to re-do my hair in a different way and managed a regular ponytail that looked halfway decent, then approached Shawn waiting patiently at his table.

"I ordered a cinnamon roll and coffee and got you the turkey sandwich and soup. I remember you mentioning before how much you loved the bread here," Shawn said.

"I wish you would have told me. I do get the food here for next to nothing." I said, sitting down across from him in the booth.

"It's no problem at all. I've got this one covered, Shawn said.

I glanced down. Was there seriously a stain on my shirt? I thought it was just on my apron, but it looked like some of the pancake batter with blueberries landed on the front of my shirt. I looked away, embarrassed, but Shawn didn't seem to notice.

"I came by to ask if you'd like to come to Glacier National Park with me and a few of the guys I work with. One of them is bringing their wife and another their girlfriend, so you wouldn't be the only woman there. We were thinking about hiking up to see Avalanche Lake. I hear it's amazing, and I've always wanted to go. What do you think? You up for a hike?"

His offer sounded like heaven to me. I hadn't been hiking for so long, since I'd been so busy with work.

"That sounds like a blast," I said. "I wish we could go right now. When are you guys planning on going?"

"Tomorrow, actually. I remember you mentioning you're off work this weekend, so I thought I'd ask to see if you wanted to come along."

"Yep. I'm off tomorrow. I was thinking about asking Marsha if I could pick up some extra hours, but I need the break."

"Great! I'll pick you up around eleven then. A lot of the guys are bringing their own picnic lunches, and I'll pack one for me and you. Do you like fried chicken and salad?"

"I haven't had fried chicken in forever. Sounds good to me. How about I bring dessert?"

"I've been wanting to watch what I eat, but I'll make an exception tomorrow. Fried chicken and dessert sound like a good meal to have since I'm splurging."

"I make the best peach cobbler," I bragged. "Marsha's recipe.

"I love cobbler so much. My mouth is starting to water. I didn't know that you were a cook."

"Kinda. Sometimes it's part of my job. Marsha trained me to help in the kitchen a little with prepping some things. I never really took an interest in it till I came here. I've learned so much about cooking, and I'm finally starting to get the hang of it."

"Well, I have to get going. I have a guy coming over to help me repair the kitchen sink, and he should be there soon. I'll catch you later," Shawn said. He left a ten dollar bill on the table. "This is for the lovely server," he grinned. Waving, he turned to leave. "See you tomorrow."

Did Shawn just call me lovely?

The next morning, I spent most of my time cleaning the apartment. I had a lot of nervous energy, and tidying up always helped me think clearer. With the dishes piled up, I tackled them first. Thinking about downsizing my dishes, I shook the thought from my mind. Wouldn't I want to save some for if I had a family someday? I'd need plenty for family dinners. Berating myself, my thoughts turned to how there was no way that was going to happen. Who'd want to marry someone like me? I had too much of a past, and no man wanted anything to do with that.

I thought of Shawn as I sorted the clean laundry that had been accumulating on my blue rocking chair for almost three days. It had been so much easier to toss it aside, rather than put it away after being pulled from the drying rack.

I liked that Shawn was a teacher at the college. Would he ever mind me visiting, or possibly sit in on one of his classes, just to see what it was like?

In high school, I remembered wanting to go to college. I'd even applied and got accepted into a few places. One was Montana State, where Shawn would have attended. Would I have run into him on campus if I would have pursued my dream? I had wanted to study creative writing or literature, and even considered teaching. Many would never believe that little fact about me.

Some high school teachers would have thought I'd spend the rest of my life selling alcohol and cigarettes at the local gas station. I'd been rough, especially in high school, and I believe that's the only side most people saw of me, letting my guards down, and allowing people see who I really was. Honestly, I had been scared. Terrified of what would become of my life if I'd continued down that path. There was the Missy that would party almost every night, hook up with guys, and dabble in drugs. Then there was the Missy that would go to the library and read some of those huge classic books, dreaming of the future and wishing I could find a good guy like in those books.

I scrubbed out the right side of the sink really hard with cleaner, so I could place the clean dishes that needed rinsed in it. There were some things caked on the side, and I had to scrub hard, which helped get my frustration out and distract me from thinking I could ever have a chance with Shawn.

Ten thirty rolled around and I was already dressed and ready to go hiking. I'd chosen a polka dot dress shirt, blue jeans, and hiking tennis shoes. Maybe not the best outfit to wear outside to sweat in, but I felt pretty for once. My routine included straightening my hair, applying foundation and concealer, liner, mascara, lipstick, and even taking the time to paint my toenails. Not that anyone would be able to see them, but it felt good I was able to take some more time on myself. Hopefully Shawn would notice I took a little extra care on my hair and make-up. Everyone knew this was a rare occurrence.

A knock came at the door exactly on time. I took time to head over and open it, taking in deep breaths.

"Hey," Shawn said. "Read to go?" His gaze rested on me longer than normal. "Wow. You ready to go? Is there anything I can help you carry?" he said after a long pause.

I invited him in. "Just my backpack with snacks and a water bottle. But I think I got it."

He smiled and turned to head to the car. I wished I had the superpower to read minds. Did he think I was pretty?

"Have you ever been up to Glacier National Park before?" Shawn asked as he pulled onto the main highway.

"Yeah. But it's been a couple years since the last time I went. I've been there just two times."

"Do you remember which part you were in?"

I stopped to really think about it, not wanting to mention the fact I was probably wasted that night and went with some drinking buddies. That trip was partially a blur, but I can remember a part of the lake. Although it was probably against the rules to bring alcohol, we had some, and remember drinking lots of it. It was my way of escaping reality, but I hadn't been drunk again since that night.

"I don't remember where we were at, but I do remember being by Lake McDonald. That's about it."

"Hmm. The lake we're going to looks like paradise. It will certainly take your breath away, I hear."

I nodded and smiled, thinking about my outfit. Was it overkill to wear a dress shirt to go hiking? Too bad I didn't think of packing an extra pair of clothes in my backpack. But I did remember to bring half a box of granola bars to share, my purple water bottle, and some string cheese in a small lunch box that had a spot for an ice pack.

Once we made it to the park, and drove down the winding roads, I see a part of a lake glistening through the trees.

"Oh. I may have went too far. How could I have missed it?" Shawn drove a few more miles before he was able to turn around. "Hopefully they have parking over there. I think it's one of the busier hiking trails this time of year."

We managed to steal a spot from a guy who was backing out with his white pick-up truck. He had his hands full with a bunch of kids in the back seat.

"No, save that for lunch when we get there!" the man yelled to one of the older kids in the back. They appeared to be diving into the back where the ice chest was located and digging through the food. The man looked behind him and slowly backed out, as Shawn prepared to take his spot.

"It is such a nice day. I love how clear it is. I'm really looking forward to just being outside." I said.

"Me too. I'm really glad you came today." He peered at the dashboard clock. "Looks like we're a little late, but they said they'd wait for us right by the sign over here. I see Patricia and Lucas waiting."

After we stepped out of the car, Shawn opened the back to reveal a large, beautiful picnic basket.

"Wow. You really went all out, huh?" I teased.

"Actually, I didn't really think about how I'd tote this thing up the mountain, so maybe I can tell them we're just going to eat here before we go. Either that or I could try and shove the fried chicken and cobbler in my backpack," he said.

I helped him carry a few things over to where his friends were waiting. "Looks like we're not the only ones who are late," Shawn says right before we walk up to Patricia and Lucas.

"Missy, this is my friend Lucas. He works next door to me at the college. He teaches upper-level English. Our office and classrooms are next to each other. And this is his girlfriend, Patricia." I reached to shake both their hands. Patricia looked me up and down, a huge smile on her face, as if there's some inside joke I don't know about.

"We found a good spot we can lay down our blankets on the ground and eat." Lucas pointed to a spot where they'd already laid out their things. He had a camera, a big backpack, and a bag of chips out. "We brought enough to share." Lucas invited us to sit down.

"Well, should we wait for the others, or start eating?" Shawn asked. "I'm starving. And maybe I shouldn't mention this in case she didn't make enough, but Missy says she makes one heck of a dish of peach cobbler. My mouth's been watering ever since she told me about it." I'm surprised and embarrassed all the attention is suddenly on me in front of these people I don't know. I didn't know what to say, so I just smiled.

"I think there would be plenty if you guys want to try a little," I said, reach into my bag to grab out forks and paper plates with the dish of peach cobbler.

"Oh my gosh," Patricia said. "That smells so good. I've been on a diet lately, but today I think I'm going to have some of that, if you don't mind. I know it probably won't help me with hiking, but I think it will be so worth it," she laughed.

"No problem." As I dished out some of the peach cobbler, Shawn grabbed out a dish of fried chicken.

"There's both white and dark. I wasn't sure what you'd like."

We dug into this feast, and Lucas also shared the potato chips and some salad with us.

Lucas and Shawn discussed some things about their job and what they're going to teach the next term. Patricia slid closer to me.

"Shawn has told us a lot about you," Patricia said, digging into the peach cobbler first. Nothing like having dessert before everything else.

"He has?" I said with my mouth full. What could he have told her about me?

She nodded. "Don't worry. It's all good things."

"Really? What did he say?"

"Mainly that he met you at the bakery where you work and how you're really close with the owner. He said you're really nice to talk to and he enjoys your company." Patricia gave me a look as if there's something I don't know about.

"That's cool." I struggled to find the words. Is that all he's told her? I wondered if he'd mentioned the times I was rude to him. But then again, I thought he was being equally rude as well.

Patricia and I enjoyed the rest of our lunch, and I stopped to look up at our surroundings, excited to try the hike. Hopefully we wouldn't be too full by the time we hit the trail.

Shawn pointed off in the distance just as were packing up our lunches.

"Hey hey!" he calls off in the distance. He approached a shorter guy and a tall woman and gave them both a high five, He chatting with the couple. Shawn introduces them as Will and Emma.

"Will works across the hall from Lucas and me. He teaches math. We like to give him a hard time for it too." He punched him on the arm.

"Hey. At least with my papers there's just one answer. You guys have to grade essays and that would be a nightmare."

"You get used to it," Lucas said.

"At least it's more fun than torturing our students with impossible problems where teachers don't even show their students how it relates to real life," Shawn joked.

Patricia and I laughed at their conversation.

"So, Missy. Shawn's told us a lot about you. I'm glad to finally meet you," Will said as we packed up the rest of our stuff. He told us he and Emma already grabbed a bite to eat, and apologized for being late.

"Oh, he did, huh?" I looked over at Shawn, who was busy packing up the picnic basket. He peered at us through the corner of his eye. I had a hard time reading his expression. Seemed like he told all his friends about me. My curiosity grew.

"He told us that he really likes you but that..."

Shawn quickly cut him off. "Hey, Will. Can you help me load this stuff into the car? That way I don't have to make two trips."

"I can help you with it," I said.

"No, you girls get acquainted. Will and I will pack this up. It's payment for being late," he joked.

Shawn said something to Will I couldn't hear.

"I'm sorry!" Will threw up his hands after they had loaded their stuff. I wondered what Will was about to say, before being interrupted by Shawn. What did he mean that Shawn liked me? With the way these guys liked to joke with each other, I wouldn't be surprised if they just liked to tease each other about the ladies. My guess was Shawn would be the only single guy at this gathering. Lucas and Patricia were dating and I'm pretty sure Will and Emma are the ones he said had been married a few years.

Will and Shawn made their way back to where we are standing near the sign to enter the trail. Loaded with our back packs, water bottles, and hats, Lucas led the way down the Trail of the Cedars.

"The beginning here is actually perfect for families with little kids. It's all a board walk. We'll come to the actual trail here soon," Lucas informed us.

The guys walked ahead of us while Patricia, Emma, and I strolled behind. I liked how shaded the path was so far, as compared to others I'd been on.

I thought it would be awkward around Shawn's friends, but I actually felt at ease around them. Patricia and Emma seemed really welcoming, and the guys kept cracking joke after joke as we hiked. The other women and I laughed as we listened to the men talk.

The guys started quoting puns, and Patricia threw a couple back at them as we approached the end of the board walk.

We stopped at a sign that showed the path up ahead and the different landmarks. I studied the trail ahead to Avalanche Lake, and it looked steeper. We climbed in the same order we walked down the board walk, with the women in the back. Not too far along the path, I already had to stop to catch my breath. We stopped at some waterfalls to take pictures and were on our way again.

Emma chatted a little with me and explained how she had been in one of Will's classes a few years ago, and how that was how they first met. She said they waited until she got out of his class till he pursued her, and were friends for like a month after that, dated for three months, and then married ten months later.

"It was kind of a whirlwind romance." She explained how her family didn't want her to marry him so quickly, and how they believed she was too young.

"I was twenty when I married. My grandmother also sided with my parents, but I do remember her saying how she married when she was only fifteen. She said you don't have freedom. How you can't really do what you want when you marry so young. She tried to convince me to wait until I graduated college," Emma said. She had to stop and catch her breath for a moment.

"It aggravated me when someone compared me with my friend who waited a long time to get married. I hated when people would do that. It always made the other one feel bad. I feel also that my parents already had somebody in mind for me to marry, but I went ahead and married Will against their wishes," Emma had a sad look on her face, as if this all had just happened.

"It's your life. You're the one who would have to deal with it, not them. They should have minded their own business. You were a legal adult," Patricia said as we pushed up the hill.

"That's what I was thinking at the time. That I was old enough and it didn't matter what they said," Emma said.

Patricia and Emma chatted a little more and I just listened. I couldn't relate at all to what they were talking about. All this marriage stuff. Feeling the green monster of envy again, I pushed it back down and distracted myself with the gorgeous scenery. We were all grateful for the shade from the tall evergreen trees on that hot day.

Chapter Forty-Five

Chloe

The issue of finances weighed on me again. What if I tried to look for a job? But not just any job. I didn't want to leave the baby at daycare or a babysitter. What if I could find a job that would allow me to take the baby with me, such as being a nanny for a family? Winter was coming and our heating bill was going to be incredibly high. I remembered that from the year before.

Grateful for a savings account, there would be no way we could pay all our bills, what with Peter working and going to school. I was afraid we were almost to the point of not having enough to cover all the bills. I was hoping we could use the savings to pay for other things such as an emergency fund, diapers, or even to fix up our car that needed a new transmission. But really we were going to be using it to pay for college classes and bills we couldn't cover from Peter only working part time.

I wrung my hands, feeling a ton of bricks on my shoulders. Peter and I decided together it would be best for me to stay at home with the baby. But was it also part of my job to find a way to help out with finances? To me, maybe a babysitting job would help, as long as the baby could be with me.

I heard a knock at the door, forgetting that Marsha said she would stop by sometime to see how things were going. Taking a look in the mirror at my hair, I tucked back some stray hairs into my pony tail, and answered the door with the baby on my hip.

Marsha greeted me with a one-armed hug since she held a throw away oven pan and covered with foil. The smell of lasagna met my nose, and I breathed in the wonderful scent. She laid the pan down on the counter. The house wasn't in order, but I knew Marsha would understand.

“This smells fantastic, Marsha. This must be your famous lasagna I love so much,” I said.

"It’s not a problem. I’m happy to share,” Marsha said, moving some clothes from a kitchen chair to sit down.

“How about I dish some out and then we can go out on the front porch? It’s so nice outside, and I could use the fresh air,” I said, grabbing some plates and forks. Marsha set up some folding chairs outside for us.

"So how are you doing lately, Chloe? I got to admit I really do miss having you around the bakery. Your smile could light up that place like no one else,” Marsha said.

"I’m just going to be honest with you, Marsha. I am grateful I get to stay at home with the baby. I think that's probably the best thing for him. But lately I've been thinking about how much I want to contribute financially, and it really bothers me. It's not that I would want to leave him in a daycare or anything while I go out and work. It's just that I’d like to find something that would allow me to take the baby with me and make a little extra cash each month."

Marsha blew on the lasagna before taking a bite. How nice it was hot out of the oven, and we didn’t need to reheat it.

"I’ve known a lot of young couples who have felt the same way you do. The Lord provides. You just see,” Marsha said.

"Sometimes we're just so tight. We have to drain our bank account to just pay for the bills. I wish we had an income that could at least cover all our expenses."

"That can be stressful. Especially for a woman. You guys have always had what you needed though, right?" Marsha said, stuffing another bite into her mouth.

"Right," I said.

"And that's something to be grateful for. I think you guys would be just fine whether you decided to try and find a job or not. I can see your point with wanting to try and help. I won't guarantee there's something out there exactly what you're looking for, but if the good Lord wants this for you, he'll show you the way. If you want, I can help you look up a few places to call. There are several daycares in the area, and some are at people's houses. It wouldn't hurt to see if they needed the extra help."

"That's a good idea. Would you mind if I laid the baby down for his nap and then maybe we could look together?"

"That sounds great. I'll get the dishes and wash them."

I knew better than to argue with Marsha about stuff like that, so I just thanked her for cleaning up for me. The older I get, the more I realized that most people just like to help, and rather than argue with them when they offer something, it's better to be really gracious and polite instead of trying to talk them out of it or saying something like, "you don't have to do that."

I put the baby down for a nap, and thankfully he didn't put up much of a fuss. Poor guy was tired and worn out.

Heading back over to the front porch, Marsha was already dialing phone numbers. I always knew I could depend on Marsha to get things done. What a breath of fresh air when all I had been doing that morning was worrying.

"The one I just called is Tiny Tots Childcare. We'll have to try that one back later." Marsha picked up her phone again and dialed the next one. Someone answered right after the first ring. Marsha asked them if they had any openings for workers, but they didn't need anyone at that time.

After Marsha and I called all the daycares in the area, we decided to try and check back the next day. Most places said they didn't need any new workers, and one place was for kids who were already potty trained. Disappointed, I slipped back down in my chair.

"What about the job service place here in town? Isn't it their job to find people jobs that fit them?" I asked Marsha.

"You could always try there, I suppose. It could be that it's just not the right time to look. Maybe you just need to take some time to enjoy the baby at this age and then try again when he's older like in about a year or so. Also, jobs will sometimes pop up when you least expect them."

"Yeah, I guess you're right," I said. Still, part of me didn't want to give up yet. "You know, there's a new nanny service here in town I saw on a flier at the college yesterday afternoon. I just remembered that. Maybe I can give them a call and find out more info."

"Never hurts to try," Marsha said. "Like I said though, it may be best to just stay at home and enjoy your baby. I know it doesn't feel like it now, but babies grow up so fast. You'll be glad you spent the time just with him," Marsha advised.

When it was time for Marsha to go, I tried to hide my disappointment. I appreciated the company.

"There is something I wanted to ask you before I go, Chloe," Marsha said.

"What's that?" I asked.

"There's a women's conference down in Texas coming up soon and I agreed a long time ago to go with one of my good friends. This was before I even knew about the job offer I'd get in Mexico. But it looks like the timing will work out. The date it falls on will work perfectly with Larry and I moving."

Marsha hadn't even found someone for sure to take over the restaurant. Were they really going through with moving?

"We'll be renting a little trailer and hauling some of our stuff down there. I'll be wanting to get rid of a lot too. Anyways, I was wondering if you would be interested in going down there with us to the conference?" Marsha asked.

I stared at her like she was crazy. Go on a long road trip with a new baby?

"I know you have the baby, but we'll make sure he's taken care of. There will be childcare provided at the actual conference, and plenty of breaks where you could go and check on him."

"I'm not worried about that. It's quite a long drive to take a little baby," I said.

"I've already thought that part out too. We would take our time. Also, my friend has an RV we would be traveling down in. There's plenty of room. My friend loves children, so you wouldn't be a burden at all. We would love to have you come along. Just think about it. It would be a lot of fun."

Thinking about what Peter would say, I almost turned Marsha down right away.

"I invited other friends to come, and some of them are considering it. They would be driving separately, of course. It is a women's conference, so Larry will just be hanging out in the RV when we get there. You would get your own room and everything in the RV, and my friend said I could bring anyone I wanted to," Marsha said.

The trip sounded more and more tempting. We wouldn't have to be stuck in a car for hours on end with a little baby, and we could spend some time looking at the country as we drove down to Texas. It might be great to get a break for a while and to just get away.

"I'll think about it, Marsha. It's awfully nice you thought of me. Thank you." A big women's conference like that is bound to have a hefty price tag attached to it. Marsha knew we were tight on funds, but I had to know. "How much is the conference and food and everything?" I asked.

"All the expenses are covered. Don't you worry about that. We've also got the meals covered, the only thing you need to buy is maybe some extra snacks you want," Marsha said.

"That sounds like so much fun. Thanks again for thinking of me."

Marsha grabbed her things off the couch, said her goodbyes, and headed out the door. I shut the door behind her.

The baby was still not awake, so I said a quick prayer of thanksgiving.

You knew, didn't you, Lord? You know how much I wanted to go and you know how much we have. Thank you so much for this opportunity. I hopped off the couch and grabbed my suitcase to pack. There was one problem, though. She didn't tell me when we would be leaving. And talking to Peter was another thing.

Chapter Forty-Five

Jesse

Zoe and I were able to bake together a lot that week. Even with all the extra mother-daughter time, she hadn't mentioned anything about the text conversation and how it made her upset. I noticed the past few days a small change with her. Right before Haley would drive her to school, I saw her leave the house with her dress-up clothes she only wears to church, along with a little bit of makeup. Nothing too dramatic. Just some mascara and lip gloss. She looked great, but Zoe is so pretty without any make up at all.

Having two days off in a row, it felt nice to catch up on chores. I'd noticed the laundry piling up, and the girls needed socks and clean shirts. They'd been so busy with school and homework, I didn't nag them to do any extra chores, other than keeping their room clean. Knocking out their laundry, I thought back to when both of them were little. I'm so blessed to be their mom, even with all their ups and downs.

Pulling some jeans and T-shirts out of the dryer and folding them on the countertop, I think about how I've never met anyone with as many T-shirts as Zoe. I stacked her basketball shirt and nicer pair of blue jeans together with some socks and walked up the stairs to deliver them to her room. I could hear Zoe's voice through the closed door.

"...even when I tried to dress up a little, she still criticized me. Right in front of everybody at lunch today. It's like she's building herself up as she tears me down. And nobody says anything to her. They just sit and sip on their drinks and chuckle here and there as she rips into me. They don't care that what is coming out of her mouth is totally degrading and hurtful." I could hear Zoe crying on the phone. My Zoe. Everything within me wanted to burst through the door, grab the phone out of her hands, and give her a hug to comfort her. But I knew the best thing to do was to just wait. Zoe would want some space, so I needed to just give her time to come to me. It's one of the hardest things I have to do as a mother of two teenage girls.

Just as I was about to turn and head back down the stairs, I heard Zoe's side of the story.

"She's just still so upset I wouldn't let her cheat on her homework. She tried to tell me Ms. Mendez said we could get help from each other, but I already talked with the teacher myself. She said it was a take home quiz, and we were only allowed to use our notes, and nothing else. If someone was absent on a day we had taken notes, it was their responsibility to get them from the teacher ahead of time, before the quiz," Zoe said. My guess her conversation was with her best friend from school, Miranda.

"Yeah. Even when I did tell her what Ms. Mendez said, she lied and told me she made an exception for her. When I told her it probably wasn't a good idea, her face turned bright red. She just stomped away. A few other people were standing there. I must have really embarrassed her. Maybe I should have taken her aside and talked to her instead," Zoe said. Long pause.

"I'm not being too nice. I'm just trying to see it from her perspective. I want to try and understand why she said all those hurtful things to me. Maybe she's having a hard time at home or something." I smiled after she said that. I'm so proud of her. Thinking of the other person, even when she had been hurt. That's my girl.

I heard Zoe talk about having to go and wanting to get something to eat. I made a dash for it down the stairs as quickly as possible, heading back into the laundry room where I unfolded a pile of clothes, to look busy. Zoe's door opened. I prayed she didn't hear me at all try and make my escape.

I refolded Zoe's laundry and head upstairs as if that were the first time. I suddenly had an idea.

I trudged with the laundry basket up the stairs. Zoe sat on her bed, writing something down, her door wide open. Seemed like an invitation to me.

"Hey, Zoe," I said, waltzing into her room, laying the laundry basket on her bed.

"Hey, mom." She looked up for a second and continued to write. Math homework again. Seemed like she either quickly recovered from her phone conversation, or she was using math as a distraction. I sat on the bed next to her, near the laundry basket.

"I've noticed you've been dressing up a bit more lately. It looks so nice. And then I saw you pulled out some of the skirts I bought you quite a while back, and I was wondering if you would be interested in going with me to get you some more clothes. You know. Ones you pick yourself and know you'll like? Not ones your lame mom picked for you," I laughed.

Zoe stopped her homework and looked up.

"I normally don't like shopping, mom. You know that. But that does actually sound a little fun. It would be nice to get away from the house for a while. I don't have very much homework tonight anyway. I could finish these in like half an hour," Zoe said.

"I still need to get ready. Why don't you finish your math up, then come down? I just need to do my hair and some make-up, and I might cut up vegetables for dinner tonight so it's ready when we get home," I said.

Zoe nodded. "Sounds great, mom." She continued her homework.

I ran down the stairs and into my bedroom to find a better outfit. Feeling like a teenage girl again, I was ready to go out shopping. That was what I'd imagined my relationship with my daughters to be like someday. Still their mom, but also becoming more of a friend to them as well. I was glad to have this time off work.

I wore my best pair of jeans, dark with a sequence on the back pockets and a purple blouse, almost like a medieval peasant dress. It's elegant because of the dark, solid shade of purple. To match, I had matching stud earrings and a silver necklace. I shuffled through my closet to find my black flats with a white bow at the end. Comfortable yet chic. I wonder what Zoe was going to wear.

Dabbing on the last bit of makeup, I heard Zoe coming down the stairs.

"Ready, mom?" She peeked into the bathroom. Zoe wore the same thing when I'd seen her. Light blue jeans with a dark blue t-shirt from her school band one of her friends gave to her. Guess the dressing up thing she'd save for school, which I'm totally cool with.

"Yep. Let me just grab my keys," I said.

In the car, Zoe said, "Mom, can we stop at Polly's Shop? Haley said they have some good blouses and dresses in my size." She pointed at the window before the turn to the store came and I turned on my blinker for the pick up behind me.

"No problem. I've actually been wanting to go there for a long time, and never have."

Polly's a local shop owned by a lady named Polly James who moved here from New York City. She was tired of the fast-paced life and decided to move out to the mountains. She still loves fashion, and has some really cute clothes. Some she even designs herself. The majority of clothes the teenagers wear at Zoe and Haley's school come from Polly's. They're more pricey then I'd like, but they can have some great sales on Saturdays.

I let Zoe have some space as she rummaged through the blouses on one of the racks displayed in the back. Shuffling over to the skirt section, I enjoyed browsing what they had for longer ones. I'd never felt comfortable in those shorter skirts the girls liked to wear these days. It was nice to sit down and not have to worry about a wardrobe malfunction of any kind.

After ten minutes of looking, Zoe approached me with three blouses and a dress.

"I'm ready to try these on," she said.

"Okay. Sounds good." I continued to look through the sales rack as Zoe tried on her clothes in the dressing room, taking her time. She didn't ask my opinion or come out to model the clothes, but decided to buy a couple blouses, and placed one back on the rack.

"Too big," she explained. "I can use the money earned from helping with Ms. Hunter's yard last weekend."

"No, Zoe. This is my special treat. It's been so long since we've been out together, and I would like to pay for them this time," I said.

"Thanks, mom." Zoe gave me a big hug, learning not to argue with me about that type of stuff.

While I paid for the clothes, Zoe shuffled through the purses for a bit. Wow, she's changed. Since when would she even look at purses? I peered at her from the corner of my eye and could see she had a sad look on her face.

The cashier waved as we left the store with our purchases. Zoe walked in silence again, with something on her mind.

We drove a few miles and Zoe wiped her eyes with her sleeve. She sniffled. I decided the time had come to speak up. Yearning so much for her to come to me first about what was going on, I put my rule aside about waiting, and broke the silence.

"What is it, Zoe?" I said, gently putting my other hand on hers as I drove.

She sniffled more and shook her head.

"It's okay. You can tell me. No judgement here. It's just between you and me."

At that point she released the flood gates, and the tears wouldn't stop. I wasn't sure whether to pull over or continue home. The clock on the dashboard told me others would be waiting at home, and I'm sure Zoe felt overwhelmed already.

I pulled over to the side right by a neighborhood park with swings and a new slide. Patting Zoe's hand, I sat and waited as she cried.

"These clothes are not me. They're not even modest. Look at this one!" She tossed one of the blouses, and I held it up. It had a low-cut neckline and would be very revealing. How could I have not noticed when I went to buy them? Would they even let her through the door at school? Then, as if reading my mind, Zoe explained.

"I was invited to a birthday party next weekend," she said.

I waited for her to continue. She looked down at the blouses in her bag. "I want so much for this one girl to like me, but it seems no matter what I try, I'm not good enough. I can't do this anymore. I can't pretend to be someone I'm not. I have to return these, mom. Please."

Chapter Forty-Six

Kate

In some ways it felt good to be home. I missed my kids. My youngest, who is three, kept saying over and over again how he was glad I was finally home. On the other hand, I missed the fresh mountain air, way less traffic, and my best friend. *Lord, please help Mark and I hash out all the details and finalize our decision to move out of here. I want to get out of L.A. so bad.* Maybe a selfish prayer, but it's how I felt.

It was time to jump straight back into my routine with the kids. I found out about a new playgroup that happened to be only ten miles from our house. One of my friends gave me the address and mentioned how the group meets on Fridays in the morning for a couple hours. I always enjoyed getting out and get a little stir crazy when I'm at home too much. The playgroup sounded like a good idea. The piles of laundry at home from the trip could wait.

I hopped in our minivan, the nicest van I'd ever laid eyes on. Marks job paid him so well, he insisted we get a new one. Super fancy ride. Extra cup holders. Lots of safety features. It even had a little T.V. in the back the kids could watch. I had to ask them to turn it down several times while driving through the busy part of L.A. Traffic was so bad, the motorcycles always weaving in and out of the cars. It's amazing I haven't seen any one of them hit anything.

When I told my youngest we were headed to a play group, he did a little jig. He knew there would be different toys to play with. I checked in the mirror to see the back seat, where he smiled and laughed.

"There be ducky, mommy?"

"I don't know, sweetheart. I think there would be lots of toy animals there. We'll just have to wait and see," I said.

He seemed fine with the answer, sitting back in his seat and watching the cars out the window. But moments later, it all changed. He decided to throw one of his toddler tantrums right as we are traveling in the middle of the highway. He screamed, shook his head back and forth, and kicked. Quite the change from his calm mood.

"What is wrong!?" I yelled.

The screaming only increased.

Last second, I saw my turn. I moved over to the right lane quickly to exit, checking my mirrors to make sure no one trailed behind me, then moved over. I heard someone lay on their horn. I just about jumped out of my skin, not seeing the car there. A shiny new red Rolls Royce drove up beside me and rolled down his window, screaming profanities as I took the ramp to the exit. Hopefully I'll never have to see him again. But I'll always remember that bright red face and the fist shaking at me. Praying none of the kids understood the words coming out of his mouth, I took the exit off the busy highway and sighed.

I pulled off to the side of the road for a second to collect myself and take some deep breaths. Our pastor always talked about how this gets oxygen to the brain quickly, and slows down stress. Thought it couldn't hurt to try. After about four of these breaths, I felt much better. The scene must have really thrown off my toddler. He sat in the back seat, totally silent. Maybe the angry driver had scared him. But no matter how he stopped the tantrum, I was glad it was over.

I said a quick prayer, asking that the playgroup would be pleasant, then gathered my toddler into my arms and scooped him out of the van. He seemed like a different little boy, so calm and collected. I wished I'd felt the same. My heart pitter-pattered, feeling anxious. I wasn't sure if it was because of the angry driver, the pregnancy, or thinking about the hassle of moving. Probably all the above.

I entered through the thick double doors and my eyes met a large, colorful room full of toys, a play kitchen, a couple tunnels for the kids to crawl through, toys that looked like a box full of tools, and so much more. Tons of empty space also filled the room, where kids could run around. At least I knew he'd be safe and couldn't open the doors.

A mother and her two-year old played near the doors with one of the tunnels. My toddler found a jumpy horse nearby, pulled it by the ears and threw it around.

"Woah! He really likes that horse!" the woman laughed as she pulled her little one out of the tunnel.

I smiled and nodded my head. "We have one like it at home. He absolutely loves it and his other animals too."

"How old is he?" she asked.

"He just turned three this last June," I said.

"He is super cute!" the woman said.

"Thanks! Your little one is too." I kind of lie. To be honest, her little boy really isn't that cute, and I felt terrible for even thinking this.

"What's your little boy's name?" I asked.

"James. He was named after his grandfather on his dad's side, who passed away only a few months before he was born."

"Aww. I am so sorry to hear that. But what an honor that you named him after his grandfather. I bet his dad really appreciates that."

"When I told him the idea, he loved it. Plus the name seemed to fit. We were going to name him Jacob, but since his daddy's father had passed, I thought it would be better to pass on the name."

"So are you from around here?" I asked the woman as she picked up her son and twirled him around in the air. She put him down and he ran for a tiny stroller in the corner that held little baby dolls.

"My husband and I actually just moved here from Ohio. We've been here a few months."

"Well, welcome to L.A.! Wow Ohio? What a change. What brought you guys all the way over here?" I asked.

"A job and family. My husband is a dentist and just got a job at a clinic a few miles away. Also, his family is from Sacramento, and we had been here for a vacation once and really liked it, so thought we might come over here to be closer to his family and have access to everything here."

I'm a little surprised a person from Ohio would find this kind of life in L.A. appealing, all while my desire was to move away from the big city life.

"Ahhh." I managed to say, not sure how to respond to her comment.

"How about you?" she asked. "Where are you guys from?"

"I grew up actually outside L.A. a couple hours, but moved here for a job a long time ago and met my husband here."

"Cool. Is your husband from here?"

"He grew up just outside Anaheim."

She nodded her head. "Is this your only little one?"

"I actually have three others who are school age, and...."I hesitated. We decided we were going to keep the pregnancy a secret from people except for close friends and family, but I shrug it off. I don't know this lady. What were the chances I would see her again? Probably very high, if I continued to come to this play group, but part of me didn't care. I preceded to tell her we were expecting a baby.

"Oh my goodness!" she glanced down at my belly, like most people do, even though I'm not even showing yet. "Congratulations!"

"Thanks. And it's not fully official yet, but my husband and I are thinking about moving our whole family to Montana soon."

The lady stopped and stared. "Montana? Wow. What a change from here. Isn't it really cold up there? And the winters really long? I'm pretty sure cows just fall over and die there."

I laughed. I had actually thought of the winters there. I'm not a big fan of cold weather, so I would have to invest in a wide wardrobe of coats, scarves, hats, and gloves. We'd also need to buy several pairs of what Chloe called long johns. I had so much to learn about that state.

"What makes you and your husband drawn to Montana?" The woman grabbed her son by the hand and led him to a huge box of toys that looked like play tools for the boys.

"One of my good friends from college has lived there for about five years. She worked at this local bakery in a small town for awhile before having her first baby, and I got to know the owner there. The lady is actually accepting a job all the way down in Mexico and offered to hand the business over to my husband and I. My background is in cooking and baking, and I've always dreamed of owning my own bakery and restaurant someday," I said with a dreamy look in my eyes. Now that I shared this out loud to someone else, it made me even more anxious and excited to get back.

To my surprise, the woman frowned. "Wow. A bakery business, huh? And with a baby on the way? That sounds like a recipe for disaster," she said.

I hadn't expected this reaction from a total stranger. "How's that?" I finally choked out the words.

"My sister had a bakery business years ago in a small town. She thought it would really take off, but now her and her husband are in the middle of filing for bankruptcy. It's actually a really hard business to be in. A ton of work you would never imagine, and all for nothing. My opinion? I think you and your husband would be better off staying here in L.A. There's more job opportunities, and if something doesn't work out, there's always something else he could try for. Better than starving your whole family in the middle-of-nowhere Montana."

I gulped. It didn't sit right with me when people shared their negative advice without being asked. Her comments felt like a punch in the face.

"Actually, there's more to it than what meets the eye. The woman who owns this place right now has been going strong for years and years. She has tons of experience and is going to be helping us oversee it from a distance. We would have all her same customers, and her place has such a good reputation, I don't see it struggling. She'll still own it. I'm basically being hired to oversee and maintain the place.

The woman peered at me with one eyebrow up. "Hmm. And doing all that with a baby, huh? Sounds like complete disaster. And not only that, but you won't be able to do what you want. Sounds like you'd be controlled by some lady who owns it who's not even there, and you won't be able to do what you want with the place. Wouldn't you want to make some changes? Have a place of your own?"

I was just about to tell her Marsha had already thought of that and how I'd have a lot of freedom to do what I wanted with redecorating and stuff. Not that there would be much I'd want to change. I loved the place the way it was, but I did have some ideas and things I wanted to add to the menu. And maybe some more special holiday events.

Before I could think of what to say in response to this woman, she turned around and was talking to someone else and distracted with her little boy showing her a toy he just picked up off the ground.

Tears formed in my eyes. What this woman had to say to me really hit home. It was actually something I'd been thinking about for three days non-stop, and now my emotions were surfacing. What if she was right? What if I couldn't handle a baby and helping to run a restaurant? And although Chloe knew Marsha really well, what made me think she would let me run the place I really wanted to? How would I be able to balance it all? Would it be just a big mistake to uproot the kids from the only place they'd ever known, and make them live in a far off place where the winter never seemed to end?

I had a sudden urge to grab my toddler and walk right out the front door. I felt out of place and wanted to get away as far as possible from the woman who had dug up so many negative emotions inside of me. What if she was right? What would I do?

I grabbed my son by the hand and quietly slipped out the door. The head lady noticed and watched us as we sneaked out, then gently waved. I wanted to get as far away from there as I possibly could.

I buckled my son into his car seat, and then hopped into the front and put on my seat belt. Right after the click, that's when the tears came. The drive home was quiet, and when I glanced into the back mirror, my son stared out the window again, seeming to enjoy the ride, which is a relief. Maybe he was able to get some of his energy out at the play group.

I pulled into the driveway and saw Mark's car back from work early. I pulled my son out of his seat and carried him in. I wanted him to lay down and rest, and checked the clock on the mantel in the living room. Only a few more hours till bedtime. Mark saw the look on my face when I walked through the door and I wondered if he noticed how stressed I looked. He immediately grabbed Dillon from me and walked him to his highchair to give him a snack while I sat on the couch for a minute to regroup.

After the snack, Mark asked one of the older kids he picked up from school to play with our youngest for a bit. Then he grabbed me by the hand and led me to our room. He had a seat on the bed, and I say on our little chair my grandmother gave us for a weeding present, which used to be her own. It's a rocking chair and recliner, and is a nice shade of blue, one of my favorite colors.

Mark held his hand in mine for a while and didn't say anything. He entwined his fingers into mine, and turned our hands over and over again. It felt like a massage. Before I knew it, he was massaging my fingers and the bones in my hand to help me relax. I leaned back in the recliner and closed my eyes for a spell while he continued to massage. After about five minutes he finally said, "so what's been on your mind? Are you doing okay, Kat?"

I sighed and pulled my hand away, not out of anger or annoyance, but so I could think of what to say next.

"You know that play group I've been wanting to go to my friend invited me to a while back? Well, I went today. And this complete stranger got me thinking..."

"Oh no. About what?" Mark pressed.

"Just about this whole move and uprooting our family, how much stress it's going to be. We have another child to think about. We're starting all over again with a new child, and here I am wanting to take over this restaurant, and how am I going to do it? I'm just so stressed right now."

Mark grabbed my hand again and held it. That night was the time we were scheduled to give an answer to Marsha.

"But you won't be doing this alone. I've actually talked to Marsha and voiced some of the concerns we would have, and she addressed every single one of them. The job that Larry's friend is offering won't start for another four months. If we decide to go through the interview process with that. We probably won't even need that income, between what we're doing at the restaurant, and because Marsha is letting us stay at her house while they're gone in Mexico. She said down the road if we're interested in buying, her and Larry wouldn't want to see their house go to anyone else. All her kids are already established and own their own houses or are paying off a mortgage of their own. There's no one else she would rather have there than us. Do you know how much we would be saving by not having to pay rent or a mortgage each month for a while? Plus, we would be selling this house too."

"What about the baby? How am I going to do all this stuff with a newborn?"

"I've thought it all out. In the beginning, I can run the restaurant and taking care of most things. I've done this all before, remember? As the baby gets older, you can bring him or her with you to the restaurant to work. Marsha also knows several trustworthy people who can pitch in and help with babysitting if need be.

I took a deep breath, some of the panic had disappeared.

"Trust me, Kat. You won't be doing this alone. We're going to have some of the best mentors I've ever met, and plenty of support as we transition. I really feel this is going to be great for our growing family." He stared at me as if looking deep into my soul. Mark placed his hand over my belly, and held it there.

"God's got great plans for all of us, including the newest member of our family."

I opened up my phone to look at the time. Only one more hour until we are supposed to meet with Marsha.

"I got one hour to shower, dress, and look pretty," I said.

"Why? It's only Marsha. She wouldn't care if you wore sweatpants. Besides, we're meeting with her on the computer. She probably wouldn't be able to see your outfit anyways."

"I want to be dressed well for this moment. Our lives are about to change and we're accepting my dream job," I said.

Talking with Mark sure did help my mood. I no longer cared what that woman back at the play group said. Maybe it was just my emotions playing havoc on me with being pregnant and all. Who knew? But one thing was for sure. Our lives were about to change forever and ever. To me, it was a thousand times more sweet, than bitter.

Chapter Forty-Seven

Marsha

Waiting on the front porch, I spotted my daughter's van pull into the driveway. "Ruth! I am so glad you guys were able to make it out today. It really does mean a lot to me." I gave my daughter the biggest hug imaginable. When was the last time I'd seen her? Maybe last Christmas? It felt like far too long. Her husband and kids drove three hours from Bozeman to help me pack. Our big move was right around the corner, and with Kate and her husband officially taking the position, I felt overwhelmed, yet my heart so full. I couldn't believe Larry and I would be taking this adventure.

"Of course, mom. I wanted to help. Tom is taking the kids out for ice cream and a movie while we pack, then they'll be over to help us with the rest," she laughed. "Tom also prefers helping with moving boxes, not packing them," she said.

"Well, of course Grandma has some sugar cookies waiting for the kiddos when they get here. Are you sure you guys don't want to stay the night here at the house? You know I always have plenty of room, and I'm sure Larry would love the company of the grandkids, as would I."

"Thanks, Mom. But we already booked a reservation. We thought about how we want the kids to enjoy some swimming, and plus you and dad are so busy packing, we didn't want you guys to have to worry about hosting us. You have way too much on your plates right now. But I would love for you to come sit by the pool tonight and we can chat while the kids swim, if you'd like. Even if it's just for a half hour."

"That does sound really nice. We'll just see how much packing we get done today, and then we can play it by ear."

It was quite a relief to think how I wouldn't be going through the house all by myself. Larry tried to help with the packing where he could, but he had a lot of other things to work on at the restaurant. He's also getting the place spick and span for when Kate and her family arrive. It was going to be hard giving over the keys, but at the same time, I felt excited to see what adventures awaited us in Mexico.

"So, where should we get started?" Ruth asked. She wore some faded blue jeans and an old T-shirt from back when she was in college.

"I was thinking we could start up in the attic and then work our way from the back of the house to the front," I said. "The stuff you guys don't want to take with you, it may be at a storage unit down the road. We don't want to take a lot with us."

"Wow. The attic. I haven't been up there since I was a little girl," Ruth said.

"So many memories up there. Do you remember when you and your sister use to play dolls up there?"

"That's one of my favorite memories. We played dolls almost every morning and you kept calling for us to come down for lunch. We went on playing, and finally, you decided to join us in the attic. You brought our lunches up to us, and we all had a big tea party with the dolls and stuffed animals. It was like we had our own little club up there in the attic."

"I remember that. You girls were so excited you got to have a tea party in the attic. When your daddy came home, we called out to him to come upstairs to the attic, and he joined us for..."

"Cranberry juice and cookies."

"Wow, your memory is better than I thought," I chuckled.

Ruth sighed and looked around the house, her hands in the back pockets of her jeans.

"I can't believe you're selling this place, Ma." She had a sad look in her eyes.

"Actually, I'm letting Kate and her family stay here, rent free. It's not for sale. But I was thinking down the road I would offer it to them if they wanted to buy it."

"Wow. That's quite a deal they're getting. I'm actually looking forward to meeting this Kate. I've heard so much about her, I feel like I know her," Ruth said. Did I hear a hint of jealousy?

"She's just the person we've been looking for to help run this place. She not only came highly recommended by Chloe, but also had shown us what a great job she's going to do. Her husband's going to be running most of it, at first. Kate's expecting a baby, and I'm sure she'll have enough on her plate. They both have experience managing a restaurant. That's how they met. The husband's mother owned a restaurant in L.A.

Ruth headed for the garage, where the entrance to the attic was located. Good thing Larry made it safe to walk up there. I couldn't handle anything extreme.

"Hopefully the boxes aren't too heavy to carry down." I pointed over to the corner where cobwebs had collected on a stack of boxes. Years and years of memories. Looking around the room with Ruth, I realized how much stuff we had collected over the years, not even realizing it. We had lived most of our married lives in that house, had raised our kids there, and some of our grandchildren. There was so much I would have to sort through and either put in a donation pile, throw away, or store in a unit. I thought of other options as Ruth and I scanned the area.

"Ruth? Would you and Darold have room for some of the stuff from when you were kids? I can't believe I hadn't thought of giving you some of this before. I know some of the kids could have used it. But whatever they can't use now, you can always hold on to for when they have kids of their own." Tears formed in my eyes. My wish was to turn back time and be standing there in that attic with my daughters, having a tea party all over again. How I missed those days.

"I'm sure we would. We have tons of storage out in the barn Darold remodeled years ago. He even told me we could use it for storage. The only other thing he puts in there occasionally are hay bales."

A few years after Ruth and Darold were married, he found a job as a ranch hand. He helped work cattle and a bit of land. The place where they were staying was an amazing deal, and included a place for their family to stay, without having to pay rent. They loved it there so much and had been there for over 15 years. I didn't blame them for not wanting to move.

"Oh. My. Gosh." Ruth stopped in her tracks.

"Is it a mouse?" I asked. We'd seen our share of mice over the years and I hated them. I thought Larry had gotten rid of all of them and closed all the possible spots where they could have come in.

"No. It's not that. I can't believe I forgot about these!" Ruth lifted some Easter baskets out of a box. They were wrapped in plastic bags.

"Remember old man Winnie? Emma and I called him Winnie the Pooh. Not in front of him, of course. He was our next-door neighbor years ago. Emma and I had learned somewhere about ringing people's doorbells on May 1st and running, leaving them candy on their doorstep. With old man Winnie, we did this about five times. He must have looked out his window, because later he commented on the candy we gave him. He thanked us for it, but I do wonder if we annoyed him ringing the doorbell over and over again. He gave us the baskets back. Said it was so that we could use them for other things." Ruth laughed at the memory. "I can remember Emma and I must have given him all our candy from Easter eggs. He was such a great guy. But..." Ruth frowned. "One day Emma and I were playing out in the back yard and we saw him fall off his ladder. We panicked, but someone from inside his house must have seen him fall, because they came rushing out. They had us grab you and Dad and asked that you call 911."

"I almost forgot about that too. It was so long ago." We both paused and gazed out the attic window over into Winnie's yard. He had died years ago. We heard about it at church. How he had some heart problems and died at the age of 85. His granddaughter lived there now, and had a couple kids that played in the yard on occasion.

"I wish I would have gotten to know him better. He seemed like a very nice guy," Ruth said, a touch of sadness in her voice.

I place my hand on her shoulder. "There's nothing we can do about the past. We can only look ahead to the future. I know a couple of Winnie's friends at the rest home. Their families live very far away, and they love the company. You guys are going to stay the night at a hotel nearby, right? You should come over with me tomorrow to the rest home and we can give them a little visit."

"Maybe." Ruth considered my offer. "I guess we'll see how everything goes with packing, and if Darold is up for watching the kids again."

"Or they could always come with us. Folks in those rest homes always enjoy young people. I bet it would just brighten their day."

"Can I think about it a bit? I'm a little nervous. When I tried to call our local rest home before about visiting the residents, I couldn't get a good answer on the visiting rules, and it kind of put a bad taste in my mouth to want to visit there."

"Well, they already know us at this one. All I would have to do is bring you in."

"Okay. I'll think about it." Ruth leaned down to pick up another box. Looked like we had more Easter baskets leftover from when they were kids than I thought.

"Has Isaiah come to visit recently?" Ruth hesitated, changing the subject. I could tell she wanted to share something with me but wasn't quite sure if she should. Isaiah is my second oldest boy. I have two boys and two girls. Or should I say two grown men and two grown women? Moses is my oldest son, then there's Isaiah, Ruth, then Emma. Emma likes to give me a hard time that she's the only one that didn't get a famous Bible name. Ruth was always close with Isaiah as well. They are only a couple years apart, and I can remember them playing a lot together growing up.

"No, not since you guys were here for Christmas. I did talk to him a few weeks ago on the phone, though. Seems they are doing well."

Ruth looked down at her hands, a sad look on her face.

"Oh."

"Ruth? Is something wrong?" I worried. Usually, my kids were very good at keeping in touch and telling me things going on in their lives, but every once in a while, the siblings will hear about something before I do.

"Let Isaiah tell you himself. I don't want to be the one to say."

This put me in a tough spot. I didn't want to call Isaiah and pry, yet I didn't want to make Ruth tell me what was going on.

"Just tell me. Is Isaiah well? Is he hurt or sad?"

Ruth hesitated. "He's pretty sad," she finally said.

I sighed. "Please tell me, Ruth. If he gets angry at you for telling me, I'll tell him it was my fault."

"I don't know if I should."

"Please. I just want to know if my son's all right."

"It's his job. He lost his job."

"At the school? He's been there for so many years."

"Yes, for twenty years to be exact. It's because he's the art teacher at the high school. The school was having financial issues for the last couple years, and art seems to always be the first to go. He'll finish up the school year there, and then he has to find another job."

"Oh poor Isaiah. I know how much he adores that school and how everyone there adores him as well. There's no way they could keep him?"

"Apparently they've tried and tried, and cutting a teacher's salary seems to be the solution."

"They don't have any other openings at the school? Maybe he could teach math or something instead."

"They might for the next school year. And Isaiah is qualified to teach that. But you know how much art his passion. He doesn't see himself doing anything else."

"I should barge right into that principal's office and give them a piece of my mind!"

Ruth chuckled. "You sound like a mother of a child in school. I want to give them a piece of my mind too. All we can do right now is pray he finds a different job in another district where he can teach art until he retires. He probably has what? another twenty years in him, don't you think?"

I couldn't answer Ruth's question. All I could think about was Isaiah and how he's taking the news. It would be hard to move his family to a new place, away from where they'd put down roots for so many years. I just wished I was the first he told. And then, as if reading my mind, Ruth spoke on the matter.

"I think he would have told you first, Ma. It's just that I happened to be over at his house visiting since we were in the area and he slipped up when he started talking about next year. He didn't even mean to tell me. It just happened. And, being the nosy little sister I am, got it out of him that they wouldn't be renewing his contract for next year. I'm sure he would have told you soon enough."

Ruth wrapped her arms around me.

"Remember when Isaiah had been bullied at school and he told Moses about it and not you? You were waiting for Isaiah to tell you about it, but a couple of weeks past, and he still didn't mention it?"

I nodded my head.

"I remember you writing a letter to him about it, because you weren't really sure what to say. You took him out on a mommy son date one night and instead of giving him the letter, he started to talk to you about it."

"Yes. I remember that. I took him to the fair and I remember riding rides with him and getting corn dogs and cotton candy. We had such a good time."

"So maybe that's what you need to do. You haven't seen him for a while. Maybe if you guys just get together sometime before your big move, you'll find an opportunity to spend some time with him and catch up."

"I was wanting to spend some time with each of my kids before we move. I even want to have you guys come and see me when I'm in Mexico, sometime after we get settled, that is. I was wanting to have a big get together with everybody here at the house before we go, but I know with the time of year and everyone's schedules, it may not work out. I might just have to work it out with each family."

"Mom, we can rearrange our schedule if you want to have everyone together. I'm sure they could make it all work. They don't have paid time off for nothing. And you are more than worth it. Just ask them about it."

I sighed and shrugged my shoulders. "Maybe. I'll have to talk it over with Larry. There's just so much going on, and we would be moving so soon. But I might be able to throw something together last minute. I just might need your help."

Chapter Forty-Eight

Missy

Panting and out of breath, I kept wondering when we'd reach Avalanche Lake. We passed people coming down the mountain saying, "It's just around the bend!" Or "only a little bit more to go. Keep going." Patricia and Em slowed the talking, each of us struggling to get up the hill.

Distracting myself with the scenery, a thought popped into my head. Probably Shawn's fault. He got me thinking more about stuff I tried to ignore my whole life. Could it be possible there was a God who actually cared? So many times I'd questioned if there was a God, and if he was good. I'd been through so much. How could he have allowed such tragedy to happen?

Shaking the thought, I looked up ahead and saw Shawn waving to us to come quick.

"I see the light at the end of the tunnel," he yelled. "It's beautiful!"

I laughed at his enthusiasm, but when the lake came into view, I understood. I'd never seen anything like it before, except in magazines. Right in front of us, lay a gorgeous view of a distant mountain with a waterfall cascading down the front. A clear lake reflected the mountain and the sky. At the corner of my eye, I saw someone running. Realizing the runner was Shawn, he threw off his T-shirt and only had on jeans. Barefoot, he ran across the beach, straight for the lake. He threw his hands up and ran as fast as his legs could carry him, I'm sure. In a flash, we hear him jump in.

"In jeans, huh?" Patricia looked over at Shawn and laughed. "I sure hope he won't be cold on the way back. That water is probably freezing cold!"

"It's hot enough outside, he just needs to sit in the sun awhile," Patricia said.

There was something about Shawn I felt drawn to. He seemed so free, not caring what others thought. He enjoyed life and wasn't afraid to share what he stood for. My wish was to be more like that. And why couldn't I? No one was stopping me. Yes, over a dozen people stood around who could probably see me, but I shouldn't have cared.

On impulse, I took off running in the same direction as Shawn, feeling the wind push me along as my feet hit the chilly water. When was the last time I let my hair down and enjoyed life like this?

I waded into where the water reached my stomach and did a somersault under the surface. Might as well get my hair wet. The cold stung me at first, but after the initial shock, it felt refreshing. I dove under a few more times, not bothering to look back at the people who came up the mountain with me. They probably thought I was crazy.

Shawn played halfway across the lake. He did the same thing; dove under and came back up again, over and over. It was as if we were in our own little mountain lake world together. No one else swam in the water.

After ten minutes of swimming, I exited the water and jogged to the rest of the group. Each of them sat on a large tree that had fallen over.

"Hey hey hey!" One of Shawn's friends called. "You really took quite a dive, huh? That water must be pretty chilly."

"It's worse after you get out actually," I said, shivering. Wishing I'd brought a change of clothes, I found a spot on the log to sit in the sun, hoping it dried me off and warmed up fast.

Relieved they didn't say any more about it, Shawn's friends continued their conversation. They were talking about the ocean and a trip someone went on.

After a few minutes, I saw Shawn jogging up to where I sat.

"Care if I join you?" He plopped down next to me and handed me a towel. "I always carry extra when I hike to a lake," he smiled.

Relieved, I grabbed the towel from him, dried my hair, then wrapped up in it for warmth. Without saying anything else, he handed me a pair of workout pants and a T-shirt out of his bag near the log where we were sitting.

I thanked him and he moved over to a spot on the other side of the log to chat with his friends. Making a mental note to always carry an extra pair of clothes, I searched for a spot in the woods to change.

After changing, I found a spot in the sun back on the log to sit and take in everything around me. Shawn and his friends laughed and took pictures of all the chipmunks hanging out all around us. One stood close enough, they could reach out and touch it if they wanted to. Patricia grabbed out her Smartphone and started recording.

"And he passes the acorn to his friend...and SCORE!" she shouted. Shawn joined in on the commentary.

"And he's back out again on the prowl! Looking for his next snack. He sniffs and score! He found the nut!" he said.

Patricia mentioned how it would be best we start the hike back down the path, since one of the guys needed to catch a train that night to visit his cousin in Chicago.

"Maybe we can grab a pizza or something before we drop him off at the station," Emma said.

"Pizza sounds good right about now, guys. I could totally go for one with extra cheese," Shawn said.

While we hiked down the mountain, I thanked Shawn for the clothes.

"It's not a problem at all. Like I said, I always carry extra."

Emma nudged Patricia, who hiked side by side. They peered over at me, grinning.

I felt curious about Shawn. Had he ever dated before and what was his type? As if reading my thoughts, some of my questions were answered a little way down the mountain. The hike went smoother going down, and I enjoyed every minute of it.

As if out of nowhere, Phil, another one of Shawn's professor buddies from the college caught up with us. Apparently, no one knew he was coming. He had driven separately when he heard some of the guys from work were going.

"Hey! I didn't know you were going to be here." Shawn punched his friend. Phil was headed up the mountain, while we were heading down.

"How was the hike going up?" Phil asked.

"Way worse than going down, that's for sure." Patricia said. "Boy, you sure are walking fast."

"You bet I am. I'm not going to miss my hot date tonight. I already had to reschedule once with her."

"Another one, huh?" Patricia looked disappointed. "I thought you were done with dating for awhile."

"Naw. I met this one on social media and couldn't say no. She seems perfect for me."

"You say that about all the girls, Phil. And don't you meet all the girls you've been with online?"

"Hey. Ain't nothing wrong with playing the field and having some fun. Live today, for we die tomorrow, that's what I always say."

"I bet you're breaking a lot of hearts along the way, though, Phil." Patricia said.

Phil shrugged his shoulders. "One-time dates are always the best. Get the girl. No commitment. Don't have to see her again. That's that."

"You mean part of you doesn't want to have a real relationship? Someone who will be by your side the rest of your life?" Patricia said.

"Eh. Someday, I guess. But right now, I want to just have some fun," Phil said.

No one else responded. We continued the hike in silence for quite some time, which was totally fine with me. I hadn't been out in nature like that in so long. Once we are close to reaching the end of the trail, Patricia jogged up next to me.

"How you doin?" she asked, slightly out of breath.

"Not bad. I'm loving this hike," I said.

"I'm glad you got to come along. It's been good to have you with us." Patricia sounded genuine and I felt grateful to have made a new friend on the hike.

"Melissa was never a fan of hiking. I'm glad you like it," Patricia said.

"Oh. Who's Melissa? I'm sorry. I can be bad remembering names and faces sometimes," I said.

"Shawn hasn't told you about Melissa?" she said.

I shook my head.

"Oh." Patricia glanced up ahead. Shawn was far enough ahead, and busy talking.

"Melissa was Shawn's fiancé."

"Was?" I asked, trying not to show how much the topic of Shawn interested me.

"Yeah. They dated for about a year or so and then Shawn proposed. They were engaged for about a month and then Melissa started talking to an old boyfriend she used to have and decided she wanted to get back together. She broke the engagement off, but only after she had...Well, you know how a lot of people are these days. This happened over three years ago.

I only nodded. Patricia had no idea about my past. I had been one of those girls back in the day. Good thing I had never been engaged before though.

"Anyways, Shawn hasn't even talked about women since that happened. That is, until you came along."

"My boss Marsha just wanted me to be friends with Shawn. She knew I was looking for people to hang out with. That's all this is, really," I said.

"Well, I can tell there's some sparks there. When Shawn first told us about you, I could tell there was a sparkle in his eye. I'm really good at spotting when a guy is interested in a woman. You could ask any of my friends," Patricia said.

"I think you're imagining things. The only reason Shawn is hanging out with me is because my boss was trying to get me connected to some people in her church. It was supposed to be a woman friend that she arranged this with, but it turned out she asked Shawn for some reason," I countered.

"Maybe she thought there would be some sparks there too," Patricia grinned.

"Are you saying my boss is trying to orchestrate something for my love life?" I laughed.

"Deny it all you want, it still doesn't change the fact Shawn has something for you. I just know these things. I've always been right. Just ask my friends who are married now. I saw it coming all along."

"Trust me. Shawn has shown no interest in me in that way. I can tell you that much."

"He may have not shown it to you because remember, he was in a relationship with a girl who he thought was the one. It took him so long to get over her. And Shawn is not like Phil over here who just dates for fun and does one- night stands. He's a real gentleman, and genuine in his faith. He's keeping his distance on purpose. He doesn't want to make the same mistake again."

I felt glad Patricia was being honest with me. It answered a lot of my questions about Shawn and his philosophy on dating. Unfortunately, the more Patricia talked, the more I realized I had too much of a past to ever date him. Shawn wouldn't want a girl like me, if he only knew who I really was.

Chapter Forty-Nine

Chloe

Socks. Underclothes. Three pairs of good jeans. Check. Check. Check. When was the last time I'd even been on a trip? I felt stoked about the trip down to Texas and to get away from the everyday things. On top of paying for the women's conference in Texas, Marsha invited me to join them in Mexico afterward to see the new place where she would be working and living. Although super sad to see her move, I prayed for the Lord's direction in their lives as they started a new adventure together. And Kate as well. It would be nice to have my best friend close again, and with her family too. My hope had been to make many fond memories with them as they moved into Marsha's house and ran the restaurant. It sure was going to be different around our little mountain town.

Right at noon, I heard the doorbell ring. "Are these the bags right here you're taking?" a tall friendly man said. "I'm Dan and my wife's name is Laura. We've heard so much about you, and we're excited you're coming with us," he said.

"I'll be doing the driving for the trip." Dan reached out his hand to shake mine and smiled at both the baby and me.

As Dan grabbed my things to pack into the RV, I locked up the house and did a quick check to make sure I gathered everything. One can never be too sure with a baby. They have so many things they need on trips, and this would be the first big one of his life.

Excited to ride in the R.V. and watch the scenery, I felt anxious to leave.

While loading up the last of our things, my jaw dropped. My mind had changed. I didn't want to go anymore because of something or *someone* I saw.

Missy stood near the entrance of the R.V, her hand in the back pocket of her jeans. She appeared to be talking on the phone to somebody. It took a lot of self-control to not turn around and march home. Who had invited her and why was she going? I thought Marsha told me it was just going to be me and her two friends and her and Larry would be joining us at all the stops. She never mentioned Missy.

My stomach did gymnastics flips, and not the good kind. I knew it sounded selfish of me, but I was hoping to have a break and not see anyone else from work.

"Great," I mumbled under my breath as I found a spot on the R.V. couch to sit and process everything. My whole perspective on this trip had changed in one split second.

"This is not happening right now," I said aloud.

"What?" Missy said from over by the restroom. I looked up to see she'd been giving me a questioning look and she finally was off her phone.

"Oh. Nothing," I said while trying to appear distracted digging around in the baby bag. What was I looking for anyways? Missy didn't appear to be mad, just curious. And surprisingly, she didn't have the normal frown I used to see all the time when I worked with her. It felt out of the ordinary to not see her in work clothes. She's dressed in khaki pants and a country looking shirt, which actually looked nice. It had gray with accents of purple, and she took the time to pick out matching earrings too. Something felt different about her.

Missy sat on a seat across from me and rustled around in her bag. She grabbed a pair of pants and shirt, paused for quite a while, smiled, and gently put it back in. I wondered what that was all about.

"That's cool you get to come on the trip too," she said. Missy looked like she meant it, catching me by surprise. Marsha knew

Missy and I didn't fully get along all that great at work, and maybe it had been her master plan to get us together on the trip and work out our differences. Who knew for sure?

I nodded my head and smiled at Missy. Not only did she look different, but she was acting different too. Who was this and what did she do with the Missy I met at work?

"Any idea what this women's conference is about?" Missy asked, opening a can of soda pop from the small kitchen counter next to her. I hadn't had pop in a long time. She offered me the one she opened, but I declined.

"Marsha didn't say much about it. I guess just talking about things like Jesus," I said. Wasn't that obvious and wouldn't Missy know it? Marsha informed us the conference was Christ-centered. Now that Missy knew, would she want to leave? Instead of looking bummed like I expected, she seemed to ponder it.

"Hmm. I think that will be good for me," Missy said, sipping on the cold can she held in her hands. I raised one eyebrow. Not something the Missy I knew would say.

I wanted to ask her questions, but she appeared lost in thought. I distracted myself with the baby and getting him to laugh.

After five minutes of enjoying the baby smile and coo, Marsha's friend Laura popped her head in the R.V. area and said, "Alright, ladies! You ready to go? We're finally ready to leave. Dan was just checking on some things with the R.V. to make sure we're ready for the road!" I heard a bit of a southern accent. Marsha had mentioned how the couple was originally from Texas.

I watched Laura jump into the passenger seat and Dan turned the key and pulled out of the driveway.

Missy and I sat in silence, looking out the window, listening to the hum of the R.V. It was one of the nicest I'd ever seen, with a living room that expanded when parked.

I glanced at Missy and noticed her staring out the window, still lost in thought. I attempted to think of something to talk about, but decided sitting in silence and just enjoying the ride would be better.

A half hour later, Dan turned on the radio to a Christian music station. I recognized the song.

"I love this Casting Crowns song," Missy said. Since when did Missy listen to Christian music? Last I heard she loved heavy metal or something equally obnoxious.

"Wow. I can't believe I didn't recognize who this was." I listened more. "Yep. You're right. It's Casting Crowns. You a fan?" I asked.

"Oh. I started listening to them like, yesterday. I went on a hike with Shawn, and it was playing in his car. He told me the artist and then played a few more of their songs off a CD he had," Missy said.

Missy's eyes sparkled when she mentioned Shawn. What was going on? Surely they weren't dating. I could never see Shawn date a girl like her. Those times I would stop by the restaurant for a visit, I could tell she had a crush on him. She seemed drawn to him, but I had no idea why they were hanging out. Wasn't Shawn a well-known Christian? Why would he date a non-believer? If I was being completely honest, I wondered why he would even want to hang around Missy at all. Whenever I was around her at work, she was like being a around a thorn.

The time on the kitchen clock matched my cell phone, and I realized it was time for the baby's nap. Gathering things from the living room, I then maneuvered through the narrow hallway, past the bathroom, and opened the back folding doors to the bedroom Marsha said would be for me and the baby. I thought about how nice it would be to take a nap too, but when I opened the back, there was a bag with stuff strewn everywhere, covering every inch of the bed. It looked like a full-size bed, with just enough room on one side for the baby's traveling bassinet. Wondering whose stuff it could be,

I pushed the large black bag to the side and sat down to adjust the baby's things. A tag on the side of the bag had Missy's name on it.

Lord, only you know Missy's heart. It seems now she may be open to what you have to say. Please speak to her through this conference. Let her know she is dearly loved and wanted by the creator of the universe. I know she's been through so much in her life. Help her see that you can be her best friend, and not to run away from you. Speak to her heart, and not just be interested in you because of some guy she likes is. Help her to truly have an encounter with you. And please give me the strength to be in close quarters with her this trip.

I sighed. Where was she going to sleep? Hopefully they had room in the living room, and everyone didn't mind a screaming baby waking them up in the night. It was going to be a very long trip.

Chapter Fifty

Marsha

It's official. I've decided apple cider is the best drink to have when guests come over. It's the most popular drink at the restaurant, and I've noticed sales on that stuff skyrocket when we finally added it to our menu. My daughter and I were able to pull off a family gathering somewhat at the last minute. I'm surprised it worked. She took care of most of it, and I just bought the food and arranged the house a bit where it would look decent for guests, despite most everything being packed up and ready to move out the door.

Larry helped me stack most of the stuff in a back bedroom, where it would be out of sight. For me, I wish it was also out of mind. I kept thinking about the move and when I would get excited about it, I'd remember that family would still be in the states, and then I'd feel a little sad. I felt grateful to have a big enough savings we could visit them. I also planned on flying back up to Montana the weekend after we moved. Kate had officially accepted the job, and I promised I would take time to show her some more aspects of the business and help them settle into their new home.

Thankfully, my job would be starting out slower down in Mexico and they said they'd be willing to work with me, knowing I'd be going through a huge transition with handing over the responsibilities of the business. They compromised and hired a temporary cook for a couple months, giving me time to transition. Larry's job however, started right away. He told me his excitement about it and his eagerness to start. It wasn't much time to settle in, but I knew how anxious Larry had been to get a break from all the moving stuff and embark on a new adventure.

I'm just thankful we were able to get all my kids together under the same roof. This doesn't seem to happen often, except maybe on special occasions like Christmas.

While drinking hot apple cider with my son Isaiah on the front porch, I talked about how we were going to miss it and the memories we had shared. I could even remember when the porch was built. It was an add-on and Larry worked night and day to make it for me. I remembered many nights of playing cards with the kids out on the rocking chairs we used to have on the porch, and a few times of hosting a square dance in our yard and using the porch for folks to sit down and put up their feet and get something to eat. My square-dancing group would be missed so much. So many years of friendships, dancing, and laughter. I doubted the area where we'd be moving would have a dancing group like that one.

The other part of the family say inside chatting and swapping stories from their childhood. I wanted to be in there to hear the stories, but I thought how important it was to have the time with Isaiah.

"I sure am going to miss that school, mom," he said.

"Well of course. You've been there for years. I'm sure all those people are very sad to see you go. You've done so much for them."

Isaiah tightly wrapped his fingers around the handle on his mug of hot apple cider, as if to symbolize his frustration and how hard it was to let go.

I remembered something I'd set aside while packing up the last of the boxes. I'd been meaning to give it to Isaiah for a while, and thought maybe that moment would be a good time, since we were on the subject.

Stepping through the front door, I grabbed the photo album off the kitchen counter.

"I've been meaning to give this to you for so long," I said.

I handed him a dark brown photo album with his name on it. He opened it to the first page, and I watched his lips form into a huge smile. Exactly the reaction I had hoped for.

"This is the first classroom I ever had as my own." He looked through the first few pages, savoring every picture he saw. He ran his fingers across the picture of him with all his students lined up outside in front of a rugged mountain background. He laughed. "There's Jace. And Maddie. And of course Cole. How could I forget Cole?" he chuckled. "That class was so much fun. So many of them moved away, but it has been so cool to see them grow and change each year. I didn't even know you had made this, mom. Thank you. I love it." He leaned over to give me one of his big bear hugs. His beard rubbed up against my face and I thought of when he was just a baby and I would hold him close. Quite a difference from his prickly beard.

We talked about some of his experiences as a first year teacher for a while and then I followed him back inside, where all my other grown children were gathered.

They all had a look on their face as if they were just talking about me right before I walked in and had to quickly stop talking when I walked through the door.

"Hmm.What are you guys up to?" I smiled, then turned to stare at Isaiah, who had never been good at keeping secrets. Ever since he was little, he would spill the beans about something right away. His face was the one that always looked guilty. Sure enough, I could see his cheeks turn bright red, even behind all that prickly beard of his. I looked from one of my children to the next. Some of the girls tried not to make eye contact with me, but one glanced over and giggled. Reminded me of when they were in pigtails. Was that yesterday? It sure felt like it sometimes.

Finally, to break the awkward silence, one of my grandsons, who was two, ran down the middle of the room. He climbed over his aunts and uncles to get to me.

"Grandma! Grandma! I made for you." He smiled proudly. I gave him a big kiss on his forehead and he ran back across the room to sit in his mommy's lap over by the fireplace.

I leaned down to grab the paper he laid on the floor right by my feet and opened it up. Part of it looked crinkled and peanut butter smudged over some of the parts where he colored with a crayon. Without warning, tears formed in my eyes, and I freely let one roll down. He reminded me so much of when my kiddos were that age.

Scribbled on the page, I see there's a picture of him, and his daddy and mommy, which is Isaiah and his wife. His mommy's belly was circled and next to it, it said" I'm going to be a big brother!" Clearly written in adult handwriting, of course. My mouth dropped open. It never gets old and the excitement never goes away, when I hear there's another one coming along. I had been wondering when they were going to have another one.

I held the paper close to my heart and each one of my children and their families lined up to give me a great big hug.

"That's not all, mom." Isaiah said. He brought over a map.

"I was totally blown away when you told me you accepted that job in Mexico. Because I had literally just heard about an hour before, that the teaching job I had interviewed for, would be right by the border of Mexico. When I looked at it on the map, we're actually going to be only an hour away from each other," Isaiah said.

"Oh my...." My heart leaped with excitement. A new adventure and I'd be able to hold my new grandbaby often.

Lord, you have blessed me tremendously. Your timing is perfect in every way.

Also by S.S. Zemke

The Loony Bride and Other Short Stories
Mommy Minds

Watch for more at https://sszemke.blogspot.com/.

About the Author

S.S. Zemke resides in the northwest with her mountain man and two kids. A teacher for children, she enjoys writing stories for both kids and adults. Her works include short stories, Christian fiction, historical fiction, and picture books.

Read more at https://sszemke.blogspot.com/.